22/11

10 MAR 2023

D0513218

04481413

Scholastic Children's Books
An imprint of Scholastic Ltd
Euston House, 24 Eversholt Street, London, NW1 1DB, UK
Registered office: Westfield Road, Southam, Warwickshire, CV47 0RA
SCHOLASTIC and associated logos are trademarks and/or
registered trademarks of Scholastic Inc.

First published in the US by Scholastic Inc, 2017
First published in the UK by Scholastic Ltd, 2017

Text and illustrations copyright © Inbali Iserles, 2017

The right of Inbali Iserles to be identified as the author and illustrator of this work
has been asserted by her.

ISBN 978 1407 14716 1

A CIP catalogue record for this book
is available from the British Library.

Printed by CPI Group (UK) Ltd, Croydon, CR0 4YY
Papers used by Scholastic Children's Books are made
from wood grown in sustainable forests.

1 3 5 7 9 10 8 6 4 2

Map art by Jared Blando

www.scholastic.co.uk

INBALI ISERLES

FOXCRAFT

❧ THE MAGE ❧

*For Peter Fraser – from the
Greylands to the Wildlands,
through the Snowlands and back .*

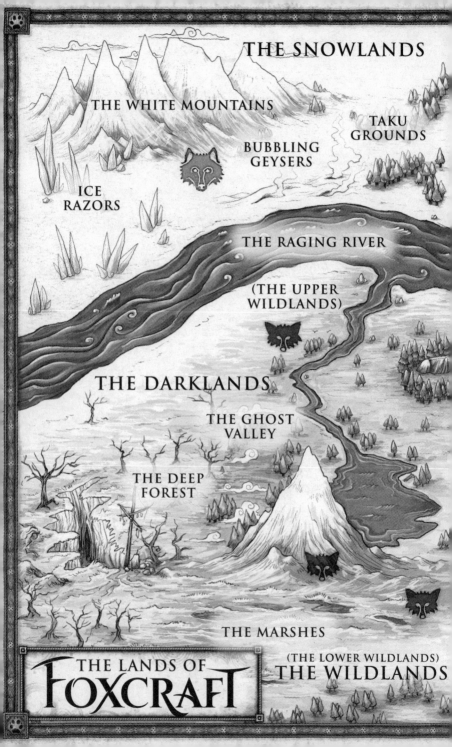

THE SNOWLANDS

THE WHITE MOUNTAINS

TAKU GROUNDS

BUBBLING GEYSERS

ICE RAZORS

THE RAGING RIVER

(THE UPPER WILDLANDS)

THE DARKLANDS

THE GHOST VALLEY

THE DEEP FOREST

THE MARSHES

THE LANDS OF
FOXCRAFT

(THE LOWER WILDLANDS)
THE WILDLANDS

Mad fox, bad fox, just another dead fox.

I couldn't shake the words from my mind. I used to chant them with Pirie when we lived in the Great Snarl. It felt like a long time ago, another age. Before the Taken arrived and my brother disappeared. When life was simpler, when days were short and twilight was filled with adventure.

When Ma, Fa and Greatma were still alive.

Before everything changed.

My paws sank into deep snow. A gale was shrieking over the tundra. Grey clouds webbed across the stars, flooding the night with an ominous glow. Wisps tumbled from the sky, ducking and darting like panicked mice. A blizzard was rising over the Snowlands.

The clamour of the Raging River dissolved beneath the

howling wind. My paw prints followed me like a shadow. I squinted into the gloomy sky. I could make out a forest of spruce trees. Tall trunks shot up against ice-capped mountains. Beneath the branches, I'd find shelter from the storm.

A shriek and my head whipped around, heart lurching against my ribs. Was it only the wind, or something else?

Someone else?

The Snowlands expanded before me in all directions, a hostile world of churning flakes and freezing air.

The realm of the snow wolves.

The screeching gales disguised their calls. The tumbling snow concealed the land in its shimmering pelt. Were wolves active by day, like dogs? Or, like foxes, could they hunt at night? I knew so little about our savage, distant cousins.

I blinked hard. If wolves were prowling, I couldn't see them.

I couldn't see much through the blizzard. I could hardly make out the spruce any more, just a faraway jumble of thick brown trunks.

I strained to catch Pirie's scent. The icy air betrayed no clues. I was alone in this wilderness. I cocked my head, my ears turning forward. Birds . . . Rabbits . . . Bugs. They had to be close. Even in the Snarl, there were always pigeons and mice, beetles and flies. There were so many different noises. The clacking of the furless, the roars of the deathway.

Freezing snowflakes stuck to my lashes and weighed on

my fur. What creature would choose to be out in this?

I gave myself a shake. My paw pads were numb with cold. What had I been thinking? That I'd arrive and somehow know where to go? Siffrin was right, I shouldn't have come here. Instinctively, I peered over my shoulder. He was impossibly far behind me now, on the distant bank of the river. Lost to the Wildlands and the Elder Wood. I only hoped he had outrun the Taken.

He'll be all right, I tried to assure myself. *He has foxcraft.*

Doubt gnawed at me. There were *so many* Taken. Worse still, I'd seen the Narral, the Mage's assassins. Unlike the Taken, they did his bidding freely. They were masters of foxcraft and would know Siffrin's tricks.

I drew in my breath. I had to believe that he was safe.

Dropping my head against the wind, I pushed harder, determined to reach the shelter of the trees. The icy gales blew back my fur to graze my skin. How long would I survive in the open air, in this deep chill? The Elders' maa had drained away. I had squandered that silver power when I'd shifted into the great bird. For moments I had sailed over the Wildlands, a creature forged of wings and feathers. Dizzily I remembered the thrill of the flight, the air that had gripped my body and lifted me high over the world.

Then the wa'akkir had failed, and I'd fallen.

Fast, deep, into freezing water.

Over the tumult, on to the bank. Into the land of bitter wind, a place beyond malinta's reach.

My paw slipped on ice. I stumbled forward, crunching through snow to strike my muzzle on the frozen ground. Whiteness wrapped itself around me and I closed my eyes.

Mad fox, bad fox . . .

Mad to enter the Snowlands alone. I hadn't thought it through – I hadn't thought at all. Crazy to imagine I'd just *find* my brother in the endless tundra. Me, a stranger to the ice drifts.

Bad to abandon the foxes of the Wildlands, when they were under attack. The Elders were weakened, the Darklands were growing. But what could I do about it? Guilt gathered at the base of my tail. I had left them to battle the Mage on their own.

I scrambled to my paws with a mewl. My flanks trembled with cold. Flurries slapped my fur and wind screeched in my ears. I struggled against it, my head hardly rising above the thick snow. My heart sank: I could no longer see any trees. Everything had vanished beneath fresh snowfall. Even the ice-capped mountains were lost to the leaden sky.

Bewildered, I whipped around. My paw prints were fading, erasing my journey from the bank of the river.

Soon I'll disappear too.

I'd only just reached the Snowlands and already the brutal land had defeated me.

No, I thought, with a surge of anger. It rolled through my limbs, warming my paws. I started again through the snow. But I no longer knew which way to go.

The wind shrilled like a fox's cry.

This way.

My ears pricked up. Had someone spoken? I started toward the shrilling. A few paces along, I bumped into a wall of snow. Flakes cascaded to reveal a low cave. Gasping with relief, I stalked inside and wrapped my tail around my flank. Out of the lashing gales, the chill was bearable. I would wait it out till the blizzard ran its course. Then I'd start to look for my brother. I didn't know where, or how. But I'd find a way.

I fell into a deep sleep, where the snowstorm rose around me, lifting me into the air and carrying me over clouds. Like the great bird, I was high over the sky, watching the Wildlands, soaring above the Snarl. The storm set me down in a peaceful meadow. Birds were peeping and trilling in the trees. Insects were clicking in the long grass. Sun tickled my nose and glinted off my whiskers. I had a strange sensation that I'd been here before, but it wasn't the meadow where the Wildlands skulk had lived. Not far from the peace of the long grass, I could hear the deathway. Furless dens hunched in the distance, grey and imposing.

It's been a long time, Isla. Greatma padded out from the grass.

My heart leaped and I ran to her.

She rested her dappled nose against my muzzle.

"I wish you'd never gone away, Greatma."

So do I. Sometimes things happen that you don't plan.

"You said we'd be all right if we stayed near the den. You told us, me and Pirie. You promised."

But you didn't stay near the den, did you, Isla? She drew away from me. Her eyes searched mine and my tail-tip shuddered.

"I was only in the wildway. I didn't mean to be there long. I didn't think you'd miss me . . ."

And Pirie?

I blinked at her. "He wasn't with me."

"But he didn't come back to the den either. Like you, he got away."

I lowered my muzzle. "I'm sorry," I whimpered. "We let you down. After all your warnings, we didn't listen. We wandered off without you."

I'm glad you did.

I looked up at her.

Of course I'm glad, said Greatma. *It saved your life.*

I lowered my muzzle. I should have been there when the Taken came. I should have done something to help my family.

None of this is your fault, said Greatma, as though reading my thoughts. *You didn't bring the Taken.*

"Why would anyone bring them?" I asked sadly.

I became aware of a deep stillness. The roars of the deathway faded. The peeps and trills of the meadow had gone. I stretched my claws, as though I might hang on to the dream by force.

"Greatma?"

Chill shot through me. My eyes flicked open and I shivered. My muscles ached against the hard floor of the cave. I looked around me, trying to remember how I'd got there. Stiffly, I rolled on to my paws. I padded to the mouth of the cave. The blizzard had swept away in the night. Golden light speared the dark horizon. Nothing stirred, not even a flake of snow.

My ears pricked as I gazed over the tundra.

Silence had a colour. It was arching, endless and perfectly white. It crept over the distant mountains, laying its pelt across forests of spruce. I could feel its bite on my damp fur, sharp and still.

The light of dawn was blinding against the snow. Crystals hung in the crisp air. My breath floated as mist, the only movement as far as the eye could see. At least the storm had passed. The wind had dropped.

The crunch of paws over snow. The thump of weight on the earth. Cautiously, I peered around the mouth of the cave. At first, I could only sense their pawsteps. Moments later, they rounded the sweeping snow. Three giant wolves with furious jowls were thumping over the tundra. I took in the sway of their shaggy pelts, the flexing of muscles at their powerful haunches. The sheer size of them amazed me. Had the wolf in the beast dens really been that large? He'd been lean, his long fur tatty. These three wolves were broad and thickset, their pale eyes shining, their muzzles clean.

I scrambled back against the mouth of the cave.

They mustn't see me!

At least the snowfall would have covered my tracks. Heart quivering, I remembered the tunnel that had cut through the mountain in the Wildlands. There had to be another way out. But as I sniffed along the cave, I met a wall of rock. I reached out a black forepaw. The rock glittered with ice, freezing to the touch.

I couldn't risk crossing the tundra, not with wolves so close. My ginger fur made me vulnerable against the vast whiteness. Here at least I had cover. I would wait it out, ears pricked in case they were close. Three giant beasts couldn't pass in silence.

Watch! Wait! Listen!

I tensed, my senses straining.

The crunch of paws over snow. A shadow leaped on the rock.

I spun around.

The wolves were at the mouth of the cave. I dropped on to my haunches and started chanting. "What was seen is unseen; what was sensed becomes senseless. What was bone is bending; what was fur is air."

Nothing happened. I looked urgently to my paws. They were black and stark against the floor of the cave.

I don't have enough maa!

I darted against the icy wall, my fur rising in spikes. The wolves had blocked the exit. It was too late to run.

The one in the centre was white as snow. "What is *this*?"

The wolves on either side of him stepped closer, their heads dropped and ears back. Their movements threw dark shapes across the cave.

One had a fuzzy grey-and-white coat. He glared at me. "A trespasser."

The white-furred wolf at the centre wrinkled his muzzle. "How dare she come here? Into *our* domain?"

"I'm not doing any harm," I gasped. "I didn't know I was in your territory, I'm not from the Snowlands."

"You stand and answer *me*, shrewling?" the white wolf growled. "Do you not stoop before a lord?" The corners of his huge jaws turned down in disgust. "This is not just the *Snowlands*, this is the Bishar of Claw, the greatest Bishar of the frozen realms. Our code is etched in the air and the earth. And you . . ." He ran his icy gaze over me. "*You* are an intruder. There is one punishment for those who trespass on our lands."

The female by his side took a step towards me. Only the silvery tips of her ears and tail disturbed the whiteness of her coat. Her large eyes were sky blue. "Shall I kill her, Lord Mirraclaw?" Her lips rose over her great fangs.

The white wolf turned away, as though already bored. "Drag her into the snow," he growled. "Let her blood be a warning to others."

2

The wolf with the sky-blue eyes grabbed me by the scruff and threw me on to the snow. I darted away, only to smack into the grey-and-white wolf.

"The shrewling is fast," he growled. "Lord Mirraclaw, might we have a little fun before we leave her to the ravens?" He slammed a huge paw against my flank, sending me spinning.

The blue-eyed wolf caught me with a claw against my throat, pinning me down. I gasped, my body frozen.

"Not much of a fighter. Look at those skinny legs. Not even sport for the pups."

The grey-and-white male stepped alongside the female. They loomed over me, their fangs bared.

"I'm not sure what she is," growled the male. "Some sort of giant rat, I guess. Lordess Cattisclaw, do you know?"

The female pressed her claw harder against my throat. "Not a rat," she said. "A strange, wingless owl? A skinny-legged hare?"

The white wolf – the one they'd called Lord Mirraclaw – shoved his broad face between the others. He glared down at me, his maw contorted with revulsion. "Fools," he snarled. "She understands. She must be one of Queen Canista's pups. An inferior breed that should have perished in the battle for supremacy. Watch as she pleads for her pathetic life." He lowered his muzzle, his lips peeling back over jagged teeth. "Aren't you scared, wretched creature? All alone here without friends?" As the white wolf drew closer, the others fell back. "Won't you beg us to spare you?"

I scrambled free, but I was surrounded. My heart was screaming against my ribs.

Bullies! They'll never see me beg.

I glared at the white wolf – Mirraclaw. Despite my terror, my voice was steady. "I am fearless. I am friendless. I am *fox*."

"She has guts." The female's silvery tail gave a wag of amusement. "I like her. What do you think, Norralclaw?"

The grey-and-white sprang forward to jab me with his paw, catching me in the chest. I rolled in the snow, gasping for breath. The moment I found my paws, the female butted me with her great shoulder, sending me flying. I tumbled in whiteness to thump against something solid – the thick leg of a wolf.

Mirraclaw was glaring down at me. "Enough!" he snarled. "It's time to get back to the Bishar of Claw. Get rid of the fox-ka!"

The female sprang forward, lips peeled so far back that her pink gums were bared.

Terror ripped through me.

The Bishar of Claw.

My thoughts leaped to the wolf in the beast dens. What was his name?

"Farraclaw!" I yelped.

The wolves froze, their eyes growing wide. I saw them glance at one another.

"What did you say?" hissed Mirraclaw.

They know him! I realized. "I'm here to see Farraclaw," I said, thinking fast. "I have a message for him."

"Who from?" asked the female.

I had to hold my nerve. "I'm not allowed to say."

"What sort of message?" spat the white wolf. Murder was written in his cold yellow eyes.

"A secret message – one I can only pass on to Farraclaw."

I expected Mirraclaw to lunge at me, but he paused. One white ear rotated. For a beat, no one spoke.

Emboldened, I cleared my throat. "I must see Farraclaw. It's a matter of life and death."

Mirraclaw glared at me. The sun was rising over the Snowlands, throwing scorched light around his broad

13

shoulders, a halo of cool flames. He turned, his hackles rising in spikes. "This way," he snarled. "Lordess Cattisclaw, make her hurry."

The female shunted me ahead of her. The wolves bounded effortlessly. It was harder for me. I had to leap over the snow, each time landing clumsily. Despite prods and shoves, I couldn't keep up. In the end, Cattisclaw closed her jaws around my scruff and scooped me up like a cub. Her clasp was not tender. I felt her teeth digging into my flesh, and every hard jolt of her paws on the earth.

I forced my eyes open, determined to see where we were going.

Through jerking leaps, I caught flashes of snowscape. Mirraclaw was in the lead, cutting a path through the rolling tundra. The other male bounded at Cattisclaw's side. Up ahead, I saw spruce trees daubed in white. It was the forest I'd spotted the previous night, the one I had lost in the blizzard. It took no time for the wolves to reach the trees. Still they kept running, as though they couldn't tire. Where they passed, birds shrieked and flapped away. A creature raised its furry head and dived into the snow.

The wolves didn't pause.

They ran uphill. I saw frozen lakes and arching rocks. Far off mountains were banked in clouds but overhead the sky was blue. The sun rose to dazzle the snow without a hint of warmth.

The wolves kept running. The female held me locked in her jaws. Pain stabbed along my neck, but I stayed quiet, doing my best to tuck my tail beneath me. I had to focus, to work out a plan. Would I really see Farraclaw? Would he remember me? The caged wolf had been nothing like these three muscular beasts. He'd lacked their confidence and power. I pictured the ribs poking out of his shaggy fur and the hairs that had worried away at his muzzle. Even if he chose to help me, what could Farraclaw really do against the Bishar's might?

Now that the wolves had slowed, I had a better view of the world around me. A ring of rocks cut through the snow, as though we were passing through giant jaws. Steam was rising up ahead. I craned to see a bright blue pool, bewildered to feel its heat. How did the pool stay warm surrounded by snow? Why didn't the water freeze?

A stream flowed from the pool. I sensed the heat fading as the water rushed along a tooth of rock. Mirraclaw lowered his head, murmured a few words, and drank thirstily. Cattisclaw dropped me on to compacted snow. I drew in my breath, woozy from the journey. I watched as she and the other male drank from the stream.

"Lord Mirraclaw," said Cattisclaw. "May I let the fox drink?"

"From the sacred stream?" he spat in reply, not deigning to look around. "Certainly not. Fox-ka is here against my better judgement. Fox-ka can die of thirst as far as I'm concerned."

I thought that, at least, unlikely, given the amount of snow that surrounded us. But as I looked at the clear blue stream, I yearned for a taste of its sweet water.

The wolves were soon on the move again but now they walked slowly, their pawsteps mindful. Cattisclaw jabbed me forward. I walked between her and the grey-and-white male, with Mirraclaw still in the lead. A golden stone shone ahead of us. As Mirraclaw reached it, he turned to Norralclaw.

"Call a meeting of the senate," he commanded.

"Yes, My Lord."

Mirraclaw stooped his head before the golden stone. The two wolves behind him stood rigid.

My ears swivelled forward.

Mirraclaw spoke solemnly. "Noble King Serren of Bishar Claw, who guards this realm and keeps our peace. Let us pass who are honourable of purpose and pure of heart." He raised his muzzle and walked on. The grey-and-white male started after him, pausing at the golden stone. He echoed Mirraclaw's words.

I glanced back at Cattisclaw.

"You must request permission to pass into the Frozen Fort," she said.

The hairs rose along my neck. *The Frozen Fort.* I wasn't sure I wanted to enter.

16

"Whose permission?"

Cattisclaw's blue eyes bore into mine. "The ancient spirit who protects the entrance."

I looked at the golden stone. Beyond it, Mirraclaw and the grey-and-white were already far ahead. I licked my lips, turning back to Cattisclaw. "I don't know what to say."

The wolf sighed. "Move aside, Fox." She stepped in front of the stone, shooting me a hard look. "Lower your head."

I did as she told me.

Cattisclaw repeated Mirraclaw's words. "Noble King Serren of Bishar Claw, who guards this realm and keeps our peace. Let us pass who are honourable of purpose and pure of heart." She leaned over to me. "On you go, Fox." I noticed that she didn't call me "Fox-ka" like Mirraclaw. I stepped ahead of her once more, and we walked beyond the golden stone between two teeth of rock.

As we padded over the snow, I saw the imprint of fresh paw marks. My whiskers bristled. How many snow wolves lived here? I could already smell them on the frosty air; seven, eight . . . I lost count. Many more than lived in a fox skulk. Was Farraclaw among them?

Jags of ice flanked us as we passed deeper into the snow wolves' territory. Light glanced off them, pearly and bright. The ice stooped over my head into a closed passage – a frozen cave. Shards of reflection shifted around us. I caught the distorted gleam of Mirraclaw's pale back across the ice ceiling as he strode ahead of us. I looked over my shoulder. Another wolf now stood at the golden stone. She watched, her ears pricked.

"Hurry up, Fox-ka!" Up ahead of me, Mirraclaw and the grey-and-white wolf had come to a stop. The white wolf lowered his muzzle in an urgent whisper: "Bow your head at all times. You will address the court with respect. You will not speak, unless invited to do so."

My tail curled around my flank.

"This way," he growled. He started forward.

Cattisclaw gave me a nudge. "You heard Lord Mirraclaw."

I looked at her in desperation. "Please, I just want to see Farraclaw. Why are you bringing me here?"

"You must bow to the prince and the court of Claw," she said. "It is our way. Only later may you talk."

"Later, you'll kill me," I reminded her grimly.

"Perhaps," she said, her blue eyes sparkling.

The smell of wolves grew thick on the air as I followed Mirraclaw along the passageway. Soon, the path before me broadened, rising over my head into a great chamber formed of ice. The sun beat against the frozen dome. The ice hummed with light, with greens and blues, violets and reds. Gazing up I felt giddy, overwhelmed by the colours.

I swallowed, my throat as dry as dust.

I pictured the clear blue water of the stream. I pushed the thought away.

Focus, Isla.

Could foxcraft help me? Should I slimmer? Karak? There was always wa'akkir . . . The Elders had taught me how to shape-shift, but I was exhausted from the journey. Would I have enough maa to change my shape?

I had to hold on to my existing maa, I needed to keep my wits about me.

I drew in my breath as I looked ahead. I knew there were lots of them – had sensed their powerful scents – but the sight of so many wolves made me faint with terror. They settled into rows. They had left a gap in the middle where Mirraclaw now passed, glaring and snapping his teeth. As the white wolf trod between the others, they stiffened. They stared at me, their snouts jabbing the air.

Trembling, I passed between the wolves, avoiding their wild eyes. I tried not to focus on their ragged claws. I tried not to think about their massive fangs.

"Keep walking," whispered Cattisclaw. "Do as Lord Mirraclaw tells you." She fell back to sit along the front row of wolves. Up ahead, the grey-and-white male took his place in the row behind her. Left to follow the white wolf, I was almost sorry to see them go.

Mirraclaw did not turn to look at me. He continued strutting between the wolves until he reached the head of the chamber. His sense of superiority was clear in everything he did – in his raised tail, his set maw, the way in which the other wolves fell back to let him pass. I scrutinized them urgently, seeking the ragged beast I'd met in the Great Snarl. But I could hardly distinguish between them. The wolves were a mass of tensed muscles, broad shoulders and flowing pelts. They all looked in better shape than Farraclaw had.

When Mirraclaw reached the ice wall at the head of the chamber, he turned to address them. "All hail the prince!" he barked.

"All hail the prince!" yelped the wolves. Their voices boomed and my ears flipped back. As one, the wolves lowered themselves to the ground and bowed their heads. Even Mirraclaw dropped to his belly.

Silence filled the chamber. The wolves were still as rock. Between them fell a shadow.

"Bow, Fox-ka," snarled Mirraclaw.

He swiped my back with a huge paw and I slumped to the ground. But I didn't bow my head. If death was coming for me, I would look it in the eye.

I craned my neck. Over the stooped heads of the Bishar, I saw their master. He moved between them with easy dominance. His white coat fell about his shoulders, flecked with silvery grey. He strode on powerful legs, his tail straight behind him. Beauty and power circled him like musk.

The wolf lowered his gaze. His eyes were like the moon. I saw fire there, a bolt of sharp red violence.

"All praise Prince Farraclaw Valiant-Jowl!" barked Mirraclaw.

"Praise!" echoed the wolves.

"Farraclaw?" I gasped. Where his maw had been scabbed and hairless, it was now slick with pale fur. His once scraggy pelt rolled off his shoulders in a glossy mane. His whole body thrummed with maa.

The wolf's ears rotated and he stared at me. His maw relaxed and he spoke. "Isla of the Greylands."

"You know this fox?" spluttered Mirraclaw in surprise.

Farraclaw's eyes never left my face. "How could I forget her? She released me from the beast dens. I owe her my freedom." He cocked his head and his tail gave a wag. "Well, Isla," he said. "You are a long way from the Greylands now. Have you come to claim your debt?"

Light glimmered from the ceiling of the ice chamber. Beneath it, the wolves remained crouched, their bellies low to the ground. But they tilted their heads and watched curiously.

Farraclaw sat before me. I marvelled at his size. If I'd risen on my back paws, I wouldn't have reached his shoulders. "Isla of the Greylands! You have come a long way." His voice was deep. "Where did you find her, Lord Mirraclaw?"

"I was guarding Storm Valley with Lordess Cattisclaw Fierce-Raa and Warrior Norralclaw Raa," said Mirraclaw. "The foxling was lurking in Nirrabar's Cave. She did not even apologize. We were about to execute her for her impudence."

Farraclaw looked at me, not Mirraclaw. "Is that so?"

Fear whispered at the back of my neck. I'd hoped that

22

Farraclaw would protect me after his promise in the Greylands, but that was a long time ago. I hadn't any idea of his status then. How would he act before his Bishar?

Mirraclaw bowed deeply. "We only spared her as she spoke your name, Prince Farraclaw. She said she had a message for you."

"Indeed?" Farraclaw's gaze remained on me.

"I . . ." My voice sounded shrill in the quiet chamber. I sensed the snow wolves craning to hear me. "I'm still looking for my brother."

Farraclaw tipped his muzzle. "The one who went missing. You never found him?"

I ran my tongue over my muzzle. "I've been searching the Wildlands. I went to the Elder Foxes; they're said to be the wisest of my kind. A local skulk helped me, but they were attacked. One of the Elders has gone bad, he's enslaving foxes, turning them against their old skulks." The words came out in a hurried muddle. My tail sank to the ground.

Mirraclaw snorted. "Trouble among the foxes. Sounds serious," he sneered.

"Silence!" barked Farraclaw, catching me off guard. I jumped back, my hairs on end. But the prince's rage wasn't aimed at me. He glared at Mirraclaw. The white wolf collapsed on the ground, his ears pointed out to the sides. Tension rippled over the wolves, palpable in the cool air. No one moved.

Farraclaw's voice was soft now, almost a purr. "Isla, you were saying?"

I glanced at Mirraclaw nervously. The white wolf's head was dipped, his eyes downcast. "I couldn't find Pirie. The Elders told me to search the Snowlands." I met Farraclaw's gaze. "It has to be a wolf. No cub of Canista is greater!"

The prince stared at me in amazement. "You've come here alone?"

"I didn't know what else to do," I said in a quiet voice. "Siffrin was going to join me but he couldn't cross the Raging River."

The snow wolf snorted cheerfully. His great muzzle dropped and I flinched. But he didn't harm me – instead, he gave me a friendly nudge. I could smell his musky scent. "You're quite a brave one, aren't you, Isla?" His tail was wagging. "I do not know how I might help you but I will if I can. A snow wolf never forgets a debt." He raised his head to address the Bishar. "All rise," he commanded.

The wolves leaped up, watching attentively. From the corner of my eye I saw Mirraclaw roll on to his paws and shake out his fur.

Farraclaw gave me a prod. "This young fox is called Isla. She is our guest, a friend to the Bishar of Claw. As you know, the furless caught and entrapped me in their wicked show dens, where many came to gawp at me. In my heart, I died many deaths there, so far from the Snowlands. I would not have survived there much longer."

There were sympathetic whimpers and whines from the Bishar.

"Isla released me, risking her own life for my freedom. I will have her accorded the greatest respect. She may roam our realms, she may take of our kill. Be as a friend to her, and protect her as our own." Farraclaw lifted his muzzle. "One Bishar, united under Queen Canista's Lights. For friendship. For honour. For ever."

"For friendship. For honour. For ever!" echoed the wolves. Their voices boomed in the ice chamber and I flinched.

Farraclaw gave a shake of his grey-speckled mane. "Come greet our guest!"

The Bishar broke from its rigid order. Wolves bounded towards us. I drew in my breath. The sight of so many wolves made my belly clench. But I could see from their wagging tails that they were friendly. They huddled around me, yipping, sniffing, their ears pointing out to the sides.

"Welcome, Isla," they called.

Cattisclaw pressed between them. "A friend of Prince Farraclaw's is a friend to all of us."

I gave a shy wag of my tail. "I guess you don't get to kill me after all."

Cattisclaw yelped in amusement. "Not today," she said

with a twinkle in her eyes.

The wolves shuffled closer, tails thrashing and heads cocked. They closed around me, a mass of pale fur above my head.

"Give the poor fox some air!" said Farraclaw. "You will all have a chance to know her better." The wolves drew back, their tails still thrashing. Farraclaw cocked his head. "You will stay for now, won't you, Isla?"

My tail quivered hopefully. "If that's all right."

"Let me show you around the Bishar so you know where you are, and you can tell me more about your search." He started briskly towards the exit of the chamber and the wolves fell back to let him pass.

"See you later, Isla," said Cattisclaw. She gave me a friendly nudge with her wet nose.

I started after the wolf prince, trotting to keep up. Light was shifting over the chamber. Glaring yellows twisted to green. I glanced among the snow wolves as they whined and growled softly in welcome. They were alive with movement now. It wasn't just that their tails wagged – they leaped up and butted against one another, licking and nudging.

Their cub-like cheer was addictive. I felt my spirits soar. The Snowlands were brutal, but at least I was safe with Farraclaw. Maybe the wolves could help me find Pirie.

As I started to turn, I noticed Mirraclaw. He stood at the head of the chamber, his yellow eyes catching the light. His ears were pricked ahead of him, his tail was stiff. His muzzle wrinkled over a long white fang.

Farraclaw paused at the entrance to the chamber to let me catch up. He looked down on me, head cocked. His golden eyes no longer seemed ferocious – there was warmth in them too.

"Well, well," he said quietly, now that we were out of earshot of the other wolves. "You are a tiny creature, scarcely as large as our pups. Small but mighty." His voice told me he was teasing me, but not entirely. There was admiration there too.

"Are there cubs in the Bishar at the moment?" I asked.

"Oh yes," said Farraclaw. "Four beautiful pups." His tail lifted with pride. "Do you want to meet them?"

I wasn't entirely sure I liked the idea of giant cubs. They might not be as quick to listen to the prince's commands as the adult wolves had been. But it seemed rude to say no. "All right," I murmured. "Is your mate in the Bishar?"

"My mate?" Farraclaw threw me a sideways look. Then understanding crossed his face and his tail started wagging. "Oh, they're not mine!"

"They aren't?"

"Of course not! Only the king and queen have pups. Though we all adore the little ones so much, it's almost as though they are ours too." Farraclaw started striding again. I hurried to keep up. He led me along the ice passage, taking a turn I hadn't noticed before. I could smell the rich scent of snow wolves marking the route, but over them was Farraclaw's musk. His dominance was etched into earth beneath our paws and the cool, silent walls. I sensed no greater wolf, no stronger maa.

"I thought . . ." I frowned, remembering how Farraclaw had commanded the whole Bishar. "Aren't you the leader?"

His maw grew tense and he looked serious. For a while, he didn't speak as he led me into the open, to a forest of aspens. Their silvery trunks shimmered against new snowfall. He stopped at the first tree and bowed, murmuring some words I didn't catch. Then he padded between the trees, sniffing deeply. "This is Claw Weald. It runs around the northern stretch of our territory."

I heard a high-pitched yip, the alarm call of a small creature. Scanning the branches, I spotted fur and small dark eyes. The creature hovered on the tree trunk, squeaking.

My belly rumbled. "Is this where you hunt?" I asked.

"Here?" Farraclaw frowned. "No . . . Our prey would never dare come this close. We have to travel to find the best kill."

"But there's prey here," I said, confused.

The snow wolf followed my gaze to the squeaking creature in the aspen. He snorted, steam rising from his black nose. "We do not chase tree rats!" His tail started wagging.

"Oh, Fox, how different we are."

I remembered that he'd mocked me in the Great Snarl. I puffed out my chest proudly. "There's nothing wrong with them!"

"Better than feasting on furless waste, I suppose," said Farraclaw. Seeing my expression, he grew more serious. "Do not take my teasing to heart, young fox. The Bishar would starve to death in no time if we tried to fill our bellies with scampering things. There is room for many creatures in our beautiful world." He gave me a shove with his nose, and I nudged him back, mollified.

I still had a lot to learn about wolves. I remembered the small wildway near my old den, where Ma, Fa and Greatma had found most of our food. "Where do you hunt?"

"Wherever our prey may be found." Farraclaw paused. "Provided that's in the Bishar of Claw. Follow me, I'll explain."

He trod a path through the aspens, his paws leaving giant prints in the snow. After a while, the space between the trees grew wider. The earth rose upward beneath our paws. We were making for an outcrop of large black rocks. "Up here, I can look out over the Bishar. I come here to think."

"Alone?" I asked.

"Usually. The rest of the Bishar may only join at my command, or on the word of the king or queen."

I stopped. "Were the king and queen in the Frozen Fort?"

Farraclaw looked beyond me towards the pale aspens. "No." He turned and climbed the outcrop. I began to follow, scrambling over the wide-spaced stones. They sparkled with ice and my paws slipped as I fought to find purchase.

The wolf had already bounded to the top of the outcrop and was peering down at me. Balanced alone on the dark rocks, he looked even more majestic, his grey-tipped coat stark against the sky. "Do you need help?" he barked.

"I'm all right," I said quickly, determined to make it up the rocks on my own. At least the wolf was good enough to look away as I slid on the stones. At last, I reached the top to rest at Farraclaw's side. From here, I could see the borders of Claw Weald, the Frozen Fort and the golden stone where Mirraclaw, Cattisclaw and Norralclaw had asked permission to pass. The tundra rolled out in stretches of white.

Farraclaw looked towards it, allowing me to catch my breath. "You are searching for your brother. I have known the terrible wrench of loss. I was torn from this land by the furless, thrown in a cage for their amusement. I would have died there." He turned to me with blazing eyes. "A brave fox saved me. Isla, know that there is nothing I wouldn't do to help you."

I shifted beneath his bold gaze. "Do you remember what I said in the Snarl? 'A fox is lost to the Elders, beyond the fur and sinew of the greatest of Canista's cubs.' It's the only clue I have."

His ears twisted. "What does it mean?"

My tail crept to my flank. "I wish I knew." *Why didn't I ask the Elders to explain when I had the chance?*

"You mentioned a Wildlands skulk. Yet you came here alone."

I sighed, my tail creeping to my side. "They were good to me. They took me in, along with Siffrin and Haiki."

"Other foxes?"

I dipped my head in acknowledgement. "I met Siffrin in the Great Snarl. He's a messenger of the Elders. I didn't trust him at first . . . but I was wrong."

Farraclaw tilted his head to watch me. "What happened to him?"

"He's still in the Wildlands. Safe . . . I hope. There are so many Taken there."

Farraclaw's ears rotated. "Taken?"

"Dead-eyed foxes, slaves to the Mage, an Elder who broke from the others and uses his foxcraft for wicked ends. He is building an army of foxes, sapping their will. Draining their maa."

The wolf frowned. "Is that the same as maha?"

"What do you mean?" I asked.

"It is the essence of all things. It is the water that runs through the Raging River, the force that makes the blizzard rise, the grass grow, the rain fall. It is the light that shines from the stars. A great warrior bursts with maha. When he or she has passed, it dissolves. It becomes part of the great whole, rejoining the earth and the air."

"That sounds like maa," I said, though I'd never thought of where maa came from, or where it went when someone died.

He inclined his head. "You spoke of two foxes. Siffrin and another. A friend?"

"Haiki." My ears twitched. There was something about Farraclaw's frank, bold manner that demanded frankness in return. "I thought he was but he tricked me. He was spying on me for the Mage, using me to get to the Elders." My tail bristled and I gave it a shake. A shadow passed over my thoughts and I stared at the tundra, no longer seeing it. I didn't want to talk about Haiki.

Farraclaw seemed to understand. He turned his attention on the view. "Most of what you see now is in the Bishar of Claw. Wolves are territorial. For us, it is all about family – for what is a Bishar if not our brothers and sisters, cousins, elders and pups?"

His husky voice was soothing. I relaxed and listened.

"Life in the frozen realms isn't easy. We are at the mercy of the wind and ice, at the will of our ancestors. We look out for one another."

I craned my neck, trying to catch a glimpse of the Raging River. I could just make out a blur of blue. "Are there other families in the Snowlands? Other Bishars?"

"Oh yes," said Farraclaw darkly. "Look to the sunrise

and you'll reach Growl Wood. There our territory ends, and the reign of the Bishar of Growl begins. It is ruled by Queen Ravengrowl. Her lands are humble but not without benefits. The Bishar faces the sea so their pups can practise hunting with seabirds and feast on eggs every day. Our pups aren't spoiled like that." He turned his head. "Now look the other way." Farraclaw's ears pricked forward and his whiskers flexed. "Beyond those low trees lies the Bishar of Fang. Our old enemies. If a member of our Bishar meets one of theirs, only one will walk away alive."

The hair trembled at the back of my neck.

Farraclaw went on. "Their territory is rich in fresh pools, and it is crossed by bison in their search for grasses. But much is inhospitable. Even a snow wolf would think twice about venturing on to the White Mountains, or the Ice Razors in the far west. There are few trees in the Bishar of Fang, few places to hide or take shelter. It makes the hunting much tougher. How can you surprise your prey when they can see you coming?"

I looked beyond the low trees. I could see clouds of blue spiralling into the air. "What's that smoke?"

"The land there is torn, and heat bleeds from the wounds."

I blinked at him. I had never heard of anything like that. I drew my gaze over the vast horizon. The sun was high overhead, a pulsing globe of orange.

I wondered what the hot, torn earth looked like up close. "Have you ever been there?"

"We do not enter their territory, and they do not cross into ours. The Bishar of Claw is the strongest in the Snowlands. We respect our ancestors and the ancient laws that govern the wolves. To enter Fang without reason or provocation would be a challenge. It would almost certainly end in bloodshed. It could lead to war."

A confrontation between so many snow wolves was a frightening thought. "You'd beat them, wouldn't you, Farraclaw?" I couldn't imagine any wolf fiercer than him.

"The bilberry does not speak of its own sweetness," he said with a puzzling flex of the whiskers. "And it mightn't be up to me."

"I thought Claw was strongest?"

"Things changed when I was in the beast dens. King Birronclaw fell ill . . ." His voice dropped. "Word must never reach Fang or Growl. King Orrùfang is brutish and cruel, but beneath it, he is a coward. He would never challenge a healthy wolf. But if he ever found out about our king . . . Our lands command the best hunting spots – long have they watched us with envy. Under the ancient laws that govern the Bishars, a king may lay claim to enemy lands – he may demand to fight the neighboring king. If his challenge succeeds, or his rival cannot fight, the Bishar falls." Farraclaw's muzzle wrinkled. "Do you know the first thing they'd do if they seized our realms?" He turned to me, his eyes burning. "They'd kill the pups. Stamp out the bloodline."

My belly flipped. It was so barbaric. "But you wouldn't, would you, Farraclaw? You wouldn't do the same to them?"

He held my gaze a beat. "I'd do what I had to." His ears pricked and he rose abruptly. "See that dark mass? It's bison."

I'd never heard of bison and wasn't sure what I was looking for. I spotted a large number of creatures trudging along the snow to an outcrop of bushes at the edge of Growl Wood.

Farraclaw rose to his paws. "Come. I promised you pups. Then I will call together the Bishar once more. The bison are on the move. Amarog must consult with the stars this night."

I wasn't sure what this meant. "Don't you make the decisions?" I asked, following Farraclaw down the icy rocks.

"I make *some* decisions," said Farraclaw carefully.

As I reached the base of the rocky outcrop, I caught a last glance of the Bishar of Fang. The blue steam was a distant swirl. "What happened between Claw and Fang to make them enemies?"

Farraclaw sighed. "Our king killed theirs when they were both young, in a skirmish over a stag carcass. They say the slain King Garrùfang's spirit haunts their realms, that he has cursed the wolves of Claw." Farraclaw dipped his head. "May the fallen rest in the peace of the forest."

"Where is the king of Claw?" I asked. "Where's the queen?"

"Queen Sableclaw is with the pups. She used to be our best hunter but she has lost interest in the Bishar. The change in the king . . . It hasn't been easy on her." He padded on to the soft snow, and I started after him.

I knew it wasn't my business, but curiosity tugged at my whiskers. "What's wrong with him?"

Farraclaw paused midstep. "King Birronclaw was the greatest wolf in the Snowlands: huge, powerful, potent in maha. The largest wolf in all the frozen realms." Farraclaw sighed. "I do not wish to speak ill of our leader; I revere and honour him." His face was troubled. "Sometimes maha fades, even in the living. A sickness takes hold, the mind becomes weak . . . The king is not as he once was."

"How did it happen?" I asked, wondering what Farraclaw meant.

He didn't answer me directly. "I had a terrible feeling, back at the beast dens. I knew the Bishar was in danger."

"But you're here now," I pointed out. "If you became king, the Bishar would be safe from attack."

Farraclaw turned his yellow eyes on me. The dark outlines made him look fearsome again. His voice was low, almost a snarl. "You must never let anyone hear you say that. Every wolf swore an oath to King Birronclaw. While he lives, I will not challenge him. All hail King Birronclaw Valiant-Oolf, Lord Protector of the Bishar of Claw, High Commander of the Snowlands." He set his jaw, looking into the distance.

"The Bishar comes first, under moon and sun. For friendship. For honour. For ever."

We padded back through Claw Weald in silence, veering westward with the sun. I could hear the yelp of wolves up ahead and my tail stiffened instinctively. Farraclaw glanced at me. "You have no need to fear."

He had ordered the wolves to treat me as a friend. Was he really so sure they would all obey him? I took in his profile and the set of his jaw. Confidence rose from his fur.

He doesn't doubt it for a second.

The yelps and snarls grew louder. A moment later, we reached a clearing. Two wolves were sparring in the snow as a circle of others surrounded them. The spectators were baying, alive with excitement. There must have been eight or nine wolves there, not quite half of the Bishar. With a crackle of unease I was reminded of the confrontation between Siffrin and the coyote chief, back in the Wildlands. The

38

wolves didn't look so different. They were like giant, magnificent coyotes. Their eyes gleamed, their jaws gaped.

But this time the fight was in play.

I recognized one as Norralclaw, the grey-and-white wolf who had found me with Mirraclaw and Cattisclaw. The other was a warrior called Rattisclaw. He had brown fur and a creamy belly.

"Lazy rat, you can't catch me!" snarled Norralclaw, squaring up to the brown wolf.

His opponent sprang at him, and Norralclaw rolled out of the way in a froth of white snow. "Too slow, Ratty." He stretched out on his belly and raised a forepaw. He started gnawing at a split claw, as though entirely untroubled.

Rattisclaw fell back on his haunches. "You'll pay for calling me that!" he growled. The brown wolf noticed me and Farraclaw. He dipped his muzzle in acknowledgement and his posture stiffened as he grew more focused. The other wolves bowed briefly before returning their attention to the fight.

Farraclaw padded between them and settled down to watch. I hung a few paces back. Already, Rattisclaw was charging at Norralclaw. The brown wolf brought the grey-and-white down with a thud, snapping his huge fangs around his neck. "Who are you calling a rat?"

Norralclaw squeezed his eyes shut, drew himself into a tight ball, and bucked, sending the brown wolf tumbling.

The wolves around him yelped in support of one side or another, their tails lashing. "Kick him, Norralclaw!" or "Watch your paw, Rattisclaw!"

Farraclaw turned to me. "Come, Isla."

Reluctantly, I padded to his side.

"Such mock fights are an important part of keeping up our hunting skills. When the pups are a little older, they will watch the fights daily. Then they themselves will be expected to spar." His ears twisted forward. "The whole Bishar will be here for the pups' first fight. It's not to be missed."

I thought of Pirie. Back in the Great Snarl we had often chased each other, though our play fights were more about who was faster and the occasional sharp nip. I watched the wolves, the power and breathlessness of their clashes. The force behind their paws and their muscular forelegs, the strength in their huge jaws. I knew they could really hurt each other.

Norralclaw pinned Rattisclaw to the ground, winning the tussle. They both fell back to the whoops and barks of the watching wolves. They licked each other's muzzles and bumped shoulders with good humour. Unharmed, they turned to Farraclaw with quick bows. Then they shifted position and dipped their heads again. To my surprise, I realized they were bowing at me.

"A good fight," said Farraclaw with pleasure. He rose to his paws. "Come, Isla. The pup den is along the stream."

"Send our greetings to the pups!" said Norralclaw. "Tell them we'll catch them a feast. They can have some juicy loin."

As we started padding away, I heard Norralclaw snarl. "Dog, come over here a minute."

I looked over my shoulder. The white-and-grey flashed his teeth at a wolf I hadn't noticed before. He was snow white like Mirraclaw, but unlike him he had skinny legs and a slim tail. He was smaller than the others, only reaching Norralclaw's shoulders. But the most striking thing about him was his ears – they flopped down at each side of his head, instead of pointing upward.

Norralclaw was watching this strange-looking wolf. "Maybe I'll fight *you* next time."

Rattisclaw padded to Norralclaw's side. "What do you say, Dog?" He dragged his claws over the snow. "Wouldn't you like to fight a warrior?"

A couple of the other wolves started growling.

"Fight!" barked the black-snouted wolf. "Go on, Dog-ka, let's see you fight!"

"Fight!" echoed the others.

The floppy-eared wolf stooped low to the ground. "I'm afraid I wouldn't give you much sport." He threw his fore-paws on the snow in a play bow. "Maybe another sort of game." He started prancing, then turned a small circle around the wolves. They yipped and whined in amusement.

"What a fool," snipped Rattisclaw, but his tail was wagging.

"There are berries in the trees!" yelped the floppy-eared wolf. "Bet you can't get them before I do!"

"Rubbish!" barked Norralclaw. "Any one of us could out-run you!"

The floppy-eared wolf started capering about, slipping clumsily over the snow. The other wolves barked in amusement. Then he scrambled to his paws and started running towards the aspens. He was much faster than I'd expected. The wolves broke into a chase. I watched them zigzag among the trees. "Isla?" Farraclaw was standing a few paces ahead. "Aren't you coming?"

I hesitated. "Who was that wolf with the floppy ears?"

"Oh." Farraclaw looked bored, and was already starting again towards the stream. "That's just Lop-ka."

"Why did they call him 'Dog'?"

"Because of those ugly, misshapen ears."

"They were all chasing him."

"In sport," said Farraclaw dismissively. "Don't worry about Lop. He's nobody, the under-wolf."

"*Under-wolf*?" My ears swivelled as I looked back between the aspens. There was no sign of the wolves any more. Their yips had faded on the sharp air. "What do you mean?"

"He's no warrior," said Farraclaw, a hint of repulsion in

his words. He picked up pace and I bounded to catch up. It was clear that the subject was closed.

Farraclaw padded along the edge of a tall ridge of rock that ran along a lake. The bank was frozen, a hard shell of frosted white hanging over the water. But further in, I saw ripples and large numbers of long-necked birds.

It seemed to have grown colder as the day progressed. A sheath of ice crept over the snow.

"Does it ever get warm here?" I asked.

"Too cold for your liking?" Farraclaw's tail gave a swish. "By the Eve of the Maha some of the snow will have melted. Flowers and fruit cover the land, at least up here – the Storm Valley remains unpredictable. We prefer the snow, though. The bison are hungry and tired . . . the hunting is better."

"The Eve of the Maha?" I asked, cocking my head.

The prince's eyes grew thoughtful. "A special time, when the Bishar reflects on those who have gone before. Our warrior ancestors, the heroes, the fallen . . ." His voice drifted. "It comes at the longest day of the year, drawing to a peak as the light fades."

"That's the gloaming!" I realized. "It means something to foxes too." I knew that from the Elders, though I wasn't really sure *why* it was so important.

We neared two wolves who stood guard at the edge of the rock. "Warrior Briarclaw, Warrior Thistleclaw," said

Farraclaw. They bowed deeply.

As we passed the guards, my ears flicked forward. I'd heard a high-pitched squeak.

Farraclaw heard it too. "The pups!" His tail gave an excited wag. He led me along the rock to a small valley with low trees. I could already make out movement down there, clutches of beige fur. Farraclaw turned to me, his expression serious. "The queen may be close," he murmured beneath his breath. "She remains our leader, even if she's lost the will to rule. You must offer her respect."

I didn't know what this meant. Was I expected to bow? To stand in silence while Farraclaw presented me? I didn't have time to ask. Farraclaw was already bounding towards the small trees.

The pups must have picked up our scent. They tumbled out from among the trees, yelping and shrilling. "Prince Farraclaw! Prince Farraclaw!" they cried, converging on him. They sprang on his paws, nipping and tussling, leaping up to snap at his tail. He licked their soft faces. "Who's this, Prince Farraclaw?" They turned their dark blue eyes on me.

"This is my friend, Isla. She's a fox from the Greylands."

The pups stared at me in wonder. One, who was grey, padded up to me boldly. She was almost as tall as I was. "Isla, do you have snow where you come from?"

I thought of the day when the sky had rained wisps and

the earth had swallowed the sun beneath ice. "A bit." I looked around. The tundra stretched in all directions, like a great white hide. "Nothing like this."

"Is it hot?" asked another pup, releasing Farraclaw's tail.

"Not hot . . . or it wasn't when I left. Warmer than it is here, though I guess that's not saying much."

Farraclaw nodded at each pup in turn. "That's Gallin, Dorrel, Lupin." He turned to the bold, grey-faced pup. "And this here is Jaspin. They're too young for full titles."

Jaspin poked her snout in my face. "What's a fox?"

"She doesn't look very strong," yipped Dorrel.

"Not as strong as us," agreed Lupin, tensing his stumpy legs.

Farraclaw caught my eye. "Foxes are strong in different ways."

"You need brawn to catch prey!" yipped Gallin. "Like me!" He bumped Jaspin off her paws and she bit him on the leg. "Ouch!" he cried.

It wasn't long ago that I was playing with Pirie like that, back in the Snarl. I felt the fizz of maa in my blood. Perhaps I had recovered from my exhaustion. "I have other skills," I said silkily. I started to chant. "What was seen is unseen; what was sensed becomes senseless . . ."

"What's she doing?" muttered Jaspin, rolling on to her paws.

"I don't know," said Farraclaw. "It must be a fox thing."

I could tell from his tone that he thought I was playing. I knew he liked me – I had proven myself in his eyes. But he didn't have much respect for my kind.

"Now you see me," I murmured. "And now . . ." I drew in my breath.

The pups whined. "The fox . . . she's gone!"

From the corner of my vision, I saw Farraclaw stiffen. "Isla!" It was easier to focus through the slimmer than it used to be, easier to hold it. I backed away from Farraclaw and the pups, silent as air, slipping between some ragged foliage.

"The grass moved!" gasped Dorrel, craning her neck towards me.

Releasing my breath, I flickered back to visibility.

Farraclaw stared at me. "By Queen Canista," he murmured.

The pups yipped and hopped about in excitement.

"She was there all the time!"

"She was invisible!"

"Can you teach us how you did that, Isla? Can you? *Please?*"

Their good humour was infectious. "Maybe," I said, cocking my head at them.

They capered around me. They must have been very young, despite almost matching me in size. Jaspin, the dark grey-faced pup, gave me a playful thump with her forepaw and I stumbled. The pups were small, but they were already stronger than me.

"Careful," rebuked Farraclaw.

"I'm all right," I said quickly, giving myself a shake.

Jaspin panted cheerfully, her short tail wagging. "I'm sorry. I've never met a fox before. You're amazing!" The pups pressed together, shunting one another out of the way, their small ears pricked up. Longing tightened in my chest as I thought of Pirie. I felt older now, weighed down by all I'd seen since my family disappeared.

"How have you been?" asked Farraclaw. "Dorrel, you're looking a bit bony. You need feeding up!"

"Yes, please!" yipped Dorrel and the other pups joined in. "We're hungry!"

I saw movement beyond the small trees. A lean, off-white wolf appeared. Her dark-rimmed eyes were round. "My Prince Farraclaw," she said softly with a dip of the muzzle.

Farraclaw bowed deeply. "I was introducing my fox friend, Isla, to the pups." He nodded at me, clearly intending to say more, but the queen hardly looked at him. She ignored me completely. Her attention was on Dorrel.

"It's time to come inside, pups," said the queen. "Rest now. You've played enough."

"But Prince Farraclaw's arrived!" whined Jaspin, as the others joined in. "He brought Isla and she just turned herself invisible! Don't you think she should teach us?"

"Come inside, pups," the queen repeated. Her voice was weary, without a ma's authority. The pups scarcely seemed to hear her. She craned her neck, peering beyond us into the tundra. "It's dangerous out there."

I remembered what Farraclaw had said. If neighboring Bishars attacked, they'd kill the pups first.

"How long will you be here, Isla?" asked Jaspin.

Lupin's eyes widened. "Are you going to join the Bishar?"

"Will you come and see us again?"

"You heard the queen," said Farraclaw. He gave the pups a hard look.

Reluctantly, the wolf pups padded away. I saw them slip between the trees in a den dug under a bush. The queen watched them go.

"You look well," said Farraclaw. It was blatantly untrue. Queen Sableclaw was scrawny. Her eyes were sunken in her long face.

"It's all right for you to come and go as you please, exciting and exhausting them." It was the first time I'd heard any wolf speak to Farraclaw without respect. The wolf queen looked exhausted. "The pups are hungry. My milk no longer sustains them. They need meat."

"And they shall have it," said Farraclaw mildly. He opened his mouth to say more but the queen had already turned to the den and was slinking off, her shoulder blades sharp beneath her fur. Farraclaw glanced at me. His golden eyes were troubled. "I must call the Bishar together," he said to me, padding away from the pup den. "What you did earlier . . ." he began.

"It's a type of foxcraft," I explained. "Slimmering."

Farraclaw didn't answer. We climbed along the edge of the rock in silence. When he reached the top, he threw back his head and howled. The tundra rang with his powerful call.

The sun was setting over the snow by the time we reached the ice chamber. Deep orange touched its western wall as wolves padded inside. The familiar fear crept down my back but the wolves were friendly, greeting me with wagging tails before taking their positions. Only Mirraclaw looked at me coolly as I approached at Farraclaw's side.

"Prince Farraclaw," he murmured with a bow. He didn't acknowledge me.

Farraclaw nudged me with his great muzzle. "Sit by Lordess Cattisclaw," he said. "I must speak to the Bishar." I did as I was told, joining Cattisclaw at the front row of the gathered wolves. She gave me a friendly lick on the ear. Farraclaw dipped his head towards Mirraclaw in a shallow bow and turned to face the Bishar.

"Friends, I have called you here because the bison are on the move. The thaw may have started in the Bishar of Growl, but it has not yet reached our lands. Soon the bison will journey west in search of grasses. Once they cross to the Bishar of Fang, they are lost to us. We must not tarry."

The other wolves murmured in agreement.

"It has not snowed since this morning. The mountains offer us protection from the wind – our scents will not travel. Conditions are perfect. It is time to hunt!"

A roar exploded in the chamber.

Farraclaw raised his muzzle. He called over the wolves. "Amarog the Wise, what say you?"

The wolves fell silent, their ears twisting. I could hear the shuffle of paws, the stiffening of tails. I waited, not knowing what to expect. Then I heard the scratch of ragged claws. The hairs bristled along my brush and I looked around. The sound was growing louder, drawing closer.

Then I saw her.

Amarog had unusually long fur and a tousled mane of pigeon grey. It fell about her face in frazzled knots. From these hung dried berries, small green leaves and jagged burrs, as though she'd been rolling in bushes. Her claws were as long as talons, dirty and unkempt. A tangy odour clung to her fur of herbs and strange vines. I could hardly tell she was a wolf – it was almost as though the forest had come to life, as though it was loping through the chamber.

I shivered, backing against Cattisclaw as the strange wolf approached, the small leaves and berries tinkling at her mane. "Prince Farraclaw Valiant-Jowl," she said with a bow.

There were silvery twigs in her tail. "Three days and nights have I walked with the dead," she said. "Three days and nights have I fasted, taking neither water nor food." The wolves watched her intently. Silently. Reverently. "The ancestors have spoken." Her body quivered slightly, as though she was suffering a fever. "Spirits circle the clouds; they stalk the night. We must leave them to their sorrow. At dawn I shall walk the edges of the Taku Grounds. I will wait for an answer, but I will not beseech them. For all in life and death has its time, and they alone know of which they speak. No blood may be claimed until the moon is an icicle in a river sky!"

She raised her head, her eyes rolling backward a moment to reveal the whites. Then she lowered her muzzle and turned sharply to look straight at me. One of her eyes was bright green – the other was brown. "Who are you?" Her tangled mane fluttered as she spoke. The tremble in her limbs grew more pronounced, with excitement or fear, I couldn't tell. "I have seen a tormented shadow racing over the hills. Was it you who watched like the black-eyed skua? Who would pierce the sacred flesh?"

My blood turned to ice.

Farraclaw took a step towards her, but he stopped short of touching the tousled wolf. "Amarog the Wise," he began. "The pups are hungry. The queen's milk no longer sustains them."

The strange wolf replied without shifting her gaze from my face. "Our ancestors have spoken. Till the river sky! There will be *no* hunt tonight."

5

Sleep wrapped its pelt around me. Memories surged through the stream of my thoughts. I saw my old den, back in the Great Snarl. The hollow beyond the copse was thatched with twigs. I stretched comfortably and rose to my paws. Greatma was curled up next to us, still sleeping. Ma and Fa were out hunting. Being careful to tread lightly, so as not to wake Greatma, I crept out of the den.

The air was damp and dark. I could hear the cackle of furless out on the deathway, and the ceaseless growl of manglers. The brightglobes weren't shining in the furless den that towered over our patch. The ginger tomcat hovered on the wooden fence that edged the yard. His eyes gleamed suspiciously.

I needed to be quick. If Greatma woke up or Ma and Fa came home, they'd be angry to find me out of the den.

They worry too much.

I wasn't planning to *go* anywhere. I wouldn't even be leaving our patch.

I looked back at the den, my tail twitching guiltily. Brothers and sisters were supposed to share everything, and usually we did. But this was mine. At least for now, until I improved. I needed to practise when no one was watching. Then I'd be ready to share what I'd learned.

The secret was not to hurry. If you rushed, it wouldn't work – I knew that from experience. I drew in a slow breath. I closed my eyes against the night. The manglers were never silent, grumbling along the deathway. I could hear the pulsing of furless songs. I let out my breath and the sounds melted away. A faint beat rose from the soil, tingling through my paw pads. My heart fell into step with the beat. There were other sounds too, like the tinkling of water in a stream.

I opened my eyes and the world had changed. My paws were gossamer, faded from view. The furless den was a hunching purple blur. The yard was a swirling mass of greens. An amber glow hung over my head.

My eyes trailed over the fence where the cat still watched. Only his eyes were visible. A yowl rose in his throat and he sprang off the fence, into the neighboring yard.

A deep calm washed over me. The sky had cleared above our patch. Canista's Lights were white against black.

The secret had been hiding inside me from the

beginning. It thrummed at my muscles. It tickled my whiskers and shot through my tail.

I was different.

The colours, the voices. The beat of the earth.

The power.

"What are you doing?"

I whipped around. The colours were gone in an instant. The beat faded against my paws. Greatma was staring at me, muzzle strained. She glanced beyond me, into the dark patch. I caught something in her face I hadn't seen before.

Fear.

"Come into the den," she urged.

Her look was unnerving. "I was only playing." I wondered how much to tell her – how much she'd seen. "I can do stuff," I mumbled. "Make myself invisible. Hear the earth speak. See the air shift."

Greatma's tail clung to her flank. "Isla is sound asleep, and you should be sleeping too." Greatma slipped out of the den, padding towards me. "Pirie," she whispered. "I worry for you. I worry for us all."

"But why?" She was beginning to scare me.

She shook her head. "Your maa," she began.

I looked back at the den. I pictured Isla with her head on her forepaws, her tail wrapped around her. Suddenly, all I wanted was to go back to the den, to curl up against her and go to sleep.

I ran my tongue over my muzzle. "What do you mean, Greatma?" I asked reluctantly.

"Your gift," she whispered. "I'm scared of your gift."

I awoke with a deep unease. Had it been a dream, or something more? A memory . . . *Pirie's memory*. Could he really have kept secrets from me? My only brother, who could speak through my thoughts. Whose heart beat with my own.

I blinked into the darkness at the sprawling wolves. I had expected Farraclaw to have his own den, as the leader of the Bishar. Instead, he slept in a shallow trench at the edge of Claw Weald. The other wolves surrounded him, not quite touching.

Curled against Farraclaw's belly, I was cosy and warm. His pelt was so thick, nothing like Pirie's fuzzy hair, with its patchwork of ginger, white and grey. Pirie had the softest fur.

I peered around the sleeping Bishar. I had a sense I was watching more than a jumble of wolves. It was almost as though they were one creature. A great wolf.

A fox is lost to the Elders, beyond the fur and sinew of the greatest of Canista's cubs.

My ears flicked back with a start. Is that what the Elders had meant? Was I looking for more than one wolf?

I shuffled upright for a better view. Farraclaw stretched, his eyes still shut. I looked around the sleeping bodies. Cattisclaw was a tail's length away. Mirraclaw lay to the other side of Farraclaw. Norralclaw and Rattisclaw were further away from the centre of the huddle, with Lop at the edge, where there was less shelter from the wind. The white fur fluttered along his back. It struck me that the higher-ranking wolves were enclosed in the middle, where it was warmer.

The black pelt of the sky revealed countless stars. It took me a long time to untangle Canista's Lights nestled among them. When I did, I felt a strange tug at my chest. I longed to reach out to Pirie through gerra-sharm. Surely it was safe here, so far from the Mage and his army of Taken? And yet . . .

The icy chill crept under my fur.

I paused, watching the wolves more closely. Amarog wasn't here. Remembering how Farraclaw had stopped short of touching her, I guessed that the strange wolf slept alone. The memory of her gaze made my heart beat faster. She'd spoken as though she knew me.

I have seen a tormented shadow racing over the hills. Was it you who watched like the black-eyed skua?

She seemed crazy, but the other wolves did as she told them.

The queen wasn't here either. She would be with the pups in the pup den. There were so many wolves, but I suddenly realized who else was missing.

My ears flicked back. Where was the king? If he was sick, shouldn't he be surrounded by his kind, protected from the wind? Safe in the centre of the huddle?

The king was the largest wolf in all the frozen realms – that's what Farraclaw had said.

The greatest of Canista's cubs.

I glanced down to see Farraclaw watching me with one yellow eye.

"Can't you sleep?" he whispered.

"I need you to do something for me," I replied. "It's important."

"Anything," said the prince of Claw.

"I need to speak with the king. Will you take me to him?"

Farraclaw opened his mouth in surprise. He glanced at the other wolves. In the faint light of the stars I saw a shadow pass his face. "Tomorrow," he said at last. Then he lowered his head and went back to sleep.

A fizzle of snow touched my nose. I opened my eyes. A grey fog in the distance hinted at dawn. Already, the wolves were rising and shaking out their coats.

My belly growled – I hadn't eaten since I'd left the Wildlands. I wondered when the wolves had last fed. How long did they go between meals? Yet none of them had challenged Amarog when she told them not to hunt. Not even Farraclaw.

The wolves stretched and yawned in silence.

"Oh no, snow again!" Lop's voice rang out over the

wolves. They cocked their heads, turned amused faces his way. The floppy-eared wolf capered around the others, dodging the snowflakes. It was impossible to miss them, of course – the snow came down too quickly – but his loping dives were funny. I watched, tail swishing, as he pounced into the air sideways, dropped to the ground, and rolled on his back.

The other wolves started woofing.

"Like this!" barked Cattisclaw, stretching out her long legs and trotting after Lop.

"No, no, more like this," said Norralclaw. He reared on to his hind legs and staggered along the den, wobbling badly until he smacked into Rattisclaw. The brown-furred wolf nudged his leg and they briefly scuffled before Norralclaw rested his head against Rattisclaw's shoulder then licked his nose.

The Bishar became energetic, eyes bright and tails swishing.

Farraclaw panted cheerfully. The mood in the den was lifting.

I heard a snort. Mirraclaw was glaring at Lop. "What foolishness," he snarled. As the floppy-eared wolf gambolled past him, the white wolf snapped at his flank.

Lop shrank back, his tail still wagging. "I'm sorry, Lord Mirraclaw."

Mirraclaw lifted his maw, towering over the floppy-eared wolf. "Stay out of my way, *Dog.*"

I glanced at Farraclaw. He was gnawing at his forepaw. The other wolves suddenly found other things to do.

No one spoke up for Lop.

Under-wolf.

Farraclaw beckoned a grey. "Warrior Lyrinclaw, relieve Warrior Briarclaw at the pup den."

The wolf dipped her head. "Yes, Prince Farraclaw." She turned and hurried away.

"Lord Mirraclaw, take Warrior Thistleclaw and Warrior Rattisclaw to patrol the west. If the bison reenter Growl, I want to know about it."

"Of course, Prince Farraclaw," said Mirraclaw with a bow.

Cattisclaw approached Farraclaw as Mirraclaw was stalking away. "Prince Farraclaw, shall I watch the eastern border?"

"Yes," he replied. "Take Warrior Norralclaw. Watch for any incursions. I don't trust the Bishar of Fang or their jealous king."

"We will, Sire." Cattisclaw lifted her muzzle and met Farraclaw's eye. I saw something pass between them before she tugged her gaze away.

The other wolves started to leave. They hurried past Lop without sparing him a glance.

"This way, Isla." Farraclaw led me away. When we neared Lop, I saw the wound where Mirraclaw had bitten him. The white wolf had drawn blood.

60

As we approached the pup den, the queen was already waiting.

Her eyes were red, and I wondered if she'd slept. "The pups are hungry," she began.

"I know," said Farraclaw quietly. "Amarog has consulted with the ancestors."

The queen ran a tongue over her muzzle. "Dorrel could hardly rise this morning."

I heard a peeping from the den. "Is that Prince Farraclaw?" came a high-pitched yelp. "Is Isla with him?"

Jaspin, Gallin and Lupin tumbled out of the den. Dorrel followed them, her tail wagging. They capered around me and Farraclaw. The queen fell back, her expression stern.

"Prince Farraclaw, are you going hunting soon?"

"Will Isla come too?"

"Can she teach us to slimmer?"

They bumped against me, nipping and licking. They were stronger than foxes, their touch clumsier. Yet they reminded me of Pirie.

"Isla, we hoped you'd come. Will you show us how to do that trick?"

I nudged them back. "Maybe I'll teach you to karak first."

"What's that?"

"Is it foxcraft?"

"Oh yes," I said. "Would you like to know how to caw like a bird? Or . . . or bark like a dog?"

"A dog?" yipped one of the wolves.

"We don't get dogs here!"

"Are they fierce?"

"Are they scary?"

I remembered the wiry dogs I'd encountered in the Wildlands. "Not compared with wolves. Though you're all scary from a fox's point of view!"

"Not us, though," yipped Jaspin. "You're not scared of us?"

I wagged my brush. It looked ridiculously long compared with their short, skinny tails. "Of course not! Well, not till you're grown-up!" I tried to picture them as large and fierce as Mirraclaw. The thought disturbed me. Jaspin, Gallin and Lupin sprang around me, a frenzy of excitement. Only Dorrel held back. She crouched behind the others. Her large eyes looked sunken. The bones stuck out along her back.

Farraclaw was watching her too.

The queen rose to her paws. "You see how it is."

"I'm doing what I can."

"What you *can*," spat the queen.

"Amarog has spoken."

The queen sighed. "I'm sorry," she said. "You're right. If they be taken from me, it is the will of the ancestors." She tipped her head and met Farraclaw's eye. "I have lost so much . . . but that is of no consequence. I bow to a greater will." She turned slowly and padded back towards the den. Her tail was low behind her.

We didn't stay long at the pup den. Fresh snow was still falling softly, blurring the tundra and the great spruce.

I hurried next to Farraclaw as he strode along the edge of the rock. "When do you plan to hunt?"

"I know what you're thinking." His eyes flicked towards me. "Your disapproval is obvious."

"The pups are hungry. They need meat."

"I'm well aware of that." An edge crept into his voice. "Amarog has walked in death. She has spoken with the ancestors."

I shuddered at the thought of the strange, wild-eyed wolf. "Who is she?"

"She's our truthsayer, our shaman. As a pup, she carried a fever for a full rotation of the moon. She walked among the dead and made of them her friends. She is our link with the past – our pathway to the future. We can only hunt when she bids it safe."

I'd never heard of anything like that. My tail flicked impatiently. I couldn't shake the image of Dorrel crouching behind the others. The pup was almost too weak to rise. Would she make it through the night?

"But you're the prince. Couldn't you just—"

"No, Isla. Whatever it is, no. I cannot hunt. Not until it is willed by the ancestors." He set his jaw. Snow clung to his thick coat, softening the sharp edges of his pointed ears. "Amarog does not rule me, she is merely a conduit. The ancestors see all, know all. To act against them is a travesty. The meat would be cursed." He strode more quickly.

I scurried after him. My forepaw slipped on the snow and I righted myself. "I'd sooner eat cursed meat than starve to death." I thought a moment. "If it's about you hunting, how about letting me catch them something? It wouldn't be much . . . a bird, maybe a squirrel."

"You don't understand. No one can hunt, not until the ancestors will it."

My ears were flat. "What Amarog said was . . ." I frowned, struggling to remember. "No blood may be taken or . . . or 'claimed.' Something like that. But it didn't bother you when Mirraclaw made Lop bleed."

"Lop?" muttered Farraclaw. "We're talking about the future of the Bishar, not some *under-wolf*."

"He's a member of the Bishar too," I pointed out.

Farraclaw's tail was stiff, his head dropped low. "This isn't about Lop. It isn't even about the pups. It's not about *any* one wolf."

I knew that I should bite my tongue. After all, I was his guest. But the blood ran hotly through my limbs. "What is it about, then?"

He slammed to a halt and stared at me. "It's about the Bishar. Wolves come and go. We are snowflakes in an infinite sky. The snow will melt but the sky remains. It is all that matters."

Despite myself, I recoiled beneath his gaze. I sucked in my breath. He didn't scare me. "But Dorrel may die."

"Pups have died before," said Farraclaw. "They will die again."

My voice was rising. "Don't you care?"

Farraclaw looked away across the tundra. "Of course I care." His tail sank low. When he spoke again, his voice was a whisper. "I have a duty to the Bishar. It doesn't matter what it costs me, or what it costs the queen. The Bishar comes first. It *always* comes first."

I crackled with anger. I couldn't believe what I was hearing – the wolves were prepared to sacrifice their own pups in the name of what? Some crazy whim?

I'd hardly paid attention to where we were going. I looked around to see low shrubs emerge from the snow. A grim-faced wolf stood guard. He dipped his head as we approached.

Without a word, we passed into a cave. Icicles dangled over our heads, dotted with light. The rest of the cave fell into darkness. A huge silhouette stood against the wall. As we approached, it came to life. Broad shoulders, a short tail, and two pointed ears.

A ripple of fear ran along my back.

Farraclaw walked in front of me. His movements lacked their usual confidence – he approached the figure cautiously. "King Birronclaw Valiant-Oolf," he said. "Lord Protector of the Bishar of Claw, High Commander of the Snowlands. Great warrior, wise leader, I honour you."

"Get away from me!" The voice was surprisingly shrill for such a huge beast. It bounced around the dark cave. "Who are you? I must be alone. Touch me, wolf, and I'll tear out your eyes!"

The prince outstretched his forepaws and lowered his muzzle to the ground. "My King, it is I. It is Farraclaw, your son."

6

Farraclaw bowed deeper. "Fa, forgive me my intrusion." He rose and took a step forward.

The wolf king shifted. I couldn't make out his features in the dim cave. All that was clear was his height and bulk. "Get back!" he snarled.

"But Fa—"

Without warning, King Birronclaw sprang forward, a flash of yellow teeth and moist white eyes. The old king may have been sick, but he was still the largest wolf I'd ever seen. He slammed Farraclaw with his massive shoulder. I darted out of the way as the prince tumbled.

The king slunk back into the shadows. "I told you to leave me alone." His voice was low now, almost a whimper.

Farraclaw gasped for breath. With a wince, he rolled on to his paws. He glanced at me, his ears pointed out to the sides.

He didn't want to take me to the king. He tried to talk me out of it.

If I'd realized King Birronclaw was his fa. If I'd understood the madness that had rotted his mind. I glanced at Farraclaw, pity tingling my whiskers. He started forward again but paused at a distance from the king. "I am sorry to trouble you, Sire."

The king began muttering. "In the morning, the blackbirds sing. They cheep in the trees, and I hunt . . . Always, the whistle of beetles. Twilight, the ravens. Black over the sky. Ravens' wings, silver thunder. Night creepers, they haunt my peace. Silence, I must find silence. I am not myself."

My tail hung low. The old wolf couldn't help me. His mind was ruined.

"Fa . . . ? My King . . . ?" Farraclaw's voice was soothing. "Tell me what I can do. Shall I bring you snow to slake your thirst?"

The king wasn't listening. "The red-tailed hawks are calling. Tearing through my thoughts."

Farraclaw turned back to me. "Always he talks of red-tailed hawks but I've never seen one this far north."

The king fell silent. I saw him crane his neck and feared he'd lunge at Farraclaw again. He shuffled forward, a strange movement for such a large creature. "Who's there?" he spat. "Show yourself." A shaft of light fell across his face. His muzzle might have been white once, but it was blackened with dirt. His eyes were gauzy, weeping at the edges. In the light, their dark centres shrank into slits. An acrid smell rose off his fur, like meat gone foul.

I backed away, my hairs on end.

"Fa, I have brought a friend to see you. This is Isla. She is a fox from the Greylands."

"A fox?" The wolf's teeth were chattering. He peered closer with his gauzy eyes. His jaw slackened to reveal the tips of his long fangs, but he wasn't snarling. Hope flickered over his face. "So cold, so far. But you have come. At last, you are here."

I stared at him. "Do you know me?"

King Birronclaw blinked hard. "I have known your kind."

He was the greatest wolf in the Snowlands – huge, powerful, potent with maha. The largest wolf in all the frozen realms.

My heart was thumping. "A fox is lost to the Elders," I recited, "beyond the fur and sinew of the greatest of Canista's cubs." I took in the hump of his shoulders, his thickset limbs. "There is no wolf larger than you."

The white eyes bulged. "The Elders? Is it almost the gloaming?"

My tail jerked up. How did he know about the Elders?

I have known your kind.

I watched the king carefully. "Have you seen my brother, Pirie?"

"Pirie." The king sounded out the word in a long rasp. *"Piiirrreee."*

I stepped closer, to Farraclaw's side. "Where is he?"

The king's head whipped around, towards the dark wall of the cave. He clamped his eyes shut, like he was fighting to concentrate. "Be very careful, Fox," he growled. "You do not know what I am capable of. I don't want to hurt you." He snarled between his teeth. "A sickness is rotting my mind."

The prince watched, speechless.

My heart was racing. "My brother Pirie isn't here, is he?"

The king dropped his massive head. "Dark places drive you to dark acts." His eyes sprang open. "Only I am here. But never alone." His gaze raced along the ceiling of the cave. Light trembled in the icicles. "Waiting, waiting . . ." Without warning, King Birronclaw sprang forward again. I scrambled with a shriek and Farraclaw leaped in front of me, blocking his fa's way. But the king was determined, his eyes trained on me. "Listen, Fox, listen well!" He reached out his forepaws, snatching at me across Farraclaw. "I can help you, but you must do exactly as I say."

"You'll help me find Pirie? You know where he is?"

"Do *exactly* as I say, Fox! In every detail! Do not question it at any time." The great wolf grimaced with pain. "My gerra is at war, I can scarcely think. Daily he attacks me, ravaging my maa, my very heart."

"Fa, please!" begged Farraclaw.

70

I barked over him. "Tell me what to do!"

The king shut his eyes again, his body trembling. He hardly seemed able to speak. "The cache," he winced. "The cache is buried far away, amid bubbling fires that reek of decay, surrounded by frozen splinters that are larger than wolves and sharper than teeth. I buried it myself. It pains me to trust a stranger, but what choice do I have? Release the cache, reverse the spell. I beg you, set me free!"

"What is the cache? What will I find?"

Spit gathered at the king's mouth and hung on the fur of his muzzle. "There isn't time to explain. Unearth cache. Do what has to be done. The Elders sent you, didn't they?"

"Yes, but—"

The king was breathless. "Don't stop for anything."

I crept closer.

"Be careful," hissed Farraclaw. "He's unpredictable."

"I need to know." I slid past him, within reach of the great wolf. Our eyes locked. "If I do this – if I find your cache – will you take me to Pirie?"

He lifted his great head. "Your brother Pirie, is his maa strong like yours?"

Excitement leaped through me. "You know where he is?"

The wolf dipped his head in acknowledgement. "I can guess."

"You will show me?"

"I will guide you there myself if it kills me. You have my

word. But only when you find the cache. I can't help you before that. I *can't*."

"Where is he? Take me where? Please tell me!"

"First, the cache. You must hurry! I don't have long. If I perish, I can't help anyone." With a jerk of his great head, he scrambled back, away from the light. He started whining. "The red-tailed hawks are back. Why do they haunt me? What do they want? I only long for peace."

"Fa, won't you come out from this cave?" Farraclaw cleared his throat. "The fresh air will heal you. We'll make sacrifices to the ancestors. Amarog will intervene. We will end this torment."

"There is only one end. The way of darkness."

"Fa, please. Won't you come outside?"

"Always, the beetles by day, by night. Always the shrieking." The old wolf curled into a tight ball. He muttered to himself. I could no longer make out his words.

"Fa . . . ?" Farraclaw stood for a few moments, watching the king in silence. Then he turned and padded out of the cave.

It was still snowing. Great white flakes masked the land. The wolf who guarded the cave stood at a respectful distance.

Farraclaw turned to me. "King Birronclaw once wielded a ferocious intelligence. The change is hard to accept." He looked away, into the tumbling flakes.

"I'm sorry," I murmured. I thought of my own fa. For the first time I wondered if death was a mercy – if there were crueler paths.

Farraclaw shook his head. "The things he was saying, they didn't make any sense."

"But he was expecting a fox to come. He told me what to do."

Farraclaw gave me a hard look. "He's raving. You can't take anything from what he says."

"He knew about the Elders. About Pirie."

"He could have guessed about Pirie, said what he thought you wanted to hear."

"But why?" My tail flicked. Hadn't Farraclaw been listening? "He knew that Pirie has strong maa."

"Maha. That's what we call it."

"It doesn't matter what you call it. It means the same thing," I pointed out. I was sorry for Farraclaw, but I couldn't give up on my brother. The king would take me to Pirie if I found his cache. He'd given me his word. "I just need to find the bubbling fires and frozen splinters . . . I wonder where they are."

"I know exactly where they are. The fires are part of the Caldron, a circle of burning lakes. The splinters are the Ice Razors."

My tail started thrashing. "But that's great! Just tell me where to go and I'll find the cache!"

Farraclaw was grave. "You don't understand. The Caldron and the Ice Razors are dangerous lands. A wolf would scarcely choose to go there and a fox could never survive. But it is worse than that. Both are far from the heart of our Bishar, an exhausting trip through open tundra. They lie at the furthest reaches of the Snowlands, deep in the Bishar of Fang."

"Prince Farraclaw!" Cattisclaw was bounding over the curving snow. I envied her strength and grace. She reached us with a bow. "Sire, Amarog the Wise is back from the Taku Grounds."

Farraclaw nodded. "We must go."

"But the cache," I began.

"We will speak of it later." I saw the tension in his muzzle and stopped myself from saying more.

Cattisclaw led us back to the den, where most of the Bishar was already assembled. It was overlooked by a craggy knoll, where Amarog sat alone. Her eyes were open but she didn't move. She seemed to be gazing over the heads of the Bishar, into the tundra.

Cattisclaw caught me staring. "She's in a trance."

That didn't really explain anything. I watched uneasily. Between Amarog and King Birronclaw, I'd had enough of strange wolves.

Farraclaw looked troubled. "Leave me," he said.

Cattisclaw gave me a nudge. I followed her around a cluster of bushes to the den as Farraclaw sat by himself beneath a tree.

The wolves greeted us with wet noses and wagging tails. Several broke off to chase one another, bolting out of the den into tumbling snow.

Amarog stood perfectly still, snowflakes dancing around her.

"She is communing with the ancestors," Cattisclaw explained. "Last night she slept at the borders of the Taku Grounds, and today she has walked them since dawn."

My ears flicked back. "Taku?"

Cattisclaw looked serious. "Forbidden. The earth is sacred where the ancestors rest. Even Amarog only wanders as far as the borders. None may cross the Taku Grounds."

Norralclaw gave me a nudge. "Are you well, Isla? You must be hungry."

My belly rumbled in response.

He glanced at Amarog and dropped his voice. "We're all hoping we'll have permission to hunt. It isn't really for us – we can go without food if we have to. But the pups are struggling."

I thought of Dorrel. The day was drifting by. How would she be coping? It struck me that the pups were Farraclaw's younger brothers and sisters. It must have hurt him to see them suffer. "Is there . . ." I struggled not to insult the wolves' beliefs. "Is there nothing that can be done? Maybe a small hunt?"

Norralclaw's jaw gaped in shock.

"No!" said Cattisclaw. "Of course not, not unless it is willed by the ancestors."

Your ancestors don't seem very caring, I thought, but I didn't say so.

Norralclaw puffed up his chest. "When the time is right, we will do our duty. In the name of the Bishar, with the courage of our ancestors."

I remembered the first time I'd slimmered to catch a mouse in the Great Snarl. It had been a thrill, and a tasty catch, but it seemed strange to speak of duty and courage. "Does every wolf in the Bishar hunt?"

Cattisclaw stretched herself out. "Not if they're sick. And the queen is too busy nursing the pups – though she was the best hunter in the Bishar once."

"Of course Amarog doesn't hunt," added Norralclaw with a respectful dip of the head. "She has taken a vow not to kill."

"But she eats the kill?" I asked.

Norralclaw gave me a disapproving look. "That's hardly the point."

It seemed like the point to me. "Do you always hunt together?" The idea was so strange. Foxes in a skulk shared their kill with the cubs, but they always hunted alone.

Cattisclaw snorted. "We couldn't hunt the bison without one another."

"How fast is a fox?" barked Lyrinclaw, the grey wolf. "Do you think you can outrun me?" She looped around me, Norralclaw and Cattisclaw, wagging her tail.

My tail twitched. "That's all right." I stayed where I was.

Lyrinclaw turned to Cattisclaw. "I guess it's true what they say."

My ears pricked. "What do you mean?"

Lyrinclaw's eyes glinted. "That foxes are lazy."

I sprang to my paws. "We are *not*!"

"Prove it!" She looped around me again, her tail almost close enough to brush my whiskers.

I reached out a forepaw and licked it casually, like a cat. "I don't have anything to prove." But as Lyrinclaw circled around again, I broke forward and snapped at her tail, yanking out a few hairs.

Lyrinclaw woofed excitedly and burst out of the den. I sprang after her, with Norralclaw and Cattisclaw at my sides. The grey wolf bounded through the snow, pausing to let me catch up, then lunging forward. The wolves stopped to watch us. Some started yelping my name.

"Catch her, Isla! You can do it!"

It was like a jolt of maa. My paws felt surer in the snow and I ran faster, gaining on the grey wolf. I knew I could never catch her over long distances – I remembered the tireless path that the wolves had beaten across the tundra. I had to be focused and quick. To play to my advantage.

Foxcraft, Isla.

I gathered my breath and karakked, throwing my voice ahead of Lyrinclaw, screeching like an angry cat. She slammed to a halt in a billow of snow, her fur on end.

The other wolves were barking my name. "Isla! Isla!"

"What was that?" gasped Lyrinclaw. She started forward again but I ran at her with a surge of pace and dived at her tail. I grasped it for a moment, swinging through the air, then released it to land at her side.

The wolves exploded into yelps and howls.

"Isla did it! She caught Lyrinclaw!"

"She tricked me!" yelped the grey wolf, but she turned to me with a bow. "I'm impressed, Fox."

The wolves crowded around us, nudging us with their snouts. It was all I could do to keep my paws on the ground. I had to admit it felt good. Their playful vigor gave me energy; I had almost forgotten my empty belly. As they stepped back I sat on the flattened snow.

"Not so fast," said Lyrinclaw. "Now it's my turn!"

The wolves yipped in agreement, tails thrashing. Lyrinclaw's ear twisted in question. Could I outrun a wolf? I doubted it. But then, I knew something they didn't. I stretched my legs, felt my tail drifting over the snow. Although I hadn't eaten, my maa felt strong.

"All right," I said. "You can chase me."

But you'll have to find me first.

I drew in my breath, reached for the quiet beyond my thoughts.

What was seen is unseen; what was sensed becomes senseless. What was bone is bending; what was fur is air.

My paw pads faded out of view. I knew how it would seem to the wolves: as though I'd disappeared before their eyes. I heard a collective gasp of amazement.

"Last one back at the den is a rat's foot," I said. I couldn't help myself.

"Mischevious foxling!" cried Lyrinclaw.

"Where is she?" said Cattisclaw.

Norralclaw was padding around her. "She's gone!" he yelped.

I started along the snow as quickly as I could. Drawing in my maa, I karakked a fox yelp between two looming spruce trees. Through the blur of my slimmer, I watched the wolves whip around. Lyrinclaw hurried to the trees, the others in pursuit. While their backs were turned, I withdrew several paces, then split off on to another path towards a cluster of bushes.

The wolves were barking, sniffing frantically. "She's not this way!"

"Don't let her beat you back to the den, Lyrinclaw!"

I picked up my pace, weaving between the bushes.

"Run for it," Cattisclaw advised the grey wolf. "She can't beat you on speed. Cut her off before she gets there!"

From the edge of my vision, I saw Lyrinclaw bounding towards the den. Frustration flickered through my fur. I had hoped she would try to sniff me out, but the wolf was losing no time.

"This way," whispered a voice. My ears flicked back. Still holding the slimmer, I tilted my head. Through the blur, I could make out the shape of a wolf. He had floppy ears. "I saw your paw prints in the snow. Follow me. It's a shortcut."

Lop turned and scrambled beneath a bush. I followed him. On the other side of the bush, the snow dipped down into a kind of tunnel. Lop stalked along it as it cut between two silvery boulders. A moment later, we were back at the den.

"You're invisible. They couldn't see you!" Lop panted.

Breaking the slimmer, I turned to him. "It's a kind of foxcraft. They didn't see you either!"

Lop's eyes sparkled. "Maybe I have foxcraft of my own."

I realized what he meant: no one sees the under-wolf.

Lyrinclaw burst into the den to find me reclined on one side, casually washing my forepaws.

"Impossible!" she yelped. "How did you manage it?"

The other wolves gathered around her, panting. Lop hung back, his tail wagging.

"Tell us, Isla!" the wolves begged.

"Please tell us, we're desperate to know!"

A howl cut over their voices. The wolves fell silent, dropping low with their heads dipped. Amarog was rising to her paws on the knoll. The sun sank low, flooding the horizon in a pink glow.

Against it, Amarog looked black. "I call upon the Bishar of Claw. I call upon Prince Farraclaw Valiant-Jowl."

Farraclaw strode towards her, bounding up the steep mount to the knoll. She bowed to him, and he bowed in return. The other wolves watched in silence. The air was charged. If felt like a storm was rising from their fur.

Farralaw dipped his head. "What say you, Amarog the Wise?"

"I have walked the Taku Grounds and communed with the ancestors. I have offered thanks." Amarog lowered her muzzle. From this distance, it was hard to know what she was looking at, but I sensed her eyes on me. A shiver ran through me. "Night laps at the edges of the tundra. The snow melts as it falls. The bison are on White Peak."

I looked up. She was right: the snow had turned to sleet. I'd been too busy playing with the wolves to notice.

"You mean . . ." Farraclaw's tail rose with a flick.

"Look to the sky!"

We all looked up. Although it wasn't yet dark, the moon was rising, a sliver of white.

No blood may be claimed until the moon is an icicle in a river sky!

"The time has come," said Amarog. "The ancestors watch over the Bishar."

"Thank you, revered Amarog," said Farraclaw with a bow. He squared his shoulders and drew in his breath. "One Bishar, united."

"One Bishar, united!" echoed the wolves.

I caught the fire in Farraclaw's eyes. "Together we stand, together we fall!"

"The Bishar of Claw is the strongest of all!" The wolves replied in unison, their voices booming.

"Let the Snowlands tremble with what we are made!" said Farraclaw.

"The wolves of Claw are never afraid."

The prince raised his muzzle proudly. "For friendship. For honour. For ever."

"For friendship. For honour. For ever!" The wolves barked back. Their tails were wagging, their ears pointed forward. Their gazes were on Farraclaw up on the knoll.

He threw back his head with a rumbling howl. The wolves howled back, a harmony of excited calls. Light leaped through me, a shot of maa.

They didn't explain why they were howling – they didn't have to. I had seen enough to understand.

The hunt was on.

7

A volley of howls rose over the tundra.

The wolves surrounded me, their heads thrown back, their muzzles angled to the rising moon. I looked to Farraclaw up on the knoll. The tip of his fur was golden in the fading light. He broke off and sprang down the knoll, wending his way to the den. Most of the wolves fell silent. They watched intently, poised to follow. Their tails rose behind them, their ears alert. A couple still howled, falling out of harmony into random whoops and cries.

Farraclaw trotted past the waiting Bishar, leading the way through the snow. He looped around a cluster of rocks and started a steady sweep uphill. Mirraclaw and Cattisclaw fell into step behind him. The other wolves took their positions behind them.

All the wolves take part.

Even Lop, who brought up the rear.

Only the queen and her pups were absent, and the mad king in his cave. Perhaps the queen would hunt again when her pups were stronger. I watched the rest of the Bishar curve an arch through the snow. Their huffing barks rose over the tundra, the occasional howl hanging in the air.

Curiosity pricked my whiskers. I started to follow.

At the rock cluster, I paused. I'd forgotten someone. Amarog still stood on the knoll, perfectly still, as though she was carved of stone.

The wolves moved at a trot, cutting a path through the aspens. Even at this pace, I worked hard to keep up with them. Somehow, their broken howls kept me going as they wove between the trees, making for the hills. Ravens rose from the branches, their black wings clapping against the wind. I remembered my time as the great bird soaring over the Raging River. The surge of excitement as I looked over the Wildlands, the Mage banked in a yellow fog. The horror as the wa'akkir failed, and the dizzying drop.

I was in no hurry to try wa'akkir again.

The aspens stretched before us, reminding me of what Farraclaw had told me. Claw Weald was larger than it seemed. The white trunks ran in all directions as far as the eye could see. The wolves passed between them, their ears pointed forward. In the lead, I spotted Farraclaw. Determination rose off his broad shoulders. I wondered for the first time what the wolves were hunting – what kind of creature *was* a bison? I'd only seen them as distant blobs. I knew it wasn't a squirrel or mouse, it had to be something larger. What could be so big that it needed a Bishar of wolves to catch it?

Eventually, the aspens thinned. The howls and yelps of the wolves faded into the quiet of the night. I looked over my shoulder. The last trail of red glowed over the tundra. Stars glinted in a flinty sky.

The wolves slowed down. They started pacing, their tails low. Far from the den or the friendly pups, I was starkly aware of being different – a fox surrounded by deadly cousins. *Wolves kill foxes for sport.* Fa had told me that once. The thought stopped me in my tracks. At the rear of the Bishar, Lop padded towards me, shaking his floppy ears. He gave me a lick on the nose. I glanced at him gratefully, my moment of dread seeping away. I was one of them now; I was safe. I watched the wolves scratch at the snow, their nostrils pulsing. Seeking their quarry.

Farraclaw wheeled around, maw to the snow-coated earth, and caught sight of me. He held my gaze, then raised his head. "This way."

The wolves prowled uphill, over sharp rocks that peaked through the snow. It wasn't easy to follow. I couldn't vault over the rocks the way they did. Lop dropped behind to nudge me on.

We rose over a hill. The air high up was sharp and clean. I stopped to catch my breath as the wolves stalked close to clusters of spiky black twigs.

Lop leaned over to me. "Sagebrush. The bison like it."

I could sense a change among the wolves. Tails gave small wags. Ears rotated, hackles rose.

I sniffed the snow. It was harder to catch scents in the chill, but I was starting to get used to my environment. Up ahead, I snatched at an unfamiliar odour: peppery, rich, with a hint of earth. My belly groaned and I ran my tongue over my muzzle. Lop looked at me with meaning. "That's right," he whispered.

Farraclaw stopped at the sagebrush, his muzzle poking between the twiglike stems. The other wolves lined up alongside him, quiet as shadows. I peered between the brush, catching a glimpse of huge black boulders. I frowned. What were the wolves staring at?

Then one of the boulders moved.

Farraclaw turned and caught my eye. "Stay back," he cautioned.

I dipped my head in agreement.

He craned forward, rising, his shoulder blades pointed. He shunted between the centre of the brush. Without a word, the wolves divided. Rattisclaw, Briarclaw and Lyrinclaw broke to one side of the brush. Thistleclaw and several other warriors streamed along the other side, while Mirraclaw, Cattisclaw and Norralclaw followed Farraclaw. Lop hung back, waiting for his turn.

A stout white wolf with one grey paw hurried after Lyrinclaw. Lop followed. "Keep behind us," he told me.

The brush appeared in dark bursts between the snow, perhaps a fox tail's distance apart. The wolves zigzagged through it, keeping low. Excitement hissed in the air, clung to their fur. But their steps were cautious. A stream of wolves looped one way, another circled the other. I realized they were closing around the bison. The huge creatures that I'd mistaken for boulders were huddled together. There were dozens of them – they outnumbered the wolves two or three to one.

As I hurried after Lop, they finally came into full view. They were the largest beasts I had ever seen. Their enormous bodies were covered in shaggy fur. Their heads were so heavy it was a wonder they could lift them. They tugged at the sagebrush, chewing in a lazy sort of way. One looked up, startled. Long grass dangled from its mouth. Its dark eye shone, wide and wild. On its head stood two curved horns. The sharp points glinted.

I couldn't imagine how any creature could bring down a bison – even a wolf.

But it wasn't a wolf hunting the bison. It was the Bishar.

As the bison raised their heads and snorted, the wolves stopped circling. They stood still, keeping a wary distance from their prey. One of the bison made as though to run at Rattisclaw but stopped midstep. Another let out a long groan, billows of mist rising from its snout. The bison reared into one another, their tails pointing to the centre of the circle, creating a wall of broad heads and sharp horns.

I hung back as I'd promised. Farraclaw was the closest wolf to the herd. He stood facing one of the largest beasts, his ears pressed flat and his tail straight behind him. For a while, no one moved. The wolves and the bison were frozen to the snowy ground. Cattisclaw broke position slightly, scraping her claws against the snow. Tremors of fear ran among the bison. Somehow, they knew to hold their nerve – to keep their great heads angled towards the wolves.

Farraclaw's paws were fixed to the ground, but I could see his eyes working, running along the herd. He seemed to spot something in one of them that made him creep a little closer. It was a brooding beast with a twitchy tail. The creature was already beating its hoof on the snow, groaning angrily.

Farraclaw took a step towards the nervous bison. His lips peeled back and a rumble escaped his throat.

Most of the beasts stood their ground, but the nervous bison with the twitchy tail shuffled its hooves and sprang back, smacking against one of the others. The dark mass of bodies shifted, and I sensed the wolves tense. Farraclaw took another step closer. Without warning, the nervous bison broke rank and charged at Farraclaw, its massive head dropped low, its horns pointed forward. Farraclaw sprang out of its path, bounding along the side of the herd. Mirraclaw and Cattisclaw glared at the nervous bison and it turned, confused, its ropey tail swinging.

The herd started swaying. Their dark eyes rolled between the wolves, their huge hooves beat the ground. Another bison burst towards Norralclaw, who dodged its sharp horns.

The standoff was over: the bison began to run.

The wolves started after them, bounding at either side of the herd. I kept behind Lop. As the beasts stampeded through the sagebrush, I saw Farraclaw, Mirraclaw and Cattisclaw dashing back and forth, darting at one bison after another. My ears rotated, my breath coming fast. What were they doing? The bison were growing angry. Cattisclaw bounded in front of Lop, sidling up to one of the dark creatures and making to nip at its legs. The bison swung towards her, tossing its horned head. It groaned, low and fierce. But in its movements, I noticed a limp. One of the bison's back legs was lame.

I realized what Farraclaw and his nobles were doing.

They're testing the bison. Looking for signs of weakness.

The herd galloped with surprising speed. Their enormous bulk gave them the advantage as they crashed through the sagebrush. The wolves were forced to dodge the sharp bushes, working hard to keep up with their prey.

I ran with the wolves. The wind whipped wild through the sagebrush, powdering snow into our eyes. I blinked, shaking my head. Straggling behind, I spotted Cattisclaw, who bounded over to Farraclaw. Mirraclaw and Norralclaw ran alongside them. For a moment, their heads swung around and they all looked to the bison with the bad leg. Then Mirraclaw and Norralclaw sprang forward, just ahead of the injured bison, scaring the herd into running faster. Farraclaw ran alongside the creature as Cattisclaw fell into step behind him.

The injured bison dropped its head and ran faster, closing the gap between itself and the herd. Sweat streaked off its back and clung to its haunches, shimmery in the moonlight. At a wide outcrop of sagebrush, it burst clear of the wolves, who had to scramble around the brush. Mirraclaw fell into its path and the massive beast dropped its head, running at the white wolf, who scrambled away just in time.

As the herd burst free of the sagebrush, the wolves lunged forward and I dropped on to the snow, panting furiously. I couldn't keep up. I collapsed on to my belly, watching between the tall brush.

Out in open tundra, the advantage shifted. The bison forged a path through thick snow. Even for such enormous creatures, it had to be exhausting. The wolves had an easier job, following the path that the bison had cut. Still, they were falling behind. The bison were getting away.

I thought of the pups back in the den. Dorrel wouldn't make another day without food. But how could wolves catch such powerful beasts? The injured bison ran swiftly, keeping pace with the others. There was no way past its pointed horns.

I sighed, glancing up at the sky. Countless stars twinkled against the velvet of the night. Among them, I saw Canista's Lights. They were larger, brighter than I'd ever seen them before. A sharp call wrenched my gaze back to the chase. Farraclaw had stopped on the tundra, head thrown back in a howl. I recognized his rich, pure cry.

The other wolves gathered around him. They started howling too, their voices rising in harmony. The howls grew bolder, impossibly loud, as though with the voice of a hundred wolves.

The wolves bounded forward.

To run as a Bishar – that's what it means to truly hunt. Farraclaw had said that, back in the Snarl. *To sprint across the frozen realms, a hundred paws pounding the snow in time, with a blizzard at your face, the bite of frost in your throat, and the spirit of your ancestors urging you on.*

The earth vibrated, like it had in malinta. Though the wolves no longer howled, the echo of their voices still trembled in the frozen air. I saw the bison falter, bewildered by the sounds that rose around them. It was almost as though the wolves were karakking, but no . . . this was something else.

I squinted, gave myself a shake.

Against the darkness of the night, a haze of silver circled the bison. The silhouettes of countless wolves. *The ancestors of the Bishar of Claw.* Their paws glanced the snow as the ghostly howls rose over the dark horizon.

A single beast, a single heart, as the hooves of your quarry beat a path like thunder.

The voice of the earth: *ka-thump, ka-thump.*

I watched in amazement. The silvery wolves were transforming. They merged together, joined Farraclaw and the Bishar. The shapes of legs, and ears, and tails faded from view. For an instant, I saw not the wolves of the Bishar, or the countless silvery figures of their ancestors. What stormed over the tundra was a solitary shape.

A giant, fearless wolf.

It tore after the herd, swift on their tails.

A single beast, a single heart.

The herd exploded into panic. Bison charged chaotically over the snow. The silver wolf blurred into the bodies of the Bishar. The predators rushed at the injured bison. The beast staggered between spruce trees and turned towards the sagebrush. It thrashed its head, unsure where to go.

Ka-thump, ka-thump.

In that moment, Farraclaw struck, launching himself at the beast's flank. Cattisclaw sprang at its tail as Mirraclaw clamped his jaws around one tough back leg. The beast came down to howls of triumph. The Bishar closed around the fallen bison. Its death was swift and merciful beneath Canista's Lights.

"May the fallen rest in the peace of the forest," uttered Farraclaw to a volley of howls.

The rest of the bison were already regrouping in the snow. They hurried away, casting doleful looks over their shoulders. But their movements had lost their frenetic pace. For now, they were safe.

The wolves had caught their prey.

There was enough juicy meat to be shared among all of the wolves, enough to be taken back to the pups, the king, and the queen. Enough for Amarog, though she scarcely seemed to eat at all.

The remains of the bison were left in the snow where eagles and ravens gathered. A lone coyote hung back, watching. Waiting for the wolves to leave. He reminded me of the coyote chief from the Wildlands, and that made me think of Siffrin.

I wished that the red-furred fox was here with me. I wished he'd seen the hunt. I would never be able to describe the beauty and power of so many wolves acting as one.

I wasn't sure how long it had lasted, or how long we had feasted on the fallen bison. As Farraclaw stood over the remains, it was still dark as pitch.

The Bishar began the descent along the frozen hill. The wolves no longer marched in formation. A lightness had entered their movements. Up ahead, Rattisclaw and Norralclaw were ramming against each other with gentle snarls.

Cattisclaw gambolled alongside me. "What did you think of your first hunt?"

I remembered the time I'd caught my first mouse, slimmering in order to trap it. A bison was very different from a mouse.

"Amazing," I said. It was true. The great, silver wolf still trembled through my thoughts. "You were very brave."

"It is easy, with a leader like Farraclaw to inspire us." Her eyes glowed with devotion.

"I guess the king used to lead the hunt?"

"Yes. Before he grew sick, King Birronclaw Valiant-Oolf was fierce. Under his rule, the Bishar was strong." She glanced over her shoulder, padded closer to me. "But he was different from Farraclaw."

I cocked my head. "Different how?"

"He didn't care for the wolves in the same way. He pushed the Bishar hard. Farraclaw's sister, Hessaclaw, was made to run up front with the nobles. For the king, it was a matter of pride. She was small for her age. She wasn't ready."

"What happened?" I asked.

"She was caught in a stampede." Cattisclaw looked away. "The king didn't even pause, didn't give rites. Amarog led the grieving that night, when the hunt was over – but it should have been the king."

"That's horrible," I murmured.

"Of course, we all wish for the king to recover. And yet . . ." Her words trailed away. She gave herself a shake. Her voice became upbeat. "You ran with us. You're an honorary wolf now, Isla."

My tail drooped. "But I didn't help."

"Of course you did." It was Farraclaw who'd spoken. I hadn't noticed him stepping up behind us. I hoped he hadn't heard what Cattisclaw had said about his fa. "You came, you shared your maha. It isn't about the individual."

I thought again of the great, silver wolf. "I can see that."

As we reached the aspens, soft flecks of light rose over Growl Wood. The triumphant wolves bounded across the snow. Most made for the pup den, eager to offer meat to the hungry pups.

Farraclaw held back. With a tip of the muzzle, he led me beneath an aspen. "Are you still determined to venture west through the Bishar of Fang?" His moon-yellow eyes stared into mine.

"I have to," I answered. "If there's a chance I'll find my brother . . ."

He drew in his breath. "Then you have quite a quest before you."

"A quest," I echoed. That's what the Elders had called my journey to the Snowlands. My tail flicked anxiously. I thought of Jana and the others, the mysterious guardians of foxlore. Enviously, I recalled their incredible grasp of fox-craft. How useful such crafts would be in finding Pirie!

"You can't go alone; it's too dangerous. I will come with you."

"I can't ask you to do that. You lead the Bishar!"

"You haven't asked – I have offered. You gave me freedom, and I cannot forsake you, knowing what it is to be divided from family."

A great warmth rose inside me and I leaned my head against Farraclaw's chest. His fur tumbled thickly around my ears.

"We'll leave at nightfall. First, we must rest long and well. The hunt is tiring, and what awaits us in the territory of Fang may be more tiring still. We will take another wolf; there is safety in three." Farraclaw nudged me with his snout. "You've spent time among us and learned something of our ways. You may pick a warrior to join us."

I drew my head away from his mane of fur, thinking for a moment. I looked past Farraclaw, where the rest of the Bishar were a disappearing blur between the aspens. "I'd like to take Lop."

"*Lop?* He's the under-wolf!" The prince didn't disguise the disgust in his voice.

"I thought every member of the Bishar mattered?"

"They do, but . . . How could Lop help in a crisis? He cannot fight. He will not lead."

I met Farraclaw's eye. "There are other qualities."

For a moment, he stared at me, saying nothing. Then he dipped his head in agreement. "When the sun is over the aspens, we will start our journey. It will be long, and especially tiring for you. You will set the pace."

"Thank you!" I gasped, throwing myself against his chest once more. For a moment, Pirie's face flickered before me. His breath rose with my own. *This quest isn't over.*

It had only just begun.

The wolves were still huddled around me in sleep, snoring gently, curled tail to paw. A navy pelt hung over the sky. Dusk. I blinked, my whiskers flexing. We'd slept all day. I remembered how exhausted I'd been after maa-sharm in the Wildlands; how Siffrin had slept after saving my life. The hunt must drain maa too. It made sense: the tension of the stand-off, the energy of the chase. The single, great wolf danced over my vision.

What is it you seek?

My head jerked around. The wolves were still asleep. Except one: Amarog sat at a distance, her bicoloured eyes on me. My ears were flat against my head – she had spoken without words. She had entered my thoughts!

"How did you do that?" I stuttered. The fur was rising along my back.

You can hear me . . . I thought you would. Her lips did not move.

I was wary of this strange wolf. Uncertain of her power. Yet gazing into those eyes, I found myself saying, "I'm looking for my brother. He's disappeared."

I have sensed a trespasser. A fox.

"Pirie?" My voice rose, but the wolves around me slept on.

I do not know his name. The wind touched the wild mane of her fur and the small leaves tinkled. *How far will you go to find him?*

"Anywhere," I said. "To the ends of the earth." Although I spoke with words, the wolves of Claw didn't stir – as though a mantle of sleep hovered over them.

And what are you prepared to do?

"I'd do anything to have my brother by my side."

Anything?

With a sickening lurch I remembered what Haiki had said. *I'd do* anything *to get my family back.*

A shadow passed the shaman's eyes. *Beware of whom you serve. Your quest is not a solo journey. Others watch. They too care how it ends.*

The hairs prickled at the back of my neck. "What do you mean?"

She tilted her muzzle. *You have the maha of a warrior.*

Have you the stomach of one? Will you carry the blood of the dead on your maw?

"I'm not planning to kill anyone," I said defensively.

Amarog didn't reply. Her gaze lingered on me. Then she rose and padded over the snow between the aspens. As she departed, the wolves started stirring. The deep breath of their sleep fell into a shorter rhythm. Eyelids fluttered and opened. The wolves started yawning and stretching. Some murmured excitedly about last night's hunt.

Farraclaw rolled to his paws, clearing his throat. "Wolves of the Bishar of Claw, I have something to say," he announced. One by one they turned to the prince. "Isla must leave us for the Ice Razors. She is on a journey of her own to find her brother, Pirie. I respect her need to be with her own kind."

Lyrinclaw whined in disappointment. "You're not going, are you, Isla?"

"I'm afraid she must," said Farraclaw. "And I with her."

Tails stiffened. Cattisclaw gave a small whimper. "You're *leaving*, Sire?"

He cocked his head. "Not for long. In my stead, I ask Lord Mirraclaw Fierce-Raa to lead the Bishar, guided by Amarog the Wise."

The white wolf bowed his head. "It would be my great honour to serve," he replied. His cool eyes trailed over me.

Norralclaw rose to his paws. "The Ice Razors are deep in the Kingdom of Fang."

"I know where they are," said Farraclaw peaceably.

"But that's King Orrùfang's territory!" Cattisclaw's tail was low. "Why do you have to go *there*?"

Farraclaw glanced at me. "Isla seeks something that's been buried there. I know it makes little sense now . . . Perhaps I can explain it better on my return."

Norralclaw stood up. "If they catch you, Sire—"

"Then I will invoke the ancient Custom of Serren, by which King Serrenclaw and King Fironfang agreed free passage for a noble cause. We do not enter to steal or dominate, only to assist our friend. The Custom of Serren applies."

I wondered where the shaman had gone, still troubled by her words.

"When are you leaving?" asked Briarclaw.

Farraclaw's ears rolled forward. "Straightaway."

"Just the two of you?" asked Cattisclaw. "What if you run into the Bishar of Fang?"

"Three of us." Farraclaw looked among the wolves, his tail straight behind him. "Lop will join us."

From the edge of the group, the floppy-eared wolf looked up in surprise. *"Me?"*

The others gasped and glanced at one another.

"Why Lop?" blurted Rattisclaw.

Farraclaw's ear twitched. "It was Isla's choice."

Lop rose warily, trotting over to me. His gait remained low, his tail drifting close to his flank. He gave me a deep bow. "It would be a privilege to join you. If you think I'm worthy of such a mission." He looked to Farraclaw. "Sire, I am honoured."

"It was Isla's choice," the prince repeated sharply.

The wolves gathered around us to bid their goodbyes, nudging us and licking our noses. "Be careful," they urged, "Come back quickly."

"Come back quickly," echoed Mirraclaw. His jaw was set, his cold eyes trained on the distant peaks of Fang. He touched noses with Farraclaw, but he fell short of bidding me farewell. The fur itched along the back of my neck.

I turned to Cattisclaw. "Tell the pups I said goodbye." I hoped the young wolves would understand.

"I will," said Cattisclaw. "See you soon, Isla."

The wolves bid their farewells.

"Run fast, be safe, live free!" I called to them, remembering how the Elders had parted at the Rock.

"Is that what the foxes say?" asked Cattisclaw.

I paused. "Yes," I replied. "It is what we say."

"Run fast, be safe, live free!" she called back. The wolves howled, wagging their tails, shunting their wet noses towards me. I felt the hum of their maa.

"Come, Isla. Let us go now." Farraclaw raised his tail. "For friendship. For honour. For ever."

"For friendship. For honour. For ever!" echoed the wolves.

Amarog appeared between the aspens. She stood silently, her pointed ears twisting this way and that. Her bicoloured eyes trained on me.

Farraclaw led the way through the aspens, winding up the curved forest as darkness closed in. I trudged after him through the snow, with Lop padding behind me. When I glanced back, the floppy-eared wolf blinked at me encouragingly.

I didn't make a mistake in asking him to come.

The Snowlands were so quiet – nothing like the rumble and din of the Greylands, or the chirping of the Wildlands. As the trees parted on to open tundra, the moon was high overhead.

Farraclaw paused to let me catch up. "We will cross the border south of the Taku Grounds. Do you see that dark mass of trees to the west? That is where we'll enter."

It was a strange route, taking us in a huge loop through the Bishar of Claw. "Can't we go straight?"

I sensed Lop stiffen.

Farraclaw's eyes flashed yellow. "We will not insult the ancestors by sullying their resting grounds."

I thought of Ma, Fa and Greatma. "They're gone. What difference does it make?" My words were sharper than I'd intended.

Farraclaw registered no offence. "The flesh may perish,

but maha never dies. It rises to the air and mingles with the soil."

My mouth opened, then shut. He'd refused to hunt because Amarog said the ancestors weren't ready. I knew the wolf prince wouldn't back down.

It was almost dawn by the time we reached the small forest at the border of the Bishar. We had rested briefly on the open tundra and drank from an icy lake. I wondered if we might rest again, but Farraclaw was keen to keep moving.

"The sun's coming up. We'll go as far as we can under tree cover. It's a shame we can't wait for the thaw. Isla, your coat will make us stand out against the snow."

My tail sank guiltily.

"The trees wind down to the Raging River. That's something," said Farraclaw. "We'll have to look out for burning pools." I remembered the blue smoke that I'd spotted from the black rocks. Looking back into the Bishar of Claw, I thought of what the prince had said to Norralclaw. "What about 'Serren'? Do we really have to hide? Won't the wolves of Fang let us pass?"

"I do not doubt that this ancient custom is known to the wolves of Fang. But I have never put it to the test." Farraclaw cocked his head and his tail gave a quick wag. "If you don't mind, I'd rather not do so today. King Orrùfang is the son of the slain King Garrùfang. He has never forgiven my fa. I hope he'd be reasonable, but . . ."

I wasn't about to argue.

As we crossed into the Bishar of Fang and the low, dark trees, Farraclaw looked back.

"I'm sorry to be taking you away from your home," I said.

"It's all right," he breathed softly. "I was once dragged from the Bishar of Claw by the furless. Now I am leaving of my own will. My heart tells me I shall see it again."

The lines between the Bishars seemed invisible. Where the furless of the Greylands would have built walls, the wolves laid scents I could not interpret. All I could see was a row of spiky willow. Yet I noticed the change in Farraclaw and Lop. Their bodies tensed as they trod low to the ground, their ears rotating. I dared not interrupt their concentration.

My mind roamed to the strange dream I'd had where I was Pirie – Pirie practising foxcraft. The colours and sounds were so powerful, much greater than anything I'd felt myself. It left me uneasy. Was it more than just a dream? It had felt so *real*.

We continued through the Bishar of Fang. The light between the trees grew brighter. Birds twittered in the branches. A hare raced over the ragged grass, disappearing into the foliage. There was the faintest whiff of petals on the cool air. But malinta's warmth had not arrived in the Snowlands. A pelt of snow clung to the branches of the trees and crunched beneath our paws.

In time, I picked up another odour. Acrid, like

something rotten. My whiskers bristled – it reminded me of the foul scent of the Taken. But no, this was different, moist . . . A moment later, I saw blue smoke edging beneath the trees.

Farraclaw glanced back at me. "We're near one of the burning pools. Be careful; they're deadly. You mustn't touch them." I spotted it between the tree trunks. The water was a deep, metallic blue. Shingles that marked the edges of the pool were scorched bright orange. Heat rose in the air in bursts of vapor. The water spurted and bubbled.

King Birronclaw's words came to me.

The cache is buried far away, amid bubbling fires that reek of decay, surrounded by frozen splinters that are larger than wolves and sharper than teeth.

Excitement touched my whiskers. We were getting closer. I tilted my head and gazed into the pool. "Why is it hot?" We were surrounded by snow, by freezing air – it didn't make sense. The Snowlands had a magic of their own, one that seemed to challenge the very laws of the earth.

"Just don't go anywhere near," said Farraclaw.

Lop spoke quietly, as though he feared to awaken the fury of the pool. "There is a restless fire beneath the soil. Some say it is the source of as much of our maha as Queen Canista's Lights. Where the fire leaks into the pools, it makes them boil with heat."

I cocked my head with interest.

106

Farraclaw sighed impatiently. "We aren't far from the Raging River. The tree cover will be gone before nightfall. Why don't you rest now, Isla, while we look around?" He turned a hard gaze on the floppy-eared wolf. "Lop, follow the path of the trees and find out exactly where they end."

"Yes, Sire." Lop dipped his head.

"I will explore the river bank. I won't be long. Isla, stay by the trunk of this tree. You should be safe here. If anything happens, call for me."

My limbs felt heavy from walking all day in the freezing cold. I couldn't keep it up as long as the wolves. I settled down against the tree, drawing my brush around me. My nose became accustomed to the stench of the pool. Its warm air was soothing. My eyes soon grew heavy and I dozed.

I awoke to the cawing of a crow. It was pecking at a branch over my head. It stretched its glossy wings and took flight. I rose with a sniff. The crow had built its nest there, a complex crisscross of twigs. By throwing my forepaws on the trunk of the tree, I could almost reach it. There was something in there . . . I craned my neck. I caught the gleam of a pale green shell, speckled brown and grey.

Eggs!

Fa had told us all about them. As a cub in the Wildlands, he had gone foraging for eggs with his brothers and sister. They were prized above other meals, rich and delicious.

I licked my chops.

I reached a forepaw towards the nest, straining to grasp one of the shiny eggs. A shrill cry and I shot around, losing my balance to stumble against the tree trunk. A crow bombed towards me. Its pointed beak grazed the top of my head. I yelped in surprise and cringed against the tree.

Circling back, the crow dropped again, a whirr of anger and feathers. Another crow darted towards me. Darkness leaped before me as the birds beat their wings in my face, beaks aimed at my eye. I stumbled backward, but they didn't let up. A blur of darkness and fury whirled around me. They dived again and again with ear-splitting shrieks. Their beaks stabbed my skin, drawing blood.

I spoke sternly to myself. *Don't panic! They're only birds!*

But I couldn't help it – the crows kept coming.

I started to run. They screeched and chased me, stabbing furiously. My paw slipped, a jag of scorching pain. I'd brushed against the orange shingle. I wobbled dangerously, the crows driving harder. With a slash to my ear I cried out. I was losing my footing on the shingle. As I tumbled backward, the bubbling waters leaped at my paws.

9

A white cloud burst between the trees. Jaws clamped the back of my neck and flung me on to a patch of grass.

I looked up at Farraclaw. His eyes were luminous, the black circles tiny against the glare of the sun. It only made him fiercer. The pool bubbled behind him, spitting up boiling water. "What were you doing?" he snarled. "Do you think you'd survive a dip in there?"

My ears pressed back against my head. "I'm sorry . . ." I glanced around but the crows had flown at the sight of the wolf. I saw Lop hurrying between the trunks.

Farraclaw breathed out slowly. "It's all right. It was an accident."

Lop trod towards me, sniffing at my paws. "Isla, are you hurt?"

I examined my singed pads. It was nothing compared to

what might have happened. "I'll be fine," I mumbled. I rolled on to my paws with a flinch.

"Can I help?" asked Lop. He shuffled forward on his belly and licked my forepaw. It was soothing. He focused on each paw in turn, and when he finished I was already feeling much better.

"Thank you," I murmured, flexing my paws. I looked around. Farraclaw had backed away. He was stalking between the trees.

He hurried back towards us. "I think wolves are close. They might have heard us."

My hackles rose. I followed Farraclaw, with Lop right behind me. We kept low as we slipped between the trees. A thick clump of foliage sprang in front of us and we edged around it. As Farraclaw reached the next tree, he froze. A moment later, I heard it: wolfish voices.

"Ambitious plan," said one of them. "With or without the king, it won't be easy."

"Easy enough," sniffed another. "You heard what he told us, the Bishar is weak. Now every wolf knows that from here to the deep sea. We've been cautious too long. Why must we wait as the bison hunker in their lands? Why must our pups go hungry?"

"Lord Raùfang," called another voice. I realized that the two wolves weren't alone. Between the trees, I could make out the shapes of two more.

"Not now, Brave Sneeglefang," growled the first wolf. "Can't you hear two lords are talking?"

"I'm sorry, Lord Raùfang. I thought I heard—"

"I said *not now*." The wolf turned back to his companion. "It isn't right how our pups have suffered."

The first wolf was quick to agree. "For that alone I would kill them in their sleep. King Orrùfang's first litter, all gone. It is upon us to avenge them."

I could hear the wolves scratching in the dirt. I pawed Farraclaw. It wasn't safe for us to stay here. I started backing away, into Lop. But Farraclaw stood still.

"Just so," agreed the second wolf. "There is no space for mercy."

The first wolf – the one called Raùfang – turned toward the other who'd spoken. "Now, Warrior Sneeglefang, what was it you wanted to say?"

I could see the wolf stoop low to the ground. "Forgive me, Lord Raùfang, Lordess Bezilfang. I did not wish to interrupt you. But I heard some rustling behind those leaves."

My heart leaped to my throat.

"Farraclaw," I whispered urgently. "We have to go. There are four of them, and they'll raise the alarm."

The wolf prince gave a small nod and sank low, winding away between the trees. In silence, we jogged between boulders. I could no longer hear the wolves. Instead, there was a misty sigh, the beating of water. It grew louder as we strode forward, swirling and crashing.

The Raging River.

As the trees parted, it came into view. In daylight it seemed even greater. Water crested white rocks, battering the shingle. The land beyond it was lost in a haze of mist and spume.

The Wildlands, the Elders. Was Siffrin safe? Had Simmi and Tao reached the Free Lands? My gaze travelled west, remembering the Mage with his acid eyes. Was that mist I saw rising over the Darklands?

Always, it longed to take physical form . . . And yet in growing it could only destroy and enslave the living. It began to take shape, a ghostly being forged of ash and dust – that is why we call it the White Fox.

I wondered what Jana and the other Elders were doing. Were they preparing to battle the Mage? How could they defeat the White Fox? It wasn't even *alive*. Not like a real fox.

Farraclaw disturbed my thoughts. "Those wolves were talking about us."

I glanced at him. Worry was etched on to his features. "They didn't mention Claw," I pointed out.

"That doesn't matter. 'With or without a king,' they said. They have learned of my father's infirmity. The king has not been seen for moons. Of course they suspect . . . And they spoke about King Orrùfang's anger. It can only be Claw."

Farraclaw had a point.

"Who do you think told them?" asked Lop.

Farraclaw turned to him sharply. "What do you mean?"

Lop dropped his gaze. "'You heard what *he* told us, the Bishar is weak.' That's what one of them said."

"You think we have a spy among our own?" Farraclaw's eyes were blazing. A growl rose in his voice. "Never."

I tried to reassure him. "Maybe it's just talk."

"Only one way to find out," said Farraclaw, rising to his full height. "I will invoke the Custom of Serren."

My ears rolled back. "Didn't you hear those wolves? They won't give you peaceful passage."

"They don't have a choice. It's tradition."

"So what?" Tradition didn't *mean* anything. It wasn't air. It wasn't earth or rain. It could be ignored.

Farraclaw gnawed at his tail impatiently. "You're a fox. You don't understand. They'll respect our ancient customs; it's a matter of honour."

"But you said yourself—"

"I was just being cautious." Farraclaw glared at me. The prince wasn't used to being contradicted. He began to turn. "I want to find out what they're planning."

Lop's eyes were wide. "But they could hear you. What if you're captured? The Bishar needs you."

Farraclaw glanced at him in annoyance and Lop fell silent.

The prince was going to get himself killed. A twitch of irritation touched my tail. "Do what you like," I snapped. "I'm going to the Ice Razors. I follow the bank of the river, right?" I started padding away, ignoring my throbbing paws.

I heard Farraclaw sigh loudly. "Very well," he replied. "I won't chase down the lords of Fang. Not yet anyway. I promised to take you to the Ice Razors. After that, we will see."

My tail started lashing. Farraclaw was brave and strong, but we were in enemy territory. Even he couldn't win against a whole Bishar.

No sooner had this thought sprung to my mind than a howl rose over the din of the Raging River. "Enemies are close!" bellowed a wolfish call.

We exchanged fearful looks. My heart was thumping.

Farraclaw started running along the bank of the river. Lop shot after him. Their long legs pounded over the snow. In the distance, spruce gathered over the tundra, but we'd have to cross an open valley before we reached it. *The wolves of Fang will see us!* I realized in horror.

Lop turned back to me. "Can you run any quicker?"

"Hurry, Isla!" hissed Farraclaw, pausing ahead.

I willed my legs to move faster, but it was no use. The howls were growing louder. The wolves would be nearing the edge of the forest. In moments, they'd see us.

I thought of slimmering.

But what about Farraclaw and Lop? The wolves of Fang

will raise the alarm. Sooner or later, they'll be caught!

Another howl rose from the trees.

"Keep going!" I urged them. "I'll see you at the spruce."

Lop and Farraclaw stared at me, making no move to run.

"Go!" I barked. I spun around and started back towards the forest. When I glanced over my shoulder, they were sprinting over the tundra. *Good*, I thought. At least they'd listened. *I can do this.* I considered karakking. In the past, I'd underestimated the foxcraft. There was so much more to it than a simple trick, a crow caw tossed into the air.

Crows . . . The angry blackbirds beneath the trees had almost driven me into the pool. Perhaps I should not underestimate them either.

My paws clattered against the shingle. I scrambled to an ungainly stop, diving behind the trunk of a tree at the edge of the small forest. I could hear the wolves quite clearly now. One howled so close that my fur sprang on edge. Instinct told me to run, but where?

They'll see me.

Better to make *them* run . . .

But how? Wolves weren't scared of crows. They weren't scared of anything.

I realized my mistake. I'd been hoping to drive the wolves away. I should try to lure them instead. I crept along the edge of the wood, drawing in great gulps of breath. I thought of Kolo, the Elder Fox who was master of karakking. I remembered his head thrown back, shaking the treetops with the power of his voice. I couldn't hope to emulate that but perhaps there was something I *could* do.

With one last gulp of breath, I raised my muzzle. Picturing the thick-furred bison, I threw my voice as far as I could across the forest. What emerged was a soft groan that floated over the leafless trees.

Dangerously close, I heard a wolf speak. "Bison!" he gasped. "I'm sure that was a bison!" There was a shuffle of paws against the forest floor as she turned away from me.

"Bison?" said another wolf. "It can't be! We're wasting time. I can *smell* strange wolves. This way, to the river."

My heart was slamming against my ribs. I hardly dared breathe with wolves so close. I tried to calm my panic, to call upon the strength of the stars. I couldn't see them beneath the sun's gaze but I knew they were there – Canista's Lights. Every hair, every whisker on my muzzle shivered with maa. I sucked in my breath and spat it out across the trees. This time it boomed, a deep, rumbling growl. The unmistakable battle cry of the bison.

"You're right, that *was* a bison!" gasped one of the wolves.

They started running. I could hear twigs crack beneath their paws and feel the thump of their weight on the earth. They ran away from me, deeper into the forest, chasing the mysterious bison.

I could hardly believe what I'd done. I allowed my tail a

wag before turning to hurry in the opposite direction, along the river bank, over the tundra.

I crossed the tundra, safe in the knowledge that the wolves of Fang were chasing invisible bison. My legs were tired by the time I reached the spruce trees but my tail couldn't stop lashing.

Lop and Farraclaw sprang on me, licking and nipping me gently.

"You made that sound?" asked Farraclaw. "You roared like a bison!"

"It's karakking," I explained. "A foxcraft."

"She must have so much maha," said Lop.

Farraclaw drew back, surveying me with yellow eyes. "Foxes are quite amazing creatures. I never realized . . ."

My tail wagged even more at that. "But I don't know the way to the Ice Razors."

"Well then, we still have some use." Farraclaw began to tread a path through the spruce trees.

Over several days we walked and walked. We were more active at night when the cover of darkness concealed my coat. Days seemed to last for ever in the Snowlands, with twilight slow to appear. The nights were short, and light blurred at the edges.

The wolves took turns keeping watch, insisting that I

slept when I could. It was a long journey . . . Where possible, we hugged the rocks, wandered through forests, or traced the path of the Raging River. Farraclaw was always tense to fight, but we met no resistance – no further wolves. We passed unseen between bubbling pools, where seething waterfalls leaped and spat. We drank from melting ice at the river's edge. The land swept north into towering mountains, disappearing into the clouds.

As a slow night finally closed above our heads, green shimmers of light danced over the tundra.

"What is it?" I gasped.

Farraclaw and Lop dipped their heads in unison. "The colours foretell Queen Canista's arrival," said the prince in a solemn voice. "They will strengthen daily until the Eve of Maha, when our ancient queen stands directly above us once more."

I remembered what Rupus had said. *The wolves thought the lights represented a great canid, the queen of their warlike ancestor spirits. In the stories of their Bishars, Queen Canista existed in our own world.*

"What is the Eve of Maha?" I asked, peering up at the green lights. They shimmered over the tundra, touching the snow flats with colour.

"The night we remember the queen of the wolves. The night we pay tribute to our ancestors." Farraclaw cocked his head thoughtfully. "We howl in memory, thanking those who have passed. For only with memory of the past can we strike boldly to the future. We are all of maha. All of the same magic pelt. It is the wolf's way."

The fur tingled along my spine. "Canista's Lights are important to foxes too. Maybe even to dogs and coyotes. The Mage is controlling Wildlands foxes. There are few left to fight him. If we could use the power of the lights. If we could somehow resist . . ."

Farraclaw tilted his head. "What do you mean?"

"I don't know." I looked in the direction of the Raging River. The haze of the Darklands was lost from view. Yet the memory of the Mage still wove itself through me. Those acid eyes . . .

It was Lop who interrupted my darker thoughts. "Hares," he whispered.

I blinked across the snow. They looked like large rabbits, but they stood taller. Their fur was white, except for the dark tips of their ears. In the moonlight, I spotted two near a stone ridge, while one tore along the grass. Already, Lop was stalking towards them. Farraclaw started edging the other way.

"I thought you only hunted large creatures like bison."

Farraclaw shot me an uneasy look. "We do what we must."

It was almost a fox's response. I watched as they stalked towards the ridge, creeping closer to the two hares that hopped over the snow.

The third hare froze. It seemed to sense that something was wrong. Standing downwind of Lop and Farraclaw, it might have caught their scents. Perhaps it heard the shush of their paws on the snow. I sank low as it started hopping my way.

What was seen is unseen; what was sensed becomes senseless. What was bone is bending; what was fur is air.

The hare was a blur of light up ahead. The light grew stronger, filling my vision. I held the slimmer. Closer, closer . . . My nose caught the hare's rich scent. Unable to control myself, I pounced. The hare gave a strange cry and leaped into the air. I sprang after it. It moved with speed, tearing past me on the snow, but it tripped in its panic and I threw a forepaw on its back. I pinned it down, breathless. The hare fought back – it was as almost as strong as I was. I gathered my maa, grappling to hook my paws around it, seeking out its throat. I bit down fast and hard. It bucked under my grip, then relaxed. A hiss in the air. A shimmer of light rose from its body and quickly faded into darkness. A few drops of blood coloured the snow.

Its maa was fading.

I released the hare, licking it a couple of times. Its eyes stared vacantly. Looking up, I saw Lop and Farraclaw, each carrying a hare in their jaws. They took in my kill with wagging tails.

"You see. A fox is good for some things," I said proudly.

We retreated behind dark crags, where we could feed without being seen.

"May the fallen rest in the peace of the forest," said Farraclaw, before tearing into the soft flesh.

I gazed over the tundra. In the moonlight, the blood on the snow looked black.

10

I didn't like the way Greatma was staring at me, worry etched into her muzzle. I wanted to pad past her to the den, where Isla was sleeping. She led me to the ivy that hung over the fence at the back of our patch. She beckoned me to follow her under its thicket of leaves.

I sat, gazing back at the den. "I was only playing." The words sounded feeble.

Greatma slipped on to her belly beside me. "Not all games are suitable for young foxes." She ran her tongue over her muzzle. "Not all games are safe."

I didn't want to meet her eyes. "What do you mean?"

Greatma sighed. "You were born early, before malinta. You and Isla both. Sometimes when this happens, it's like a knot of maa has lodged in the cub's heart. It unfurls as they growl. Such cubs are rare, you understand. They have more life source in them than a full-grown fox. They are able to do things that others can't."

My tail flicked and I turned to her, remembering the quiver of power that ran through my limbs. "What kind of things?"

"Their talents differ. Perhaps they run faster, climb higher than others. Some may be stronger. Others find their gifts lie in unknown lore. Untaught, yet by instinct they stumble into foxcraft."

My fur spiked at my neck. "What's that?"

Greatma's stare cut deep. "I think you know."

"What you saw just now . . . it was only play. I can make myself disappear if I try really hard. I feel a link with the earth and the air. I'm *connected* somehow." I feared Greatma's disapproval but I had to admit it felt good to share what I'd been feeling. Most of all, I wanted to tell my sister. I wasn't really sure why I hadn't. *I'll surprise her*, I said to myself. *When I'm really good, I'll teach her what I know.* But it wasn't that, not really. I'd enjoyed having a secret. "Why isn't Isla like me?" I asked. "She was born the same day."

"Don't underestimate your sister," said Greatma. "Her maa is strong. Though not like yours . . . You have the touch of Canista in your eyes. I have seen it." She gazed warily under the drooping ivy. "Others may see it too."

"What does it matter if they do? It's harmless really. I turn invisible. I make colours jump into the sky. Sometimes

I think I can sense the edges of thoughts – Isla's thoughts, not my own."

Greatma stiffened. "You sense her thoughts? Yet in the same breath, you tell me it's harmless."

"I wouldn't do anything bad. I don't *listen* to her thoughts, if that's what you mean." I sat up, offended. "I'd never do that!"

Greatma stared at me a long time. I held her gaze. Eventually, her ears relaxed, pointing out to the sides. She stretched a forepaw – ginger, grey, and gold – just like my own mottled colours. "No, you wouldn't. You have a good heart, Pirie. You don't realize how it can be out there . . . You think everyone is like you."

"What do you mean, Greatma?"

"You cannot know how others will respond to your gifts. What they might think. What they may do. You need to exercise caution. I don't want you playing around with your maa any more. I don't want to see any foxcraft, any strange colours." An edge had crept into her voice. "Do you understand me, Pirie?"

Oh, I understood. Understood she was trying to deny my gift. Trying to stop me from having fun. "You don't get it," I whimpered. "I *have* to do it. It's part of me. I can't just ignore who I am."

"I'm not asking you to. Just . . . be careful. Are you aware that a light was hanging over you as you played with foxcraft? A strange, amber glow . . . Some might see it from far across the Greylands. You never know who's watching."

How could she take this away from me? "I'm only a cub. No one will care what I'm doing."

"You are certainly young. Too young to realize the truth of this brutal world. There are those who will look upon your maa with envy. You must stop these games, Pirie. No more foxcraft."

Anger rose in my throat. Why should I stop? I launched my maa through my thoughts, a tangle of ambers and reds. Colours started weaving through the ivy, lighting the green leaves. "You don't know what it's like to be different. To have this power, and then be told not to use it. You don't know!"

Greatma's eyes widened. "Oh, don't I, Foxling?" A strange light pulsed in them, flashing white. The tip of her tail was silvery.

I sprang to my paws. Sparkles leaped off Greatma's mottled coat, curling about the amber of my thoughts. Her voice echoed around me.

I was like you, Foxling. I was different too. But I learned to hide it, to protect my family. Foxcraft is dangerous: that's what my own greatma told me. Be careful, Pirie. You don't even know what you have. You don't understand what it can do.

I gasped, scrambling back against a tangle of ivy. The colours fell away. The light faded in Greatma's eyes. She approached me to nuzzle against my shoulder. I pressed closer to her, relaxing into the warmth of her coat.

"You're like me," I murmured.

"Yes . . ." Greatma whispered. "I have hidden it a long time. I do it to keep you safe. You're all that matters, you and Isla, your ma and fa." She started washing my ears very gently.

Suddenly, I was exhausted. All I wanted was to sleep by my sister's side. I relaxed as Greatma wrapped her tail around me and led me back to the den. "No one must know of our gift," she urged. "Not Ma or Fa. Not even Isla. It will be our secret."

I sat up between Lop and Farraclaw in the hollow beneath a spruce tree. From this position, I could see the dark outline of the tundra.

I lowered my muzzle. I felt closer to my brother – closer than I had since he disappeared – and yet I understood him less. All this time, he'd been hiding his talents from me, confiding in Greatma . . . Leaving me out. I'd thought of him as my double, my shadow; how well did I really know Pirie?

If I squinted, I could just make out the smoke that rose from the pools. How had Lop explained them? A restless fire beneath the soil. It still didn't make much sense to me, out here in the freezing cold.

I drummed my paws in frustration.

There are too many things that don't make sense.

What was I even doing here? Seeking some buried cache for a mad wolf king. How could I trust him to take me to Pirie? A wolf who had once been the greatest of his kind but now rambled about beetles and ravens, and hawks that didn't even exist in the Snowlands.

My gerra is at war, I can scarcely think. Daily he attacks me, ravaging my maa, my very heart . . . I am not myself.

What exactly was wrong with the king? He had known of the Elders, had spoken of malinta. I flexed my forepaw. There was something familiar about him.

Something I couldn't place.

Almost unwillingly, my mind returned to Pirie. I already knew he was in the Snowlands. Hadn't the Elders told me as much?

I pictured Mika frowning, one long ear craned forward, the other twisted back. Her whiskers trembling like breeze-ruffled grass. *The winds have spoken. He lives.*

Alive, but where?

King Birronclaw had known that my brother had strong maa.

"Maha," Farraclaw had corrected. "That's what we call it."

"It doesn't matter what you call it," I'd snapped back.

But I'd been wrong.

It does matter. A wolf would never say "maa" . . .

The dawning of a dark notion. Pirie playing with maa,

exploring a power he did not understand. Greatma urging him to stop. *What if he hadn't stopped? How far would he go?*

For a moment, I was back in the Wildlands, in Karo and Flint's den before it was attacked. They were talking about the Taken, guessing at how the will might be stolen from a living fox. Karo had heard there must be flames.

I don't believe it, said one of the old vixens. *Foxes do not burn their gifts.*

That was true. Foxes didn't burn valuable things. *We bury them.* Like the king's cache buried beyond the Ice Razors.

I jumped up. Specks of silver glittered in the frozen snow.

A fox is lost to the Elders, beyond the fur and sinew of the greatest of Canista's cubs.

A whimper escaped my throat.

"Isla, are you all right?" Farraclaw was looking up at me. The blacks of his eyes were huge in the darkness. Not like they'd been in the glare of the sun. Then they'd shrunk to tiny dots.

I opened my mouth but no sound came out. Foxes had eyes like cats. Under beams of light, the circles contracted to slashes of black. I frowned, my heart thumping harder. With a jolt I remembered the king as he'd lunged towards me in the cave. His eyes were gauzy, weeping at the edges.

In the light, their dark centres shrank into slits.

Fox eyes.

I recalled what Amarog had said to me.

Was it you who watched like the black-eyed skua? Who would pierce the sacred flesh?

"What's a skua?" I asked.

Farraclaw gave me an odd look. "It's a bird." As an after-thought, he added, "It snatches its food from other birds. Even among its own kind, it is a thing without honour. An imposter, a thief."

A chill sank through me. I thought of that rare and dangerous foxcraft . . . It should only be performed by the Elders. But the Mage knew how to do it. So did the Narral, his loyal inner guard. What if my brother had guessed at its secrets? What if he'd wanted to try it for himself?

Would Pirie really do something like that?

Staring out across the tundra, I had to admit that I no longer knew.

"You look troubled." Farraclaw was watching me intently.

I ran my tongue over my muzzle. "I think I know what happened to your fa."

I felt Lop stir on my other side.

"An illness," said Farraclaw sadly. "It came on suddenly."

"Not an illness," I replied. "A . . ." I struggled to find the right word. "An accident . . . a game that went wrong. The melding of gerra between wolf and fox. A rare and powerful foxcraft, where one mind weaves with another. It can be used to control another's will. They must have fought to

129

overwhelm each other, neither winning, both growing weak and confused. Of course it was never going to work. Foxes and wolves are too different."

"What are you saying?" asked Farraclaw.

I swallowed hard. "I think the king was pleached."

I remembered what he'd said in the cave.

Only I am here. But never alone.

Farraclaw was eyeing me strangely. "I don't know what you mean."

Lop tilted his head. "Isla's saying that a fox has somehow joined his thoughts with King Birronclaw Valiant-Oolf. That they've both become stuck, each presence vying for control."

Farraclaw's ears were flat. "Really, Isla? Can that be true?"

Greatma's warning to Pirie came back to me. "I'm scared it is," I admitted, looking down at my paws. "Your fa became sick at the same time that my brother disappeared. Pirie was good at foxcraft, but he didn't know foxlore – he had never been taught about the dangers."

Farraclaw stared at me. "So my fa was the wolf in your riddle after all – the greatest of Queen Canista's cubs?"

"I think so," I said quietly. "I think his mind may be trapped alongside my brother's. It's Pirie who sent me to the Ice Razors. He used words only a fox would, like maa and malinta. He'd heard of the Elders."

Silence, I must find silence. I am not myself . . .

Farraclaw's ears were flat. "The king mutters in confusion. He acts like he doesn't even know who I am. But now and then there are sparks of clarity."

I couldn't meet his eyes. "Imagine hearing two sets of voices, conflicting thoughts."

"No wonder it's made him mad," said Farraclaw.

I didn't know how to answer. *What if it's made Pirie mad too?* I couldn't bear to think about that. Slowly, I raised my muzzle to look at Farraclaw. I feared that the prince would be livid with rage. That my confession would fill him with revulsion – that he'd refuse to help, might even seek to harm my brother. But what I saw in his gaze was just sadness.

"My fa was not a popular king. His leadership was . . . ruthless."

I remembered what Cattisclaw had told me about Farraclaw's sister.

The prince flicked a look at Lop, who lowered his head. "But he was strong and brave. And he was – *is* – still my fa."

"I'm sorry," I murmured, reaching up to lick his nose. "Sorry that my brother could be so foolish, and that it's taken me so long to understand where he was. But we're close now, and it's going to be all right. I'm going to unlock the secret of pleaching. I'm going to set them free."

11

"Up ahead!" he yelped, beginning to run. "I think it's the Ice Razors!"

It was late at night. We had walked through the frozen tundra under cover of darkness as the moon set in a velvet sky. At last, a shimmer of silver rose over the horizon. The Ice Razors gleamed like giant fangs, jagged and deadly. They stretched ahead of us into the darkness, twinkling against the night sky. Farraclaw paced towards them, his tail flicking.

"They look sharp," said Lop warily.

Farraclaw paced the other way. He edged a forepaw through a gap between the Ice Razors. The space was too narrow for a second paw. Ears back, he shuffled out on to the snow. "I don't understand. My fa said the cache is here. He buried it himself. He must have found a way through."

Lop's voice was soft. "The king never left the Bishar."

Farraclaw opened his mouth, but paused. When he spoke, it was to me. "The fox – your brother – did he come here to bury King Orrùfang's cache? I cannot see how a wolf could manage it. If anything, he must have come here exactly because he knew wolves wouldn't be able to reach the cache." Farraclaw drummed his paw against a patch of frozen snow. "That is why my fa needed you to find it."

"That makes sense I suppose." It still seemed extreme. Such a long journey, just to make sure that whatever was buried was safe.

"What do you think was in the cache?"

"I'll know it when I see it." I hoped that was true. I placed my forepaws on the ice.

"Careful, Isla!" begged Lop.

With a light pounce, I was between two columns. Beyond them, I saw further jags of ice. How far did they continue?

"There's no alternative," I said quietly. "I'll have to go on alone."

It was hard leaving Lop and Farraclaw behind. I had grown used to their company – to the solid, comforting presence of the wolves. They promised to hide out by a cluster of nearby spruce for as long as it took. At least the wolves of Fang couldn't pass where I was going.

I trod carefully over the ice, bracing myself so as not to slip. The razors were sharp enough to slice flesh. The columns wound over the land in a frozen maze. Where would I find the cache?

What has Pirie buried?

It still stung to think of all he'd kept from me. *We were so close.*

Eventually, the jags of ice stooped lower. Some splintered into deadly, pointed flowers, twinkling in the starlight. Others broke into steps that stooped closer to the earth. I slid down them, relieved to be off the Ice Razors. The land was grainy like sand. Instead of snow, the soil was crowned in frost.

I looked around. Smoke puffed up in clouds, concealing the sky. Steaming pools dotted the land, their burnt orange outlines just visible. White froth rose on them and from nowhere they spat molten water. I knew at once these were the bubbling fires. The cache must be near. I wrinkled my nose. I would need to be wary not to stumble into one of the frothing pools. There was the hiss of steam, the gurgle of water. But when the gurgling stopped, it was eerily silent. I saw no signs of life. No creatures dwelled in the wastes beyond the Ice Razors.

Warily, I crept through the Caldron. I sensed the heat under the frozen earth and veered away from it, winding between the scorching pools. Pale rocks rose between them.

I sniffed at one, scared of burning my paw, but the rock was icy against my whiskers. I climbed up it to see further. The smoke from the bubbling fires prickled my eyes. I blinked, my heart sinking. I saw rocks and pools stretching out in all directions. Where would I start to search for the cache in this barren wilderness?

Why did Pirie choose such a hostile place? Did he really go this far just to hide the cache from wolves?

A wind sliced through the Ice Razors. It picked up the gravelly sand and spun it in low patterns. For a moment, the smoke was blown away, revealing the night sky. Beneath Canista's Lights, I spotted a lone tree. It was huge, dark, stooped in a clearing between two burning ponds. Its branches hung low, like dangling limbs. It wasn't like the white-barked aspen, or the green-leafed spruce. Its trunk was ruddy, almost red.

It was a strange sight so far north, but I knew it at once.

A blood-bark tree.

A frosting of light hung around the tree. A thrumming of maa. *That's why the cache was buried here.* It was beneath its branches that I'd find the hidden treasure.

My heart was thumping as I sprang off the rock. I started running between the burning pools, ducking away from water that spat and scorched the earth.

I'm coming, Pirie!

I skidded to a halt under the blood-bark tree. Without

catching my breath, I started to dig. The sandy soil was frozen. It slipped between my claws, and I growled with effort.

I kicked up dirt, found nothing, and moved to another spot, repeating this over and over beneath the branches of the tree. With a scrabble of paws, I felt a change in the earth. All of a sudden it was softer – more yielding. A moment later, my paw pads touched a muddle of long white hairs.

I drew in my breath. *Fox fur.* The very tip of the tail.

Nothing was more valuable to a fox than their brush. It was balance, warmth, comfort. It was the very essence of our kind. I had seen how the Elders' tail-tips glowed silver when their thoughts united, when they spoke with one voice – when they practised foxcraft.

I knew then that the Mage really *had* chewed off his own tail, or at least the tip. He could not risk his own thoughts being invaded. As an expert in pleaching against a fox's will, he must have been fearful of the same fate.

I sniffed, but the stench of the pools disguised more subtle smells. I prized out all the white furs with my claws, resting them gently on the earth. I had released the cache, just as the king had said.

I sat, waiting to sense a change. A shift in the air, a murmur from the earth. I scanned the rugged land for my brother. Where would he appear? How would he be?

A dark thought clawed at the back of my mind. *If the*

pleaching has harmed a great wolf, what has it done to a young fox?

My tail tapped lightly. My ears twisted back and forth.

Nothing happened.

The smoke still rose on the pools. The frost clung to the earth. The ball of white fur tipped in the breeze. But beyond the burning pools, it was silent.

I slammed my forepaw on the sandy ground, sending up grains of dirt. Why wasn't it working? Frustration bubbled inside me, like the stinking water of the pools.

I sank to the ground and yowled. "Where are you, Pirie? Why are you hiding from me? You lied to me about your gift! You made me think we were the same. It isn't true. You're better than me! You were always better." My ears were flat, my voice shrill like wind. "I trusted you! I never kept any secrets. But you . . . you and Greatma . . ." I shook my head violently, as though to shake the memory of their conspiracy. Deep down I knew they meant no harm. But that did little to dampen the fire inside me.

I scraped at the dirt. I missed him. I missed them *all* – my family.

With a long sigh, I let out the anger. Beyond it I sensed a vast emptiness, worse than anger, much worse. This time when I spoke, my voice was a whimper. "Why would you pleach with a wolf? Didn't you know you could never control him? Some furs should never mingle."

I sat up sharply. My gaze shot to the ball of white hair. *Fox hair.* So where was the wolf's pelt? To pleach, wouldn't there need to be both?

I crept back to the trench where I'd dug out the white hairs. I started to burrow with my forepaws, doing my best to be careful this time, to slow down, despite my thumping heart. I kicked away the earth, feeling nothing but dirt. Then something soft tickled my paw pads. Stepping back, I saw it – a tangle of silvery fur. Hairs from the wolf king's tail.

I could hardly believe it – I had uncovered the secret of pleaching. The furs were buried together, one on top of the other. My brush started thrashing. I looked around excitedly. I didn't care what my brother had done. I didn't care if he'd kept secrets. I just wanted to see him again.

I paced under the blood-bark tree. A couple of times, I barked Pirie's name. I looped between the pools. Why couldn't I see him?

Light touched the base of the Ice Razors, slowly creeping along the columns. The night was fading.

He didn't come.

Wearily, I returned to the trench. I sniffed the wolf and fox hairs, discovering nothing. I tapped my paw against the dirt. What was I missing?

I thought of Siffrin, who knew so much more about fox-craft. Not that he'd taught me wa'akkir. Even when I knew the chant, even then he was reluctant to help me. My ears pricked up. That was it! A chant – there had to be a chant. There was one for all the higher arts. Had the Elders guessed that Pirie had pleached with the wolf? What else could their riddle have meant? Why hadn't they told me what to do?

I tried to remember what I knew about pleaching. Siffrin had told me it could be undone.

Not easily, he'd said. *The thing that's stolen must be released.*

I'd asked him if he meant the fox's will. Of course, he'd meant their fur – but he didn't say so. Instead he whispered the same words the Elders said when they parted. *Run fast, be safe, live free.*

If only Siffrin was here, if only he could help . . . The Elders' farewell was bittersweet. "What's the point in being safe – being free – if you're alone?" I'd already said enough goodbyes. My spine stiffened. I wouldn't give up on Pirie. I was close now, I knew I was.

Siffrin had looked so guilty when we spoke about fox-craft. Torn between helping me and staying loyal to Jana. I closed my eyes. The bubbling of the pools seemed to grow louder.

A thought slowly dawned on me. *Siffrin knew he mustn't reveal the secrets of pleaching. But he wanted to help me. What if he told me in a way that wasn't obvious?*

When I opened my eyes, the light against the Ice Razors had brightened. A shiny pink glimmer crept over the sandy earth. I stood above the fox and wolf fur, raising my eyes to the blood-bark tree. Although I was alone, I spoke out loud.

"Run fast, be safe, live free."

A tremor of movement shifted beneath my paws. A hiss of white froth rose on the pools. The pink light pulsed red. *Something's happening!* I drew my brush along my side.

The white tip was silver.

My heart was thumping against my chest. I started darting between the pools, racing towards the Ice Razors. The great gleaming columns shifted with colour. My claws scrabbled against the ice, but I couldn't slow down. I slipped and slid between the columns, smacking bars of ice that chilled my fur. I didn't care – I was close now.

I could sense the change in the air. As I emerged between the columns on to the tundra, the light was so bright and low that I could hardly see. I paused, blinking. I knew where to go – towards the foothills, where the sunrise dazzled the crags.

"Isla?" It was Lop trotting over the snow.

Farraclaw hurried behind him. "You're back!" He paused. "You're alone."

"Not for long." I cocked my head towards the foothills. "They're free now," I said. "The pleaching's reversed." I didn't wait to hear the wolf's reply. I ran over the snow, glaring into the sun. Searching for signs of movement.

My breath caught in my throat and I slammed to a halt. A silhouette stood against the sunrise – a black figure with a slender muzzle and a long, puffy tail – the unmistakable shape of a fox.

"Pirie!" I called, starting to run again. I bolted over the tundra, my legs pumping wildly, my paws scarcely touching the earth. As the sun broke over the frozen land, I reached the craggy foothills. I blinked furiously, blinded by light. "Pirie! Is that really you?"

The voice that replied was cracking with age. "You are mistaken," he said. "My name is Métis. They call me the Black Fox."

12

He was a slight fox. Up close, I could see that he was old. His legs were bony, his forepaws splayed. His brush was long and thick. The white tip shone in the morning light as it floated over the ground. Silvery furs dappled his forehead and shoulders. The rest of him was the same dark sheen as a raven.

The Black Fox.

I stopped in my tracks. "I thought . . ." My words faded as Farraclaw and Lop drew near.

Métis cringed away from the wolves. The silvery hairs rose on his shoulders. "Another step and you die," he hissed.

Farraclaw looked amused. "You know this fox?" he asked me.

It isn't Pirie. It was never Pirie.

I grappled for words. "He's an Elder."

"Not just *any* Elder," he replied. "And who are you?"

I didn't like his tone, or the wrinkle in his muzzle as he peered at me. "My name is Isla. I'm from the Great Snarl – the *Greylands*." I blinked at him, still trying to put it together. "Who did you expect? Jana?"

"Did she send *you*?" The fox glared at me, though his eyes flicked nervously to Lop and Farraclaw. He blinked hard, as if he couldn't focus.

I thought about his question – wondered how wrong I'd been to think I would find Pirie here. I'd been a fool. *A fox is lost to the Elders* . . . Not my brother. It was Métis they'd wanted all along. I remembered Brin's uneasiness, and Shaya's words of warning. They hadn't agreed with Jana's plan. Yet Jana had conspired with the other Elders to send me out here. To search for the pleached fox and release him. She'd known all along that I wouldn't find Pirie in the Snowlands.

A chill crept deep under my fur.

She'd used me.

At last I spoke, my voice as icy as the frozen earth. "The Elders sent me. Though I didn't realize it until now."

Farraclaw frowned. "Where is your brother, Isla?"

My shoulders sagged. "I doubt he ever came this far north. The Elders tricked me. They sent me here to find Métis." I paused. "Though I'm not sure they knew it was Métis who was pleached with the wolf. Another Elder has also gone."

Métis looked at me. "Keeveny." He didn't seem surprised.

Waves of disappointment crashed over me. "Do you know anything of my brother Pirie? He disappeared from the Snarl. One of the Narral was there, and the Taken. They caught the rest of my family, but I think he escaped. Where could he be?"

"Your brother?" His ears flicked back. "A Greylands foxling . . . Why should I know him?"

My throat was dry. I had no response.

"What are you?" barked Farraclaw.

Métis recoiled. "Back away, Wolf. I have already warned you."

"Warned *me*?" snorted Farraclaw. He sprang towards Métis.

The Black Fox stumbled backward, chanting. "Feel my gerra, share my glance – calm your terror, enter trance."

Farraclaw threw open his jaws, then shut them slowly. He lowered his muzzle to meet the Black Fox's eye. A calm enveloped him. He reclined on to his belly, as though taking a nap, though his eyes stared vacantly ahead.

"What have you done to Prince Farraclaw?" snarled Lop.

Métis wheeled around to face him. I saw his tail flicker with a silvery gleam, then fade. He was grasping at foxcraft, but it wasn't working. He gritted his teeth. Trembling, he collapsed on to the snow.

"What's wrong with the fox?" asked Lop.

I trod closer to Métis. "He's injured." I sniffed his coat, sensing a deep weariness. I glanced at Farraclaw. He was still lying on his belly, his breath coming slowly. "Whatever you've done, undo it right away!"

"And have that beast kill me?" panted Métis. "It's only pakkara, a trance state. It will not hurt the wolf. But if I release him, he will hurt me."

"He won't." I looked at Lop and he nodded stiffly.

With a sigh, Métis raised his head towards Farraclaw. "When you feel my gentle claw, you will be in trance no more." Gingerly he outstretched his foreleg to touch the wolf on the nose.

Farraclaw blinked, then rose with a shake. "What did you do?" he snarled.

"You are unharmed," said Métis quickly. He tried to rise, staggered backward, then slumped down. His legs seemed unable to hold him. Already, he was out of breath.

I studied the old fox. "You pleached with King Birronclaw." It was a statement, not a question. "You were trapped."

Métis panted. "I meant only to see what might be done with the wolf's power." His eyes slid away, towards the White Mountains. "I shouldn't have tried it. A wolf's will cannot be tamed." He rubbed his eyes with an angry forepaw. "I acted against foxlore. It is not for the Elders to pleach another creature against his will. I have broken from foxlore, and I have suffered the consequences."

I sensed it – the exhaustion that gnawed at his limbs. "Your maa . . ."

"It's sapped beyond repair. My gerra is in shreds."

"King Birronclaw Valiant-Oolf is my fa," growled Farraclaw. "He has lost his mind."

I placed a paw on his foreleg. "I promised Métis you wouldn't hurt him."

The Black Fox looked up at Farraclaw. "Forgive me," he mumbled. "I meant no ill to befall the wolf. True, I would have used his brawn to our cause. After that, I would have seen him freed. It was reckless. An act of desperation." He drew in a quivering breath. "Keeveny grows ever more powerful. I thought . . ." his voice dwindled to a whisper. "I thought if we had a wolf to fight with us, that would be something."

My whiskers bristled. "So Keeveny is the Mage?"

Métis dipped his head in acknowledgement. Face knotted with effort, he rolled on to his paws.

"Cunning, wicked fox! You risked my fa's life! You thought you would try to seize his power with your . . . your *foxcraft*." Farraclaw's eyes were bright with anger. "Don't worry," he snarled, glancing at me. "I won't hurt him. I wouldn't dignify this shrewling by touching him."

Lop cocked his head. "Isla said that the Mage is controlling foxes in the Wildlands. There are few left to fight him."

"It is so," said Métis quietly. "In times of peril, sacrifices must be made. I regret the harm to the wolf king. You must know that I risked my own life as readily as I risked his." He looked from Lop to Farraclaw.

Farraclaw's head was stooped. "My fa will not recover."

I padded closer to him and licked his muzzle.

Métis spluttered in astonishment. "These wolves . . . Are they your friends?"

I turned to the old fox. "I wouldn't have made it to the Ice Razors without them. They are Farraclaw and Lop from the Bishar of Claw."

Métis stiffened. His ears twisted forward. "Did you bring others?"

Farraclaw frowned. "The rest of the Bishar remained in our territory. Why do you ask?"

I followed the Black Fox's gaze. There was a flicker of movement between the distant spruce. It took a moment to work out what I was seeing.

"Wolves of Fang," I gasped, my hairs rising in spikes. They ran in formation, their white tails bobbing as they zig-zagged between the great trees.

"Quick," whispered Métis, "Over here." He clambered around the boulders that circled the foothills. Anger flashed across Farraclaw's face. He wasn't happy to be told what to do by a fox he'd only just met – a fox who had sought to snare his fa's mind. I looked at him wide-eyed, beckoning him to follow. Jaw set, he slipped behind me as I edged around the boulders. Lop took his cue from Farraclaw, hiding just as the white wolves of Fang broke over the tundra.

Métis hunched against the grey stone. Lop pressed close to my side while Farraclaw peered around the boulders.

"It's a watch party," he whispered. "A lordess, warriors, and an under-wolf."

I wasn't sure how Farraclaw could tell all that at a distance. There were codes of appearance and conduct that were only clear to a wolf's eye.

Farraclaw's ears were flat. "We will have to wait until they pass," he whispered. "The sun is up now. We can't cross to the trees without being seen."

I shuffled alongside him to watch as the wolves ran over the snow. They were coming closer. Did they know we were here?

"It's all right," said Farraclaw. "They're stopping."

The prince was right. The female in the lead was slowing down and the others followed. At the back of the group was a wolf so stooped to the ground that he barely reached half her height. He hung back from the others, tail between his legs. Even I could now see what Farraclaw had already observed: this was obviously an under-wolf.

The female turned to look around. The others watched her carefully.

I could just pick up her words. "And the Ice Razors too. By order of King Orrùfang Valiant-Raa."

"No one comes here, Lordess Bezilfang," said a white male with a single grey paw. *Bezilfang.* Wasn't that one of the wolves we'd dodged earlier?

"I know," the lordess agreed. "But this close to the attack, we can't be too careful." Her muzzle crinkled. "Ratok, clear a space."

The under-wolf sprang to attention, dashing to a mound of snow and hastily digging a shallow trench. The others ignored him.

"It has to be before the Eve of Maha," the female went on. "Their ancestors are powerful. They've held that land for generations. We cannot cross the soil as their spirits reawaken."

The wolf with the grey paw shook out his fur. "Is it true that their king is dead?"

"Not dead yet . . . ailing," said the female. "It's the perfect time to strike. None in his own Bishar would launch a challenge while he lives, and meanwhile he's too weak to defeat us."

Crouched beside me, Farraclaw let out a low growl.

I nudged his shoulder with my nose. "It's just talk."

"No." Farraclaw's voice was choked. "She's right. We are vulnerable. They are free to attack."

I tried to remember what he'd told me back at the Bishar of Claw. I hadn't long arrived and it was all a blur. "I thought . . . Aren't the wolves of Claw stronger? You could beat them in a battle."

"Silence," hissed Métis. "They'll hear us." He edged along the boulders.

Farraclaw threw the Black Fox a withering look. He spoke to me in a low voice. "I don't think you understand. The leader of a Bishar may challenge a rival king to fight. If the other king refuses – if he is too weak, or too scared – if he cannot be found, the fight is surrendered."

Now I remembered. "You mean . . ."

"I mean," replied Farraclaw, struggling to control the panic in his voice. "That the wolves of Fang have learned that our king is sick. Their king will challenge my fa to combat. You have seen what that fox has done to him – he will not be able to fight. The Bishar of Fang will seize our lands and none will be able to stop them."

Cold crept through me. I thought of the pups in their den.

The female wolf was addressing the others. "I was only a pup when King Birronclaw killed King Garrùfang."

"A terrible thing," uttered the male with the grey paw, and the other wolves echoed their agreement.

The under-wolf had finished digging. He approached the female at an angle, belly sweeping the ground. He lowered himself in front of her. "Lordess Bezilfang, I have dug a space."

The female wolf spoke over him, as though he was invisible. "Our revenge has been a long time coming," she told the other wolves. "If it hadn't been for our helpful defector, we might have been fooled. Their king would have died, and the prince anointed before we had time to attack. But fortune shines on the Bishar of Fang."

The under-wolf dropped back. At length, the lordess padded over to the low trench. As she passed him, she called out absently. "Ratok, survey these lands." The under-wolf dipped his head. He started sniffing around the Ice Razors, shoving his head between them, then retreating.

The lordess made herself comfortable as the male with the grey paw, a perfectly white male, and another female with a dark face sat down next to her. The four wolves huddled in the trench were still talking, but I could no longer hear what they said.

The under-wolf was sniffing along the columns of ice, but was unable to pass between them. He wound back towards the spruce and disappeared from view.

There was thunder in Farraclaw's gaze. He started to rise.

"Sire, what are you doing?" whispered Lop.

"'*Helpful defector*,'" spat Farraclaw. "You were right, Lop. One of our own Bishar told the wolves of Fang about my fa. If I hadn't heard it with my own ears, I would never have believed it." He shook his head. "I must find out their plan.

I need to know who's betrayed us." He started around the back of the boulders.

"Wolf, are you insane?" snapped Métis. "You'll bring death to all of us!"

Farraclaw turned on him angrily. "To you, I'm Prince Farraclaw Valiant-Jowl, the eldest son of Queen Sableclaw Valiant-Jowl and King Birronclaw Valiant-Oolf. It is he who is mad, and it's *your* fault. Your fault he cannot defend our realms. Your fault the Bishar of Claw will fall."

Métis flinched, dropping his gaze. His long brush curved around his flank.

Farraclaw shoved past him.

"Stop, it isn't safe!" I bit his tail gently, trying to tug him back.

He shook himself free. "I'll be careful."

I scampered in front of him to block his way. "Let me go," I begged. "I can slimmer. They won't be able to see me! Let me find out what they're planning."

"More foxcraft?" The look he gave me chilled me to the marrow. "I don't think so."

But someone else had pounced in front of Farraclaw and was creeping around the boulders.

Lop.

The under-wolf looped around the crags. To my amazement, he padded down them, in plain sight of the watch group. His ears were pricked – a casual glance would reveal nothing unusual about them. His tail curved between his legs.

He sniffed around the edge of the Ice Razors, just as the other under-wolf had. I saw him pause, his head slightly cocked, before creeping on a little, his snout close to the frozen columns.

Farraclaw's eyes were fixed on Lop, though he stayed beside me, concealed behind the boulders.

I found I was holding my breath. How long could Lop's luck hold out? But the lordess ignored him, and so did the other wolves as he appeared to busy himself at the Ice Razors.

No one sees the under-wolf.

Lop was following the columns in our direction. With a glance over his shoulder, he trod alongside them to slip between the crags. A moment later, he stood between us.

Farraclaw stared at the small wolf. "That was brave," he whispered. A new respect crept over his face.

"Just doing my duty, Sire." Lop drew in his breath. "The news isn't good. They intend to attack. The whole Bishar will be there. They believe they'll have the element of surprise. King Orrùfang will challenge your fa. They know he cannot fight back."

"The fiends," spat Farraclaw.

"Soon. They didn't say exactly when."

"Where will they launch the attack?"

"I don't know," Lop murmured.

"Who betrayed us, did they say?" pressed Farraclaw.

"They didn't."

"I need to find out more." Farraclaw stepped past me.

"Sire, please don't go," begged Lop. "They will see you!"

"I'll be careful," muttered Farraclaw.

I started after him but felt a paw against my flank. "There's nothing you can do," Métis warned. "The fool will get us all killed."

I watched helplessly as Farraclaw edged away from us towards the Ice Razors. If the wolves of Fang turned, they would spot him. With his proud stance and the thick tumble of his mane, he looked nothing like their under-wolf.

I shuffled back behind the boulders, exchanging an anxious look with Lop. He gave me a comforting lick on the head. I craned my neck. I could see the white female was still talking. I caught only the occasional word. "Claw . . . Ruin . . ."

Farraclaw appeared behind the group of wolves. *He's too close.* But the wolves of Fang didn't look his way. I saw his ears prick forward and a dark look cross his face. He must have heard more about their plans. I hoped he would leave it at that.

Howls rose from the wolves, sharp on the morning breeze. Were they laughing about the Bishar of Claw? Bragging about what they'd do to their rivals?

154

To my horror, Farraclaw was moving towards them, tracing the jags of ice. *Don't go there! You can't fit between the columns.*

Suddenly, the female sat up with a growl. The wolf with the grey paw raised his muzzle, then paused. His eyes darted to the Ice Razors. "Intruder!" he barked in shrill staccato.

Their heads shot around and they stared at Farraclaw. Panic ripped through me. There was nowhere for him to run.

The wolves of Fang bounded up to him, hackles sharp, lips peeled back so far that their gums were exposed above giant fangs. They closed around Farraclaw as Lop and I watched in horror.

"Well, well," snarled the white female. "A trespasser. Speak fast, if you wish to live."

Farraclaw stood tall. His body did not betray the fear he must have felt. "I am Prince Farraclaw Valiant-Jowl. I seek peaceful passage through your lands. In the spirit of Noble King Serrenclaw, I invoke the Custom of Serren."

The snow wolves were awestruck.

"Did you hear that?" yelped the grey-pawed male. "Prince Farraclaw himself! This far into our territory. How did he manage it?"

The lordess snorted. "Peaceful passage? The Custom of Serren? I don't think so." She sprang forward and landed a bite on Farraclaw's back leg. Her jaws tore deep, and I cringed against Lop. To my surprise, Farraclaw didn't fight back.

The grey-pawed male followed her lead. He sprang on Farraclaw, sinking his teeth into his neck. "Spy on us, would you? You'll pay for that!"

"We have to help him," I whimpered.

Lop's paw tensed on my shoulder. "We can't do anything now."

I watched as the wolves of Fang circled and tormented Farraclaw, nipping, barging and snapping at him.

"King Orrùfang will be pleased to see you," growled the white female. "An honour for all who have caught you." She looked around. "Are there others here? Surely a Prince of Claw wouldn't travel without attendants?"

"I am alone," said Farraclaw in a loud, clear voice. "I do not require a whelping ma."

"Don't believe him," snarled the other female, springing forward to snap her teeth around Farraclaw's leg. "Where are the others?"

"I have already told you. I am alone."

"Liar!" Another bite and Farraclaw stumbled. But he didn't cry out, and he didn't fight back.

"Where are they?" hissed the white lordess.

"I have already told you. I am alone. I have invoked the Custom of Serren. I have nothing more to say."

The white wolf slammed against him. He stumbled but quickly rose to his paws. "Well, that is a shame for you," she spat. "A bold wolf, no doubt, and arrogant with it. But even you cannot win against all of us. Though I should like to see you try." Her ears flicked back as she baited Farraclaw. With a pounce, she landed another cruel bite on the prince's flank as the dark-faced female butted him.

The wolves fell back with a snarl. Bites at the prince's shoulders and flanks gushed red with blood. It was ghastly against his snowy coat. He set his muzzle. "You are breaching the ancient customs that bind us as neighbors and kin."

"Alas, he will not fight," said the lordess, addressing the others. "Not yet, anyway . . ." She ran her tongue over her bloodstained teeth. "King Orrùfang will know what to do with him. He is not inclined to mercy."

"I should gladly speak to your king," said Farraclaw.

"Then show some respect to his lordess!" roared the grey-pawed male, slamming his head against the prince's muzzle. The wolves closed in on Farraclaw, snapping at him, shunting him towards the aspens. For a moment, I saw him in profile. His gaze was set over the tundra. He didn't cry out or ask for help. He never glanced back at the boulders where I trembled in terror – where Lop whimpered and Métis watched in silence.

Though they bullied and beat him, taunted and mocked him, Farraclaw didn't betray us.

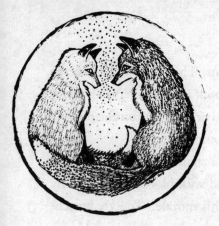

With a stretch, Métis rose to his paws. "So long, Wolf," he said to Lop. "Foxling, come. We need to get back to the Wildlands. I've been away too long."

My muzzle wrinkled. "I'm not going with *you*."

The old fox scowled. "You must. You have good maa, don't you? We shall need it. Why do you think the Elders sent you?" He gave his brush a shake. "A foxling. I still can't believe it," he muttered to himself. "They might at least have sent Siffrin."

My heart pitched. "Siffrin's back in the Wildlands. Jana wouldn't let him come." Had the red fox known of Jana's trick? For an instant I held my breath, thinking hard. Siffrin had argued against my journey to the Snowlands, and later offered to come with me. I doubted he knew any more about it than I had. I let my breath out slowly. "I'm not going with you. I'm going to find Farraclaw. We can't just leave him to be killed!"

Lop was gazing beyond me across the tundra. "We'll have to track them at a distance. We have no idea where they're taking him."

"Rubbish," snapped Métis. "What fools wolves are. I know exactly where they're going." He extended a black fore-leg. Perhaps it was glossy once, but the fur was tatty, clumping in dirty tangles around his paw.

Lop turned to him. "What do you mean?" There was a warning glint in his eyes I'd never seen before. He may have been the under-wolf, but he was huge compared to Métis.

The Black Fox swallowed. His dropped his paw. "The lordess said they're taking your master to their king. He rules over the Ice Palace at the heart of the Bishar. It's circled by a scorching stream. Below it the wolves have dug out a dungeon – a frozen cave where their enemies are tortured and killed. That's where you'll find your wolf prince."

I started forward. "We have to go there."

"And do what?" I sensed the depth of judgement in Métis's green eyes. "Think for a moment. The entire Bishar will be there. Your prince of Claw is a prized prisoner. Guards will be watching his every move." His long ears twisted forward. "You cannot save the prince. And why would you wish to? Have you failed to grasp the peril we face in the Wildlands? Do you care more for these wolves than your own kind?" His snout crinkled, though his eyes flicked warily to Lop. Beneath his contempt, I sensed fear.

My voice was a growl. "I already told you, they helped me across the Bishar of Fang. If it wasn't for Lop and Farraclaw, I wouldn't have made it to the Ice Razors. I wouldn't have freed *you*."

Métis limped to the edge of the boulders. "Consider me grateful," he rasped, sounding nothing of the kind. He paused, his forepaw trembling. With a wince he swung around to face me. Exhaustion was etched on his face. "Give me maa," he said suddenly.

I blinked at him.

Lop was treading warily beyond the boulders. "They're almost out of sight. We have to start trailing them."

Métis spoke over him. "Hurry up, Foxling. I must get home." He looked at Lop. "There's no point trailing them – doing so will only get you caught as well. I told you where they're taking your prince. You can't free him, give it up."

"We *will* free him," I said. "Come on, Lop."

We started bounding over the snow.

"Stop!" yelped Métis. "I must have maa. I won't survive without it. They need me – those foxes back in the Wildlands. I can't let them down."

I froze in my tracks. Flint and Karo had been pleached. Simmi and Tao had run to the Free Lands . . . Others like Rupus and Mox were killed by the Mage's skulk.

"I'll help you," he added quietly. "If you give me maa, I'll help you free the wolf."

Lop glared at him. "What can *you* do?"

Métis swallowed. "Foxcraft. If I have enough maa."

I stood uncertainly. The Black Fox was supposed to be the wisest fox of any age. Farraclaw was in trouble. I hadn't been near the Ice Palace, but if it was anything like the Frozen Fort it would be impossibly well guarded. How would we enter without being seen? How would we lead Farraclaw past the guards?

With a shake of my head, I padded back to Métis. "If I give you maa, do you promise to help? No tricks."

"No tricks," he conceded.

Lop had turned, his floppy ears catching the breeze.

Métis blinked his green eyes. "Why have you stopped, Wolf?"

"You said . . ." Lop scanned the tundra, where the watch group had disappeared, taking Farraclaw with them. "You said there's no hurry, that we already know where they're going."

"To the Ice Palace." Métis stared at Lop as though he was an idiot. "But you aren't going there. You couldn't get close before they caught you." Métis gave him a hard stare. "You're not royalty. You're not even a warrior. What are you, the Claw under-wolf?" How did he know? "What value are you to the wolves of Fang? They would kill you before you could even howl."

"How dare you!" I hissed. "Lop is the smartest, fastest wolf in the Snowlands."

Lop's floppy ears sank even lower. "I cannot leave my prince to their mercy," he growled.

"Neither should you," said Métis wearily. "Can't you see? You are needed now more than ever. This foxling says you are fast. Are you fast enough to warn your Bishar before the wolves of Fang arrive? You are perfectly white, and the snow hasn't thawed. You have the benefit of camouflage. Can you run along the foothills without being seen?" Métis spoke with purpose. I couldn't help but lean forward, and I saw Lop do the same. "Leave the foxling, she will only slow you down. The wolves of Fang don't know that you expect an attack – they won't waste time looping over your domains. They will strike head-on, where the territories meet. Your Bishar must be prepared. They should all be there as a show of strength, or Fang will think you weak. You must call upon your king to reach the boundary between the Bishars. If he fails, your lands are forfeit."

The truth of this struck me.

Lop nodded slowly. "And you will free Prince Farraclaw?"

"We will," I found myself saying, though I had no idea how.

The under-wolf raised his muzzle. "One Bishar, united under Queen Canista's Lights. For friendship. For honour. For ever." He turned abruptly, without even saying goodbye.

He tore over the icy ground, a streak of white fur at the foothills.

Métis sank on to his belly. "Maa," he said. "Hurry."

Although I'd received the Elders' maa, I had only shared my own with Siffrin. That was different . . . I hardly knew Métis, and what I knew, I didn't like.

"We don't have time for your doubts," he snipped, as though reading my thoughts. "I won't take much. We need you strong. Just enough to get by . . . Look at me."

I turned to the Black Fox. His green eyes sparkled with light. I started to chant: "With my touch, I sense you; with my eyes, I heal you. By Canista's Lights, I share what I have, we are knit together and you are whole."

With a lurch I was tugged into his gaze. I tumbled into iridescent green. The earth gaped, a sheer drop into darkness. I fell, legs thrashing. Wind lashed at my fur. My tail flicked up behind me. I landed on a bed of moss. Green light whirled over my head. I looked around wildly: I was in the Elder Wood. The ancient trees crowded in, their branches thick with leaves. Birds warbled, warmth touched my whiskers. I was running beside a brook. The thick trunks gave way to slender fruit trees. Brambles trellised between them and dapples of green-and-white ivy. Power flexed through my limbs. A sharp smell caught my nose. Up ahead I saw flames rising over the trees. Smoke billowed, the crackle of splintering wood. I ran towards it, knowing no fear. Air filled my chest. I sped over the mulchy ground, fast, faster, almost flying—

Métis blinked.

I slumped on to the snow. I waited for exhaustion to wash over me, as it had after maa-sharm with Siffrin.

I felt fine. Just the same. If anything, a shimmer of maa flickered at my tail-tip. I rolled on to my paws with a shake.

Métis was examining his paws. He raised each in turn, nibbling at his claws. Then he swept his tail close with a sniff.

I tapped my paw impatiently. "Aren't we going? You saw what they were doing to Farraclaw." The hairs shivered along my back. What if he refused? Métis looked up. His shrewd eyes were sharper now. "Very well." His gaze trailed to the tip of my tail. "You are not without maa. Perhaps I underestimated you." His voice was not conciliatory. "We will need it for what you must do. I will lead you to the entrance of the Ice Palace. From there, you will be on your own. I will not have the energy to help – I would only hinder you and risk your capture."

Panic rose inside me. "But how can I free Farraclaw alone?"

"You can slimmer, can't you?"

"Farraclaw can't," I replied. "Even if I reached the dungeon without being seen, how would I get him out?"

Métis padded around the boulders, on to the open

tundra. The sun was already high overhead. I pictured Lop storming through the snow. Would he make it past the watch parties? Would he reach the Bishar in time?

"Come, Isla," said the Black Fox. "I have made you a promise and I do not intend to break it. Let us hurry to the Ice Palace. I'll explain on the way."

The journey was painfully slow. Even with my maa, Métis struggled. We kept to the shadows beneath patches of tree cover, keen to conceal our stark coats from watchful eyes. Métis stopped frequently. While he rested, I managed to catch another hare. Métis picked at the kill without enthusiasm. In the end, I finished most of the meal myself.

It was twilight by the time we reached a swathe of pines at the outskirts of the Ice Palace. I could see it rising from billows of mist on a glistening shaft of rock.

"It's a glacier," said Métis. "A mass of ice."

"Doesn't it melt in the heat?"

His green gaze told me I was foolish. "Heat never arrives this far north."

As we crept closer between the pine trees, steam rose from the earth. A stream ran around the base of the glacier, spewing scorching water. Narrow paths cut between the stream, and along these stalked white wolves.

Métis raised his muzzle. "You will need to slip past the guards to reach the dungeons. Feel your way."

165

I glanced at him. I had no idea how to do that.

"I will wait here," Métis went on. "You must find me. I will need you for the journey home. Remember your promise." One black ear twisted forward. "I can help you get the wolf back to his territory without being seen. It won't be easy."

I nodded solemnly. *If I get out*, I thought.

"Trust in your maa. Do not hurry, for if you do your heart will beat faster and the foxcraft will fail. Yet do not tarry, for a seized breath will bring you back to visibility." His green eyes were cool, but he added almost kindly, "I have felt your maa. You can do this and much more. Reach deep – find your inner stillness."

I opened my mouth to reply, but he snorted impatiently. "Go now. The night will not wait for you."

I trod to the edge of the tree cover. Wolves paced the passages between the roiling stream, guarding the entrance to the Ice Palace. A howl shuddered over the snow and my fur rose in spikes. I coaxed it down. I had to stay calm – my survival depended on it. I shut my eyes. I pictured Lop racing over the snow and my breath leaped to my throat.

"Calm," said Métis. I turned to look back at him. How did he know? "The chant will help."

I drew in my breath. "What was seen is unseen; what was sensed becomes senseless. What was bone is bending; what was fur is air." My whiskers tingled. I closed my eyes. The world of my thoughts was green. A verdant forest expanded in my mind. I opened my eyes. The palace on the glacier was a blur of cool edges and bubbling water. I looked down at my paws. They had dissolved from view.

I stepped out from between the trees. Slowly, slowly, my paws crunched over the snow. I made my way to the foot of the huge glacier. With careful steps, I approached one of the entranceways.

My gaze drifted behind me. I'd left prints . . . The wolves could find them; they could track me to the glacier. A guard was pacing up ahead, his thick paws thumping the ground. Panic crept along my spine. My raised foreleg flickered into view.

I repeated the chant in my thoughts.

What was seen is unseen; what was sensed becomes senseless.

The wolf was close now, turning towards me. His shoulders were squared. Through the murk of the slimmer, I saw his muzzle crinkle. Perhaps he'd caught a whiff of my scent. His huge head turned one way, then the other. With a snort he marched on, passing me on to the tundra. It was dark now. I hoped that my paw prints would be lost to the night.

I trod the path over the burning stream. My senses expanded around me. Scarcely seeing through my eyes, the long hairs at the back of my forelegs warned me of the seething water. My twisting ears caught shuffles of movement. My long brush hovered, keeping me steady. Where the

167

heat from the stream fell away, an arch drifted into view – the entrance to an icy cave. Still chanting, I passed through its white mouth.

What was bone is bending; what was fur is air.

As soon as I was inside, I sensed the presence of wolves. *Lots of wolves.* They were everywhere, almost close enough to touch, their breath warming the air. I heard the murmurs of their voices. Tunnels drifted in and out of view, stretching in all directions. Where would I go? Two pale shapes came closer. *Guards!*

Panic clawed at the back of my neck.

Reach deep – find your inner stillness.

I drew the chant close to me, felt the words slip through my thoughts.

What was seen is unseen . . .

My vision faltered. My thoughts tumbled backward, into the verdant forest I had seen in maa-sharm. I smelled resin, firs and rich soil. I heard the twitter of birds. I started walking. Without sight – almost without thought – I must have slipped between the wolves. I was passing through the central tunnel. My invisible paws scarcely touched the ground. Although I trod on compacted ice, I felt the yielding softness of grass. I passed another wolf, no more than a hovering whiteness. A faint tension in my legs told me I was walking down. The path lurched deep under the Ice Palace. The light faded.

But the darkness did not scare me. I did not need my eyes. My other senses explored the shadows. My whiskers bristled and expanded. My brush stroked the edge of the tunnel. My snout rose. Among the jostling scent of wolves, I detected one I knew.

This way, Isla. Yes, that's right. Keep going. You're almost there.

I sensed two figures up ahead.

Pass between the guards. Don't stop for a moment.

I kept going. My brush swept against fur. I sensed one of the wolves shift position. His great head turned towards me.

Keep moving, Isla. Don't stop!

I stole forward. The wolves dropped behind me. Lower, deeper I went, into blackness. But all the time I walked in green.

My paws trod lightly over the frozen ground. I followed the path that plunged under the Ice Palace. The air grew musty and damp. Only now did I become aware of discomfort. It scratched at my throat, growing more insistent. *Scratch, scratch.* Deep in the dankness, the need to breathe seized me. I swallowed a cough, the greenery fading from my thoughts. I couldn't hold the slimmer any longer! Terror burst through me. I clutched at breath. Almost choking, I collapsed. Panting desperately, I looked up. Through the blackness, I picked up a tremor of movement. A wolf was standing over me.

My mind whirred, a jumble of panicked thoughts. The slimmer was broken! They'd caught me!

"Get away!" I snarled. My voice was shrill, bouncing off the walls. From somewhere overhead I heard water tapping on to ice. *Drip-drip-drip.*

"Isla, is that you?"

My heart lurched against my chest. "Farraclaw?"

I threw myself against him, feeling the comforting warmth of his fur. I had trusted my maa – and I had found him.

14

Farraclaw licked my ears as I buried my muzzle in the warmth of his fur. I pulled back sharply. I'd smelled blood.

"You're hurt!" I remembered how the wolves had bitten and tormented him.

"It's nothing," said Farraclaw. "I can hardly believe that you made it here without being seen. Foxcraft, am I right?"

"You are. I slimmered. Métis taught me a new technique. I was able to hold my breath longer, and disappear more. If that makes sense?"

"I was a fool to approach the watch party," said Farraclaw. "It is just as I feared. Their whole Bishar will storm our western boundary. King Orrùfang will challenge my fa. When the challenge fails . . ." Farraclaw swallowed. In time, he spoke again. "I cannot slimmer, Isla. I cannot escape."

"I'm going to help you."

"I know you want to," Farraclaw sighed. "But what can you do?"

"I saw it done once, back in the Great Snarl. Siffrin threw a pelt of slimmer over me. I'm going to do the same for you." I didn't add that Siffrin was much more experienced in foxcraft than I was. I didn't confess that he'd slimmered while frozen to one spot – whereas I would have to find a way to work the craft while we escaped.

Métis had coached me on the journey to the Ice Palace.

Stay close to the wolf, he'd told me sternly. *You must move as one. Let the slimmer fan out around you so it covers him completely.*

I'd pointed out that Farraclaw had greater strides then me.

The black fox had looked thoughtful. *I have never slimmered with a creature that wasn't a fox. I've never had call to . . . But if you wish to live, you must find a way.*

"You can do that?" asked Farraclaw slowly. I heard the uncertainty in his voice. No, it was more than that – *distrust*. He didn't like the idea of foxcraft, especially knowing its effect on his fa.

I didn't have the chance to reply. There was a shuffle of paws along the tunnel. "Who are you talking to, *trespasser*?" The voice echoed down the narrow walls.

"I was repeating the oaths to my ancestors."

The guard snorted. "Your ancestors can't help you now. Keep it down!"

Farraclaw didn't reply. We waited as the guard's paws thumped along the tunnel out of earshot.

When I was sure it was safe, I turned back to the prince. "Lop has run ahead," I whispered. "He's going to alert the Bishar so your fa can be there to repel the attack."

Farraclaw was quiet. We were probably thinking the same thing – picturing the raving king and wondering how he could possibly fight.

I pushed the thought away. "We need to go. We'll be passing right next to the guards. Walk slowly. Don't run. They won't be able to see you, but they might still sense you. The stiller you are, the less they can glean."

"And you?" asked Farraclaw.

"I'll be chanting in my head." I remembered what Métis had told me. "I will fan out the slimmer, letting it roll over you. But it can only work if we're very close. Whatever happens, stay by my side. Once we're outside, we'll make for the pines where Métis is waiting. I'll do my best to hold the slimmer."

I guessed Farraclaw was chewing this over. He must have known there was no alternative for him. Sooner or later, they would kill him. "When will we go?"

"Now." Doubts clamoured for attention. *Are you crazy? You can hardly even slimmer. You're no expert in foxcraft.*

You're not as good as Pirie.

I cleared my throat, mumbling over the chant. "What was seen is unseen; what was sensed becomes senseless . . ."

It was so dark in the dungeon that I couldn't check if the slimmer had worked. I couldn't see anything at all. But I sensed a change. My thoughts grew light and the doubts ebbed away. The ground beneath my paws felt soft like moss.

I leaned against Farraclaw. I imagined our pelts weaving together. In the eye of my thoughts, the slimmer was growing. It trembled over Farraclaw's flank and shoulders but stopped short, leaving a pale glow along his side.

I took a step forward and felt him slip from the power of the foxcraft. He moved his foreleg but overstepped me, shuffling back awkwardly. The pale glow broadened. It would leave him exposed.

Reach deep, Isla.

I mouthed the words of the slimmering chant.

What was bone is bending; what was fur is air.

Doubt rose again and my thoughts stumbled over the chant. The slimmer was failing.

Find your inner stillness.

I lowered my muzzle and relaxed against Farraclaw's shoulder. I could feel his warmth. The world faded to green once more. I felt myself leap deeper into the folds of its undergrowth, its ferns and moss, where all was quiet.

Even in the darkness, I was aware of the change. The silence expanded around us. Slowly, I raised my forepaw and sensed Farraclaw do the same. We stepped together in a smooth rhythm. Somehow, the great difference in our sizes didn't matter, as though we'd merged into one. Together, we started up the steep path out of the dungeon.

I was scarcely aware of pressure against my legs as we climbed up the tunnel. Our claws easily discovered the tiny pits in the ice that gave us purchase. Though the ground beneath us was freezing and hard, I pictured myself back in the forest. Light glanced between the trees. Up ahead, I saw the contour of a wolf guard, pacing towards us. As one, we shifted to the side of the tunnel, liquid against the narrow walls. We slipped past the guard. Soon, another was up ahead of us. I could just make out the outline of his long muzzle. Farraclaw followed my movements as we eased towards the other wall.

What was seen is unseen . . .

We drifted through the tunnel, as though floating, zig-zagging between the guards. The light grew brighter but the world remained vague, a green mossy light for a half-closed eye. Even as the scent of wolves gnawed grooves through my thoughts – even as yellow eyes turned to look towards us, and whiskered muzzles crinkled into growls – my fear did not rise. Somewhere at the back of my awareness, I knew the wolves were barking to one another. But my thoughts remained green. I heard my own voice chanting and the steady pounding of a powerful heart.

My wolf heart.

Out at the mouth of the Ice Palace, we passed along an icy bridge across the bubbling stream. Orange colours grazed the edges of my vision. The vague hiss of water. Two wolves were marching along the path up ahead. I could make out the shape of their tails. Deep in my throat, a yearning for breath.

Keep going. You're almost there.

I reached for the words of the chant. *What was sensed becomes senseless.*

The hiss of water broke my concentration. The stream spat against my leg and I gasped, breaking the slimmer.

"Isla!" breathed Farraclaw. Suddenly, he was in view. The guards up ahead were turning.

Leap back! Now!

I sucked down my breath and hurtled back into the forest of my mind. I was one with Farraclaw again, one with the chant and the rhythm of the slimmer. A guard was thumping towards us, but she was no more than a halo of light. We sidestepped her easily, drifting over the ice, past the other guard. Soon we were crunching on to snow, into the darkness, and the safety of the pines where the Black Fox was waiting.

*　　*　　*

I collapsed on to the ground, panting breathlessly.

"Isla, are you all right?" whispered Farraclaw.

"She will be in a moment." I looked up to see Métis's green eyes fixed on me. "Foxling, you have done well. I feared you wouldn't make it."

My breath still raked my throat. I was panting too hard to speak. *You helped me*, I thought. *I heard a voice while I slimmered, encouraging me. Telling me what to do. It was you. You brought me to the forest. It was the place I saw in maasharm. It was your home . . .*

Métis looked back towards the Ice Palace. If he'd heard my thoughts, he gave no sign of it. "I understand now. Jana saw something in you. That is why she sent you. That is why you are needed."

I wanted to ask him what he meant but I didn't have the energy.

"What now?" said Farraclaw.

Métis's ears twisted back and forth. "Any moment, the wolves will find out that you've escaped. They will not rest until they hunt you down. We'll have to make for your Bishar."

Farraclaw stiffened. "They plan to attack at dawn after the full moon." He turned towards the pines. "We'll follow the path of the trees as much as possible, to loop down to the edge of the Raging River. It's a longer way, but at least we'll have cover."

"No," said Métis sharply. "They'll guess that's what you'd do. Of course you'd try to hide among the trees. They'll comb every trunk and shadow till they find you."

"What alternative do we have?" There was a growl in Farraclaw's throat.

Métis shrank back, his ears flattened. But his voice carried authority. "We must cross the open tundra and hope they don't discover our tracks. It's the only way we'll get to your Bishar in time."

Farraclaw gasped in astonishment. "Are you crazy? They'll see us."

"Not if we slimmer." Métis turned his green eyes on me. "Come, Foxling. Your work isn't over. Together, we must cross a great distance with this ungrateful wolf between us. You will need your maa now more than ever."

I struggled to my paws.

"Hurt me, Wolf, and you hurt yourself." Gingerly, Métis stepped around Farraclaw so we flanked him on either side. "Isla, when I say the word, we will both start chanting. We will weave our thoughts together, carrying the wolf within the slimmer."

"I can't make it that far!" I spluttered in amazement.

Métis spoke over me. "We'll go as far as the spruce in the distance. There you can rest, but only briefly. Then we'll start again, over and over, day and night. Do you want to help the wolf or don't you?"

I glanced at Farraclaw. His troubled eyes glowed like the moon.

"Of course I do," I said quietly.

"Good," said Métis. He drew in his breath. "What was seen is unseen . . ."

I began to chant.

We drifted through the night, three bodies melded into one, passing invisibly through the heart of the tundra. At the edge of my awareness ran parties of wolves, howling in fury and searching for Farraclaw. Deep within the safety of the slimmer, I did not dwell upon their presence. If I felt my awareness shifting, Métis called me back, his voice in my head, repeating the chant.

What was sensed becomes senseless . . .

Only when we stopped to rest between stout bushes or outcrops of rocks did the audacity of our escape strike me. We passed the wolves with no effort to hide. Our slimmer was the only disguise we needed. Farraclaw dissolved beneath the pelt we wove around him.

In the mist of the slimmer were claw-pricks of white. Canista's Lights stood between the colourful display, illuminating the forest of my mind.

No, that wasn't right: it wasn't of *my* mind.

Métis had created a world of safety, his own pelt of slimmer. His own forest. I stepped through it, flanked by

Farraclaw. Hidden between the trees, the hostile wolves couldn't touch us.

Still they howled.

Moonrise.

Moonset.

Their voices drifted away.

While the slimmering drew no maa from Farraclaw, the journey was also taking its toll on the injured wolf. He limped between us, favouring his front paw. We paused less and less. Only when the breath rose at my throat – when I knew I could hold the slimmer no longer – did Métis allow us to rest.

As another night gave way to a grey sky, we slipped between some rocks. I gasped for breath, rolling on to my side. My limbs were quivering with exhaustion. Farraclaw stood over me, licking my muzzle while raising his gaze above the rocks. The slim light of dawn hung over the tundra. I could make out the patches of blood on his silver-flecked coat.

Métis was quiet, breathing more slowly.

When my breath calmed down, I finally managed to speak. "I'm not sure I can do this much longer," I confessed.

"You won't have to," said Farraclaw. I followed his gaze, rising to my paws on quivering legs. I saw the spiky willow that marked the border of the Bishar of Claw.

A volley of howls rose over the tundra. I wheeled around. The wolves of Fang weren't here yet but they were moving fast, storming towards the Bishar of Claw. The three of us broke cover to scramble towards Farraclaw's home. No sooner had we entered than Cattisclaw and Norralclaw hurtled towards us. The rest of the Bishar were standing in formation, heads lowered in threat, prepared for battle.

Cattisclaw covered Farraclaw's muzzle with laps of her tongue. "Sire, you're hurt!" she whined. "Little Isla, what happened? Lop got here last night almost dead from running. He warned us of the attack."

"We have gathered the Bishar, Prince Farraclaw," said Norralclaw. "Is it true?"

"He did well," said Farraclaw. "It is true." The prince stood boldly, despite his injuries. "The wolves of Fang know the king is ailing. They are coming to claim our realms. I need Mirraclaw here immediately. Where is he?"

I looked along the rows of wolves. The warriors' jaws were set to snarls, their tails straight behind them. Among them was Amarog, whose face was sombre. Métis cringed against me, but the wolves weren't interested in him.

"Mirraclaw's not here," I murmured.

Farraclaw stiffened.

"Sire, I dread speak," said Norralclaw, lowering his muzzle. "He left after you did. We hoped he'd gone to aid you, yet he sent no word."

"It can't be . . ." The Bishar of Fang were close now, too many wolves to count. Farraclaw swallowed hard. "Prepare to defend the realm!" he barked.

The wolves of Claw strode forward. Lords and lordesses led the Bishar, followed by the warriors. Even the pups were there, watching in fear and fascination behind the queen.

In the distance I spotted Lop. He was pounding towards us.

But another wolf was missing.

"Where is my fa?" barked Farraclaw urgently.

Lop collapsed before Farraclaw. His flanks were heaving. "Sire, I have failed you. I could not rouse King Birronclaw Valiant-Oolf. I have been with him since moonrise. He hardly moves, he does not speak."

"It is not Lop's fault," said Amarog, stepping closer. "I have communed with the ancestors. I have waited at the entrance to his cave. The king cannot be saved. He yearns only for peace."

Farraclaw turned back towards the tundra. Shapes were gliding over the snow. At their lead came a great white wolf with a stripe of black along his snout. He slammed to a halt in the snow, and the rest of his Bishar lined up behind him.

"I am King Orrùfang Valiant-Raa," he howled, "Son of Noble King Garrùfang Valiant-Snee, who was felled by King Birronclaw Valiant-Oolf. In the name of the lords of Fang who have passed to the shadowlands, I have come to take my vengeance. I shall fight your king, or I shall have your lands."

Farraclaw drew in his breath. I looked around sharply. King Birronclaw wasn't there – and neither was Métis.

15

Silence fell among the wolves. The Bishar of Fang and the Bishar of Claw faced each other with less than a clear run between them. Standing just behind King Orrùfang, Lordess Bezilfang glared at me. She must have wondered what a fox was doing beside the prince of Claw.

Next to her was Mirraclaw.

His hard eyes stared ahead, unrepentant. I shuffled closer to the prince, thinking of Haiki.

Farraclaw locked eyes with King Orrùfang.

A sly look crossed the king's face. "I see you escaped," he snarled. "Well, young prince, that makes no difference. Your lord has been of great assistance to us – from now on, you may call him Lord Mirrafang, for he has rejected your failing Bishar in favour of the many rewards we can offer. His loyalty to Fang will not be forgotten."

Farraclaw's eyes shot to his old friend. The handsome white wolf raised his muzzle boldly.

"I will call him Mirra the Deserter," spat Farraclaw. "The tundra will run with his traitor blood." Suddenly, he sprang forward, charging towards the Bishar of Fang. Ignoring their king, he made straight for Mirraclaw. Farraclaw's lips were pulled so far back that his gums were bared above his long teeth. The surrounding wolves retreated at the site of him, and Mirraclaw gasped, caught off guard.

Farraclaw crashed into the white wolf, throwing him on to the ground before King Orrùfang. But Mirraclaw recovered quickly, twisting out of Farraclaw's grip to scramble on to his paws. The two great wolves faced each other, snarling.

The wolves of Fang and Claw started barking. They pressed forward to circle the prince and the lord. I wanted to beg them to stop. Deep wounds stained Farraclaw's fur, blotches of red that hadn't healed. He was already exhausted, but I knew he wouldn't stop.

Farraclaw was stalking towards Mirraclaw again, his ears pointing out at the sides, his face contorted in rage. "Traitor!" he growled. "Despicable rat!" He lunged but Mirraclaw ducked. Only the edge of Farraclaw's paw clipped the white wolf's flank. Mirraclaw spun around and landed a deep bite on Farraclaw's shoulder. With a roar of pain, Farraclaw threw his weight at Mirraclaw and they started rolling. Red spots smeared the snow.

The wolves of both Bishars were chanting and howling. The tannin whiff of blood sent them wild.

Standing a few paces away, King Orrùfang alone watched with cool eyes. Had the king seen the exhaustion etched on Farraclaw's body? He must have guessed this brutal fight could not last long.

He doesn't care what happens to them. He'll claim the Bishar anyway.

The wolves were growing frenzied, just as the coyotes had on the rocky plain in the Wildlands. They reminded me of dogs, wild eyed and bent on violence. "Kill him!" barked the wolves of Claw. "Fight back! Make the prince sorry!" yelped the Bishar of Fang.

I backed away, my heart drumming. I couldn't look at them – not even my friends. Norralclaw, Cattislaw . . . the whites of their eyes glowed with the lust for blood.

"Stop!" I yowled. "Farraclaw, please! It won't help, can't you see?" My words were lost beneath the furious barks.

The wolves of Claw pressed closer to the fight and I hung behind Lop, catching only glimpses of fur and teeth. Mirraclaw was springing at Farraclaw, aiming for the open wounds at the back of the prince's neck. Searching for his weak spots, as the Bishar had tested the bison. The white wolf fought cruelly, biting and ripping. To my horror, he pinned the prince to the ground.

Mirraclaw will kill him!

If I could only share my maa . . . If there was something I could do. Heart jolting, I pressed between the wolves of Claw.

"You were always so superior!" snarled Mirraclaw. "But look at you now! You're no better than anyone else! You're *nothing*."

The white wolf launched his fangs at Farraclaw's throat. I started to shove between the Bishar of Claw. But as I grew closer, Lyrinclaw spotted me and forced me back with a forepaw. "Are you crazy? They'll kill you just for being a fox!"

"Please," I begged. "Let me go!"

A shrill cry and we both turned back to the fighting wolves. Mirraclaw grasped for Farraclaw's throat but the prince shoved him away. Quick as a flash, Farraclaw snapped his teeth on a glossy white ear. Eyes squeezed shut, he clamped down. The tussle of paws, a flurry of fur.

A scream of pain.

Farraclaw rolled on to his paws with a snarl of victory.

Mirraclaw collapsed on to the ground, exposing his belly. I realized with a snap of dread that his right ear was missing. "Mercy!" he barked. "Mercy, Sire, mercy!"

Farraclaw's eyes shone with hatred. He spat out the long white ear.

I looked away, giddy with horror. All around me, the wolves of Claw were howling. "Kill him, Prince Farraclaw! Kill! Kill!"

No . . . I silently begged. No more . . . Please . . .

When I dared to look, Farraclaw was in the same place, standing bloodied but proud in a circle of wolves. Mirraclaw was creeping backward, mumbling in terror. "Forgive me, Sire . . ." He spun around and bolted over the tundra.

Cattisclaw hurried to Farraclaw's side. "Prince Farraclaw, shall we hunt down the coward?" Norralclaw and Rattisclaw ran up behind her, champing to chase, to capture and kill.

The prince gave the smallest movement of the muzzle. "Let him go. His disfigurement will for ever stand as a mark of his treachery. *Mirra the Deserter.* He will roam the Snowlands a lone wolf, spurned and despised till the end of his days."

Snarls and howls still filled the tundra.

"Enough!" roared King Orrùfang. Instantly, his Bishar fell to attention, gathering behind him stiffly.

Farraclaw turned to face him.

King Orrùfang took a step closer to Farraclaw. "I hope the fight gave the wolves of Claw some sport. It is the last they shall enjoy. What becomes of your Lord Mirra is no longer our concern. He has served his purpose." I noticed that he'd dropped the "fang" from Mirraclaw's name. The king's teeth glinted. "You cannot save your Bishar. Only a king may fight me, by the ancient laws that bind our lands. Laws etched in our ancestors' blood."

"Like the Custom of Serren?" growled Farraclaw.

"A custom is not a law," replied the king easily. "We are not obliged to follow it."

"Wolves have done so for generations."

"Even so." King Orrùfang's lip rose over his teeth. "We were not bound. But you *are*. Both our Bishars are witness to this. Our truthsayers can speak to the ancient laws."

From the edge of my vision, I saw Amarog's ears twist forward. She didn't argue.

The wolves of Fang licked their chops. The fight between Farraclaw and Mirraclaw had awakened their bloodlust. The whimpering pups huddled closer to the queen.

King Orrùfang smelled victory. His tone was taunting. "I ask you now, once and for all: Where is your king?"

Farraclaw opened his mouth but did not speak. He looked over his shoulder, his gaze sweeping across the anxious wolves of Claw. Standing by Lyrinclaw's side, I caught his sharp intake of breath.

One after another, the wolves of Claw were turning. They dropped on to their bellies. A giant figure stalked among them.

It took me a moment to recognize the wolf. The last time I'd seen him he was raving. Gone was the filth and the reek of decay. The beast that strode among his Bishar was brilliant white. His massive paws kicked up puffs of snow. His pointed ears were alert.

I had never seen a wolf of such power and size.

King Birronclaw trod between me and Lyrinclaw. His muscles strained with brooding tension. His long fangs glinted. Despite my friendship with the wolves of Claw, fear of their king overwhelmed me. I cringed as he passed.

Farraclaw's head tilted. I saw a moment of confusion cross his face. Then he lowered himself as his fa approached.

King Birronclaw stopped in front of the prince, facing off against the king of Fang.

King Orrùfang was no longer standing tall. The arrogant snarl fell from his muzzle. The slightest tremor touched his forepaws. Gasps escaped from the watching wolves of Fang.

"King Orrùfang Valiant-Raa, you have called me, and I have come. I am King Birronclaw Valiant-Oolf, Lord Protector of the Bishar of Claw, High Commander of the Snowlands. You have crossed into our lands and you have dared to challenge me." King Birronclaw's voice boomed over the tundra. Yet to my ears, it sounded strange. It made me think of crows, of thunderclaps for storms that didn't come.

Karakking, of course!

I craned to look closer at the king. His body was perfectly still as he stared at his challenger but his pointed ears swivelled forward and back. Briefly, he looked over his Bishar. In the morning light, his huge eyes glowed.

Green, not yellow.

The centres were slits.

Métis.

The Black Fox had seen the king before his decline. He was able to shift into what the great wolf had once been.

But the king is desperately sick.

I remembered the danger Siffrin faced when he'd mimicked the dying coyote back in the Wildlands. I stared at Métis in the shape of King Birronclaw. If the real king died, he would die too. The Black Fox knew the risk he took. I was impressed by his courage.

The kings stood off against each other. The wolves of Fang faced the Bishar of Claw.

No one moved.

King Orrùfang spoke. "King Birronclaw Valiant-Oolf, I revere you. Lord Mirra told us of your coming demise. Wicked rumours – nothing but a pack of lies." He swallowed hard. "Please forgive us, Noble King. We came to protect your Bishar from ruin. We feared that, without your wise guardianship, the bison would run wild, destroying the grasses and trampling the brooks. We did not wish to see such a glorious realm fall to harm."

King Orrùfang dropped to the ground, bowing deeply to Métis in the form of King Birronclaw. His Bishar did the same, lowering their forepaws and dipping their heads.

"Go in peace, My Lord of Claw," said the king of Fang. "May you reign long in your beautiful realms."

King Birronclaw bowed graciously in response. "Go in peace, My Lord of Fang."

The wolves of Fang watched their king avidly. He raised his black-striped muzzle, backed away a few paces, then turned and fled back over the tundra. His Bishar ran after him, tails tucked between their legs. No howls of triumph accompanied their departure. Only the thump of their paws on the snow caught the air. I watched as their pale coats swept over the snow-mottled grass. They rounded a peak and disappeared from view.

The wolves of Claw still bowed. Even Farraclaw kept his head low. I wondered what he thought was going on – how much he suspected.

The great white wolf took a couple of paces forward. I heard him mumbling beneath his breath. "I am King Birronclaw. I am changing. I am the Black Fox." Then he dropped to his belly, the last of his energy spent.

His broad limbs shrank, his short tail grew. The head that lolled back in the snow was no longer a wolf's.

"Métis?" I yelped, running to him. "Métis, can you hear me?"

The Black Fox stirred very slightly. His mouth opened, but I didn't catch his words. I crouched by his side, my ear near his muzzle. "The gloaming," he rasped. "That is the key."

"The longest day?"

192

"The maa," he rasped irritably. His eyes opened a crack. "We must return to the Elder Rock by the gloaming."

Excitement was breaking out among the wolves. The attack had been averted. The Bishar was safe. Cattisclaw bounded to Farraclaw, licking his wounds. Other wolves circled Métis.

"Where did King Birronclaw go?" whined Jaspin.

"That wasn't the king. It was foxcraft!"

"Did Isla do something?"

"Not Isla – that black-furred fox over there."

I stared at Métis. When was the gloaming? Wasn't it soon? "I'm not sure we can make it back in time," I told him. Was the Black Fox listening any more? His eyes had closed and he no longer spoke.

I reached out to him with my thoughts. *Don't die!* I begged him. *The Elders need you.* It surprised me how much I cared. I reminded myself that Jana had tricked me, that Métis had pleached with a wolf. But I couldn't think badly of them, not really. Skulks were falling to the Mage, free foxes were forced into his army of Taken. My heart ached when I remembered little Mox, killed because he hadn't been strong enough to fight for the Mage. If Métis could do something to help Wildlands foxes . . .

A howl rose over the Bishar. Amarog had thrown back her head. Silence fell among the wolves.

"Amarog the Wise, what is it?" demanded Farraclaw.

The wolf shaman whimpered in lament. "I feel it in my whiskers. I feel it in my bones. King Birronclaw Valiant-Oolf has let out his final breath. He walks in shadow, but never alone. Gone to the land of our ancestors, where he will hunt and run with the Bishar for ever."

The queen gave out a long sigh. "Then he may rest at last."

Amarog dipped her head. "He is at peace, My Queen." She shifted her gaze to Farraclaw. "My prince, you have returned from fire and ice. You have faced dangers and over-come them. You are ready."

Farraclaw's ears swivelled forward. "I could not have done it without Isla," he said. "Nor Lop, who always gave good counsel and ran the fastest when it was most needed. He did us proud. Lopclaw, I should say. For if ever a wolf showed loyalty to our Bishar, it is he."

Lop's tail wagged at this rare praise. The other wolves looked at him with new respect.

Amarog spoke to the attentive wolves. "As the eldest son of King Birronclaw Valiant-Oolf and Queen Sableclaw Valiant-Jowl, Prince Farraclaw Valiant-Jowl is the natural heir to the Bishar of Claw. The ancestors have judged him fit for leadership." She turned to Farraclaw. "Will you accept their verdict, my prince?"

The queen padded to his side. She gave him a reassuring nod. Her tail rose behind her in a small wag. "Son, it is your time." An ease had entered her movements. Perhaps the mad king's death had finally brought her some relief.

Farraclaw's whiskers quivered. He didn't seem prepared for the speed of this news: his fa's death and what it meant for him. But his voice was calm as he spoke. "I accept the role gratefully." He turned to the shaman with a nod. "I consent to the verdict of our ancestors, Amarog the Wise."

The wolves let out a great roar.

Farraclaw threw back his head. "The king is dead!" he howled.

The Bishar howled in reply. "Long live the king! Long live King Farraclaw Valiant-Jowl!"

The moon had shrunk to a sliver of white and swelled into a lidless yellow eye. With the start of the melt, Fang's defeat, and Farraclaw's rule, a lightness had visited the Bishar. I had lived among the wolves since Farraclaw became king. During the day, I played with the pups, slimmering or karakking for them. Already they stood over me, though they ran on clumsy paws. At night, I rested at Farraclaw's side, or watched while the wolves went hunting.

Farraclaw's rule coincided with the first bloom over the Bishar. Seed cones appeared in the spruce trees. The snow began to thaw, revealing patches of damp grass. Tiny pink flowers dotted the tundra. A sweet smell hung in the cool air and a new sound awakened, the buzzing of insects.

I padded through the Bishar, digging out earthworms where soil was revealed between the snow. This amused the wolves. "Still hungry?" teased Lyrinclaw, watching me gulp down a long pink worm. "Isn't freshly caught bison enough for you?" She batted me lightly and I nipped her on the leg. She gave me a nudge. "Strange creatures, foxes," she said affectionately.

Métis recovered slowly. Most of the time the old fox slept in a hollowed tree trunk lined with moss. He would scowl when I approached, shunning my company. Still, I visited daily, feeding him torn up chunks of bison caught by the wolves. Grudgingly, he let me help him to the stream, where he drank slowly.

Pleaching with the wolf had wrecked his maa. The fox-craft that had followed had further weakened him. I could see it in his weary limbs. How long would the Black Fox last? Yet his green eyes sparkled. Unlike the wolf, whose gerra had rotted before his death, Métis was still sharp.

He huddled by the bank of the stream, little more than fur and bones. His gaze trailed over the patchy snow. "The gloaming is coming," he said. "We must leave."

I looked at him doubtfully. He could hardly stand. "Not until you're stronger. You'll never make it over the tundra. It's a long way to the Raging River from here. And you . . . You're not well."

He glared at me. "Don't presume to speak to me of my health." He jutted out his muzzle like a stubborn cub. Still, the truth of my words must have reached him. With a wince, he rose to his paws and limped back to the hollowed-out tree. "The gloaming won't wait for us."

I knew he was determined to reach the Elders. But I wondered what help this old fox was really able to provide.

"It isn't just about *me*," he spat.

My ears flipped back. He had a spooky ability to guess my thoughts.

"Don't you care about anything but your own comfort?" he added cruelly. "Have you lived among the wolves so long that you've forgotten what you are?"

"I promised I'd help you, and I will," I said stiffly. "You don't need to insult me. I was only thinking about you."

"Rubbish. You were avoiding what must be done." He drew his long tail around him. "What happens to the Elders affects all foxes," he said, echoing what Siffrin had said back in the Great Snarl. "The White Fox's first rise was thwarted by the Elders, a group of foxes of exceptional skill and dexterity. Among them, the Black Fox took the lead, as master of all arts. And so the tradition has passed through generations."

I ran my claws across a thin patch of snow, revealing new grass. "Jana said that the White Fox isn't a real fox, not even a cub of Canista."

It is not alive – not in the sense that matters.

"That is true," said Métis. "The White Fox cannot make claim to our soil. Not alone."

My ears pricked. "What do you mean?"

"What I mean," said Métis through gritted teeth, "is that someone must be helping it. Someone with more ambition than sense."

Suddenly, I understood. "The Mage."

Métis wrinkled his muzzle. "That is what he calls himself now. Keeveny of the western Wildlands. He is leeching maa in his efforts to raise the White Fox, offering himself as its link to our world. He calls it skree-maa but it's really tu-maa-sharm – a reversal of all that is intended by the foxcraft, all that is good. He thinks he can control that *thing* as a means to untold power. He will fall victim to its quest to feed and grow. Keeveny always was a fool."

My thoughts snapped back to the yellow haze that had risen over the Darklands. I pictured the den of the Wildlands' skulk, trampled and smouldering after the Taken attacked. They'd killed the old foxes. They'd killed Mox.

My ears pointed out at the sides. So much bloodshed . . .

And another image – Pirie. Only then did I realize I had pushed him away. I had fought to forget him, to erase him from my heart. Now his face floated in my mind's eye.

My tail drooped. Métis was right. In the Snowlands, so far from the Snarl and dangers of the Wildlands, I could almost pretend there was nothing wrong.

"When do you want us to leave?" I said at last.

Métis didn't hesitate. "Tonight."

*　　　*　　　*

I passed a group of warriors on my way to see Farraclaw. They were huddled around Rattisclaw and Thistleclaw, who were sparring at the centre of the circle.

"Isla, come and watch!" called Norralclaw.

I paused as the wolves yelped, cheering on one side or another. Lop padded behind them and lay down on his side, grooming his forepaws and watching from a distance.

He was still the under-wolf.

A part of me had hoped that the trip would have changed that. At least the others didn't torment him any more – not since Farraclaw had thanked him before the whole Bishar. Some, like Cattisclaw, made a point of calling him Lopclaw.

The floppy-eared wolf greeted me warmly, his tail wagging. We watched the mock battle, catching glimpses of action between the other wolves. Thistleclaw appeared to be winning, using her superior strength and speed. Briarclaw raised her voice, urging Thistleclaw on. "Quickly! Go for his flank!"

A moment later and it was over. Thistleclaw pounced at Rattisclaw and pinned him to the ground.

"Is something wrong?" Lop had turned to look at me. "Aren't you happy here, Isla?"

I kept staring ahead. Rattisclaw and Thistleclaw exchanged bows. Thistleclaw trod a short victory loop for the other wolves, who yapped and cheered. Rattisclaw started grooming his coat.

"My brother is still missing."

Lop sighed. "And this isn't your home."

"No . . ." But what was? My earliest days in the Greylands seemed a lifetime ago. My family weren't there any more . . . "I have to go back to the Elders with Métis."

Lop rose to his paws. "Are you on your way to Farraclaw? I'll walk with you."

I glanced at him gratefully. The floppy-eared wolf always knew the right thing to do.

As we walked side by side through the territory, I looked across the Bishar's lands for the final time. The view was arresting. Pink flowers were popping open in every patch of damp grass between the melting snow, though further south, in Storm Valley, the thaw hadn't arrived. High overhead, flocks of white birds flew in formation.

We walked in silence. We both knew where Farraclaw would be. The wolf king's powerful musk guided our journey uphill to the base of the large black rocks.

Lop stopped at the first rock. "I'll wait for you here."

I touched his nose with my own before clambering up the rocks.

Farraclaw was standing at the peak, looking out over his Bishar. He tilted his muzzle as I approached and waited patiently until I was standing before him. The wind blew against his silvery ruff. His eyes shone like the moon. Power rose off him as waves of amber light.

He closed his eyes and let out a long breath. "You're leaving." He had seen it in my face.

"We must reach the Elder Rock by the Eve of Maha – what we call the gloaming."

He dipped his head in acknowledgement. "Does Métis have enough maha for the journey? You know the lowlands are rugged and cold. Even now, a blizzard can race over the mountains. Winds get trapped in the Storm Valley. It is no place for an ailing fox."

"I'm not sure," I answered honestly. "Or how we'll cross the Raging River."

Farraclaw spoke solemnly. "When I was captured in the dungeon of Fang, I could think of no way to escape. I was surrounded by enemies, far from home . . . Not for the first time." He peered over my shoulder and I remembered how I'd first seen him, trapped in the beast dens. "I reached out to Noble King Serrenclaw. He told me not to fear the dark – that the shadows were my friends. He told me help was coming." Farraclaw turned back to me. "Those who have passed do not forget. They watch over us."

I padded towards him and he rested his head against my shoulder.

"Look across the tundra," he said. "Do you see the narrow path between the birch?"

I followed his gaze, spying the pale-barked trees. They sat in the shadows of a curved hill, still banked in snow.

They were almost invisible against the backdrop of white.

"Follow the path between the birch. Where the trees meet the river, there are stepping stones. Tread lightly, and they will take you to the far bank in safety."

I looked up at him. I didn't want to ask but the words tumbled out of my mouth. "Won't you come with us? The White Fox is rising. He'll enslave free foxes and ruin our lands." A note of desperation had crept into my voice. I could feel my ears pointing out at the sides. "You said there was nothing you wouldn't do to help me."

Farraclaw raised his head. He stared over the tundra, refusing to meet my eye. "I would do anything, you know that . . . even for Métis. Despite his trick with my fa, he saved our Bishar from bloody defeat. But do not ask me to desert my realms on the Eve of Maha. It is the night that we howl to our ancestors. No wolf may leave the Bishar. As dawn breaks on the longest day, we will make our way to the edge of the Taku Grounds. As twilight falls we will start our lament. I have a duty to my kin. It is tradition. It is etched in the land." His voice was almost a whisper. "I am sorry."

There was nothing I could do. I followed him down the black stones where Lop was waiting. Together, the three of us padded through the Bishar. The day was drawing to a close. It was time to say goodbye.

17

The sun sank over the Bishar of Fang. I cocked my head, picturing the Ice Razors and the faraway land of burning ponds. Métis padded to my side. We had both travelled a long way to reach the Snowlands. It was hard to believe we were leaving.

The entire Bishar had arrived to wish us well. They gathered around us, tails wagging excitedly. The wolves were careful to avoid touching Métis, not sure what to make of the scowling fox. They shuffled between us and bounded about, licking me on the nose and shunting me gently with low growls. Even Amarog was there, though she stood at a distance from the others, gazing towards the sunset.

Farraclaw raised his voice. "As you all know by now, Isla is leaving us, and taking Elder Fox Métis with her. The arrival of foxes to our Bishar has heralded much change." His eyes moved from me to Métis. "Not all change is bad."

Cattisclaw dipped her head and gave him a meaningful look. He blinked back at her. I wondered how long it would be until she was queen.

"Endings and beginnings," murmured Amarog. "You speak sagely, Sire. Change is not to be feared. As there is darkness, there is light."

Cattisclaw nudged me with her muzzle. "I'll miss you, Isla. You have taught us much about your kind."

The pups jumped on to me, weighing me down with their large paws. "Don't go!" whined Jaspin.

"Stay a little longer," begged Dorrel.

"I can't," I said sadly. "I made a promise to Métis, and to my brother, Pirie. It is time to honour it."

"Do you hear that? She speaks of honour," said Rattisclaw, his tail wagging with gentle amusement. "Pups of Canista aren't so different after all."

The last to press between the throng were Lop and Farraclaw. The floppy-eared wolf licked my whiskers gently. "Thank you," he murmured.

"What for?" He had done so much for me and Métis. I should have been thanking *him*.

Lop drew back, his tail low. "I'll miss you."

Farraclaw touched my nose with his broad snout. "Go safely, Isla. We are with you in spirit. I will look to Queen

Canista's Lights and think of you. May you defeat your enemies and find your brother."

My mouth was dry. I wanted to beg him to come with us.

Métis glanced at me, then turned to Farraclaw. "I wronged you by pleaching with your fa, yet you have forgiven me. I hope in some small way I was able to make amends." He tilted his head. "You're a fine king," he added with disarming warmth.

"Even if I am a wolf?" Farraclaw roared with amusement.

The wolves howled and yelped as we turned and started over the tundra. The damp grass revealed by the melting snow was soft beneath our paws. I glanced back at the wolves. Lop had cocked his head and was staring at me sadly. Farraclaw dipped his muzzle with respect.

My chest tightened. I would never see my friends again.

I noticed Amarog. There was something about the shaman's stance that unsettled me. While the other wolves still looked our way, Amarog stared towards the White Mountains. I followed her gaze. Low clouds were drifting over the foothills. What did it mean?

A chill ran through me.

"Foxling, are you coming?" Métis called. I was surprised to see how far he'd gone, even at his hobbling rate. I wrenched my gaze from the wolves and followed. They yipped and howled as we hurried over the damp grass, but I didn't look back again.

*　　*　　*

We picked our way downhill on a rutted path. We did our best to avoid the large clumps of snow that still hung on the soil. Long frozen, they had taken on a dirty sheen.

"The birch trees are far south, towards the bank of the river."

Métis grunted. He was panting heavily. He shuffled as he moved, barely raising his paws.

The sun brushed the Bishar of Fang. Great billows of pink light drifted across the Snowlands. Shimmers of green and blue lit the darkening sky. Beyond them, endless stars winked down on us. A murmur rose from the earth, reminding me of malinta's beat. Was it the gloaming calling to us – what wolves called the Eve of Maha?

Métis had stopped up ahead. His chest was heaving.

"Do you need maa?" I asked carefully. I felt uneasy about sharing my life source, but I doubted he would make it to the Wildlands without help.

"Keep it," he said stiffly. "You haven't enough to spare." He lowered himself on to his belly, wrapping his tail around him. "I just need to rest a moment."

I ran my tongue over my muzzle. "I promised to get you back to the Wildlands."

Métis cursed, dragging himself up. "I said I don't need it!"

Stubborn old fox.

He shot me a dark look.

I watched as he wound between the patchy piles of snow. I had to admire his determination. I followed a few steps behind him. The grass squelched beneath my paws. My legs were tired from tensing to spring downhill. Peering ahead, I thought I caught a glimpse of the distant birch trees. I picked up my pace, hopping past Métis. As long as I kept sight of the trees, we would be all right.

Still . . .

I would have felt better if the wolves had joined us. If only Farraclaw was here, or even Lop. Where we scarcely dared to tread, they ran with confidence. Wolves were so bold, so sure of their power.

I gave my fur a shake. It didn't help to think that way. Farraclaw had a duty to his Bishar. Already, the wolves would be making the journey north, uphill to the edge of the Taku Grounds. There they would wait until dawn, to start their daylong lament to their ancestors.

A cool fizzle touched my nose. I looked up. It was starting to snow. Colours had faded from the darkening sky. Pigeon-grey clouds concealed the stars.

That's what Amarog saw as she watched the mountains. The coming snow.

I wondered what this meant for our journey. Turning, I realized that Métis had fallen far behind. I hurried back to him. He was hunkered low between two frozen mounds of snow, his muzzle contorted with strain.

"I'll be all right," he snapped as I approached. He started to raise his paw, then dropped it again. With a crinkle of his nose, he finally met my eye. "All right. A snap of maa, no more. I don't want to take what you can't spare."

"I can spare it."

He narrowed his eyes. "Don't overestimate yourself."

My whiskers twitched, but I kept my eyes fixed on his. I started to chant. "With my touch, I sense you; with my eyes, I heal you. By Canista's Lights, I share what I have, we are knit together and you are whole." The tumble into green was almost instant. A fox was running through a forest. He took in the familiar scent of resin and firs. He paused, his ears pricking up. He had heard a twig snap. Hushed voices reached him. He crept around a tree trunk, listening.

"This way," hissed a vixen. She was leading a skulk through the undergrowth. Her paws crunched over the forest floor. Her thickset shoulders muscled between dead branches. Her small ears swivelled back and forth.

Karka.

She had reached the edge of the forest, where the tall trees bowed, their trunks turning black with decay.

Amidst a huddle of Taken, a pitiful voice arose. "Please, let me go. My family will be worried."

"Your family are lucky to be alive," snarled Karka. "The Mage welcomes new recruits to his skulk."

That silenced the young fox. He lowered his brown head, his long brush drooping behind him.

Karka disappeared between the trees. The other foxes trudged after her. Ravens cawed overhead. Several of the Taken looked up, watching the blackbirds with wary eyes.

The captured fox seized his chance. He turned to one of the Taken in appeal. "Please, won't you let me pass word to my family? You must have a skulk of your own? My name is Liro. I've never done anything to you . . . Where are you taking me?"

Karka bounded back into view. "Did the traitor dare to speak?" she spat. She shunted through the foliage, reaching the Taken, who cringed away from her. "Vile rat, you will learn the folly of idle words." Her lips peeled back. Her single grey eye shot across the forest. "The Elders!" she yelped suddenly. "I sense one of them watching. *Quickly*." They shoved and shunted the young fox to where the trees were dead and the long vines closed around him.

I blinked and collapsed in a heap of snow. The power of the vision had awakened a terror deep inside me.

The Black Fox was watching me. "Are you all right, Isla? I couldn't pull away. I tried . . . I couldn't do it." He lowered his head. "That's why I refused your maa. I am a husk now. I'm empty, like a dusty furrow that used to hold a stream. You could pour in all the maa you have and watch it seep into the thirsty ground. It will never be enough."

I gave myself a shake. "The captured fox, the one I saw in maa-sharm . . ." I frowned, remembering. "His name was Liro." My voice quivered. The maa-sharm had tired me. Snow was falling more rapidly, tumbling down in clumps. It clung to my whiskers.

"A young fox from the Wildlands." Métis cocked his head. His tail-tip quivered, lit with a silver glow. "You knew him?"

"I knew his skulk. They had no idea where he'd gone." My ears flattened. "Liro was captured, but not pleached?"

"The Mage had other plans for him." The old fox looked out over Storm Valley. "We need to keep moving. A gale is rising. The snowfall will hamper us."

I started to move. "Liro had strong maa." My legs quivered and my head felt groggy. "My brother has strong maa," I added quietly.

"Is that so?" muttered Métis. He was already padding ahead. Snow dappled his dark fur.

I stumbled behind him. The maa-sharm had reversed us, as though I had aged rapidly and he was the younger fox. It seemed like such a selfless foxcraft, the gifting of life source. The hairs prickled along my back. Could it, like pleaching, be performed against the will? What was the term? Skree-maa? *Tu-maa-sharm.* A dark fear crept over me.

Any foxcraft might be twisted. Haven't you worked that out yet? Why do you think the Elders exist? To oversee its practice. Without foxlore, the arts can be abused.

211

Métis was speaking to me through my thoughts. I gave my head a shake. I hadn't invited him in. "You said the Mage was leeching maa?"

Métis pressed forward. "What's that?"

"This morning. What did you mean? Where is he taking it from?"

Métis turned back to me. Through the thickening snow, I caught the light in his eyes. Suddenly, I knew. "Foxes," I mumbled. "Foxes of exceptional maa. They're not pleached."

"That would be a waste," said Métis. He turned back to the steep path over the tundra.

"Not Pirie! He wasn't killed with the rest of my skulk. He's not one of the Taken. He got away."

"How do you know he got away?" asked Métis.

My ears flattened. "In gerra-sharm, I sensed him running. He moved through the Snarl, to the winged furless."

"He was alone?"

I tried to remember. I sensed a blur of movement, of foxes in pursuit. Pirie had made it to the winged furless. Was that where Karka's skulk had caught up with him as others, led by Tarr, followed me? "Maybe not . . ." I said slowly. Then I recalled how Karka had continued to track me, even after I'd reached the winged furless. So she couldn't have found Pirie after all. "Karka followed me through the Snarl to the edge of the Wildlands. She was looking for Pirie. That proves he got away!" It was what I'd rested my hopes on – that my brother was still safe. Now that I spoke the words out loud, I realized how uncertain they sounded. "Why else would she be following me?" I said in a small voice.

Métis paused, panting heavily. "Do you really need to ask?"

My maa . . .

"I imagine that was the original plan–to trap you for your maa." Métis started over the slippery ground. "But once you were in the Wildlands, and a friend of Siffrin's, Keeveny hoped you'd lead Haiki to the Rock."

"How do you know that?" I asked suspiciously.

"I've spoken to the other Elders. You know of gerra-sharm: you've used it yourself." Métis gave me a sharp look. "Of course, Keeveny's an Elder. It wasn't the Rock's location he was seeking."

My tail hung low. "He needed the Elders to lower the shana. He knew that Jana would let me in, so he had Haiki come with me." I spat angrily, "I should never have trusted him."

"Keeveny would have terrorized Haiki into doing what he did. He must have had something over him."

"His family." I crunched over the snow.

Métis coughed. "I've been wondering about you, Isla, and your brother's disappearance. I couldn't imagine that the Mage would bother with a Greylands foxling. But perhaps the Narral have broadened the scope of their search, to feed their master's hunger for power. Perhaps your brother's maa was worth the journey." Métis paused, drew in his breath, and kept trudging. "I take it Pirie is special?"

"Yes," I answered quietly. My heart throbbed for him – my playful, affectionate brother. My paws fell giddily on to the earth. I'd run to the Snowlands with so little thought, had left on a mission that led me to Métis. Half-formed ideas were blurring and reshaping. "You shouldn't use gerra-sharm," I warned. "The Mage may be listening. That's how he tracked me. Every time I spoke to Pirie through my thoughts, the Taken appeared." I longed to reach out to my brother, but even here in the Snowlands, I didn't dare.

Métis slammed to a halt. There was a strange look in his green eyes. "Only if one is caught. Only if those thoughts are intercepted."

I knew then – knew for certain.

Pirie is in the Mage's lair. That's how the Mage could spy on us.

My throat was so tight it was hard to breathe. "Pirie was in the Wildlands all along."

"We don't call them that any more – not the part where your brother must be."

I swallowed. "The Darklands."

Métis drew in his breath. Through spinning snow I caught the restless movement of his ears, back and forth, back and forth.

Anger rose off my fur. "That's why you showed me Liro's capture. You *wanted* me to see what the Narral are doing. Why didn't you just tell me where Pirie was? I've wasted so much time in the Snowlands waiting for you to recover. I should have left right away!" My ears flattened. I shouted over the wind. "I guess the other Elders knew too? Can't you be honest with me? They knew that Pirie had been taken by the Mage, didn't they?"

"No," said Métis sharply. He turned and caught my eye. "What you witnessed in maa-sharm I saw before the last gloaming. I was alone in the fir forest where I live. The Darklands have crept closer and closer. The Deep Forest suffocates leaves and life with its clawing branches. I considered challenging Karka, but even the Black Fox cannot fight off so many Taken when they're with one of the Narral. When I guessed what they were doing with the foxling, I felt sick to my core. I needed more strength. I needed something Keeveny didn't have . . . I made straight for the Snowlands in search of the wolves. I didn't tell Jana, or the others. They would have tried to stop me." He shook his head. "I should have sent word. They must have feared for me. They must even have wondered if I was the Mage . . . Once I'd pleached with the wolf, I couldn't reach them. All my foxcraft failed." His voice was brittle. "Don't you see? I let them down." His head dropped and he started trudging again. "I've let everyone down."

I stared back at Métis. It was true, the Elders hadn't

known whether he or Keeveny were the Mage. Which meant they hadn't been included in his plan.

Métis drew his long tail around him. His paws slipped on ice. "I still can't be sure that's what happened to your brother. I showed you my memory of Liro because my mind is wearied from fatigue. Because yours is quick. Because you'll catch things I don't . . ."

I was shocked into silence by the proud fox's frankness.

"I've wondered if the Narral captured your brother. Of course I have . . . Yet something in all this troubles me. Keeveny is from the Wildlands, as are all the foxes of the Narral. They would hardly imagine that a fox of great maa could dwell in the Greylands. I cannot think what would have led them to Pirie." He blinked into the sky. "We mustn't tarry – to do so is to freeze here. Come, Isla."

I opened my mouth to protest but no words escaped. Slowly, I padded after Métis. We walked for a time without talking, struggling through the wind that whipped up the snow. The silver of Métis's tail-tip paled. His pace wearied.

I was tiring too. My limbs were stone. I focused on setting one paw in front of another. I hadn't noticed that the Black Fox had stopped until I smacked into him.

"What's wrong?"

He slouched on to his belly. "I must rest."

I blinked the flakes from my eyelashes. Fresh snowfall

covered the tundra. Trees, bushes and rocks disappeared beneath its white touch.

"The birch," I gasped. I had completely lost sight of the trees. "Métis, I can't see the birch! How will we find the stepping stones?" I craned my neck. "Métis?"

The old fox had closed his eyes. He didn't reply.

Exhaustion shuddered through me. "*Métis? Don't leave me! I can't do this alone.*" I'd shared my maa with the old fox, but it wasn't enough. Now we were both shattered, unable to continue. I slumped on to my belly. Icy wind ruffled my fur as wisps spun overhead. The vast Snowlands stretched in all directions. I had come to this brutal terrain for nothing. Now Métis would die. The Elders would lose against the Mage, and I wouldn't see Siffrin again.

The White Fox would rise.

Pirie would never escape . . .

The blizzard whipped around me. In that swirling, brutal wilderness, hope vanished.

My head sank into the snow. Shivers juddered down my back. I yearned for my family. I tried to picture Ma and Fa. To remember Greatma with her mottled fur and her stern, kind face. She was the wisest fox I had ever known. If only I could feel the warmth of her tail wrap around me.

Faintly, I remembered what Farraclaw had said about his ancestors.

Those who have passed do not forget. They watch over us.

They were just words. Greatma was gone – like the rest of them.

The wind shrilled in my ears, the biting cold sank its claws through my fur. My heart clenched in terror and grief. I shut my eyes. *I'll fall asleep . . . I'll drift away and never come back.*

The shush of the wind and snow. The chatter of my teeth. Shivers like shockwaves racking my body.

Fear is your friend, but it must never be your master. It will leash you just as surely as the furless do their dogs, and drag you to an even darker fate.

The wind dropped. Warmth swathed itself around me. I opened my eyes.

"Greatma . . . ?"

Fresh prints in the snow. I stood up, blinking hard. I spotted a huddle of dark fur a short distance from me. Flurries were falling on his back, disguising his pelt. "Métis," I called. "Métis, wake up!" I gave him a shove. With a groan, he opened his eyes.

The paw prints dotted the path before us. New snow was already falling, threatening to conceal them. "This way!" I started through the drifts, with Métis limping behind me. We fought against the blizzard. My eyes were fixed on the delicate paw prints, which seemed to appear from nowhere. When I finally looked up, I gasped to see silvery white trunks.

"The birch trees!" With a burst of energy, I bounded

down to the trees. I could already hear the thundering of the river. Where the last tree met the high bank, I spotted a large flat rock. Further stones appeared between the water. "This way!" I barked. It seemed like an age before Métis made it down to the bank. There was no time to fret about the dangerous current. With a deep breath, I sprang on to the first flat stepping stone.

Gritting his teeth, Métis followed.

We leaped from stone to stone. The snowfall lightened as we left the bank behind. The sky was brightening.

I focused on each stone in turn. When I reached the shingle I yelped in amazement. We were in the Wildlands!

Métis landed at my side. "How did you do it?" he gasped. "How did you find the path to the crossing?" My gaze darted from him to the far bank. A slim shape flitted into view – an old fox with a mottled pelt. She stared at me, her outline faint against the snow.

Greatma! I called you and you came.

I watched her fade into blizzard and ice.

18

Clouds scudded across the Raging River. Squinting over the rapids, I could barely make out the tundra. The White Mountains peaked above the clouds, pointed as fox ears.

I turned back to the edge of the Wildlands. The Elder Wood lay in darkness, though a faint yellow haze rose from the west. Trammels of white coiled through the eerie halo.

Métis sat heavily at my side. "It's happening."

My heart sank. "We need to get you to the Elder Rock." I wasn't sure what I'd do after that – how I could begin to save my brother. But hope had kindled inside me in the worst of the blizzard, and I knew I would never give up again.

Thank you, Greatma.

Métis's ears pricked up, but he didn't speak as he started hobbling over the shingle. His movements were jolting. His muzzle clenched in pain.

My frozen limbs were starting to warm up. The shingle was a relief after the icy tundra. With my ease of movement came a quickening of thought. What was it that Métis thought he could do at the Elder Rock? How could he help in this state? "Do you plan to challenge the White Fox?"

His green eyes flicked my way, then focused up ahead. He grunted, climbing over a mound of shingle. "The Mage is leeching maa. He has stolen an army of Taken. There is only one thing the Elders can do to compete with his power." He cast another look at me. I sensed he was deciding what he could say.

Tell me. I need the truth.

He sighed. "We can pleach."

My hairs raised on end. "But that's how the Taken's wills are stolen! That's what you did to the wolf king. You said it was wrong, against foxlore!" Heat rose from my whiskers. "How can you even think about doing that again? Didn't you learn anything from—"

"I'm not," he cut in. "Foxling, you have misunderstood. Pleaching is a dangerous foxcraft. Its practice is protected by the Elders. Yet just like any foxcraft, it *can* be a force for good."

I pounced over the shingle and shook a pebble from between my claw pads. "Against the will of another creature?"

"No. This is different. This is pleaching as it *should* be performed. By the Elders, together, of their own free will."

I continued towards a rising hummock. I wasn't sure I understood. "So you all pleach, and then what happens?"

Métis's restless ears sprang forward. "Our minds will fuse. Our thoughts and maa will flow freely between us. While we are pleached, we are not alone. We will be six foxes of great power in one." He paused, cradling his injured forepaw. "With the strength of the Elders, I will leave to find Keeveny. I will stop him, whatever it takes."

The ailing fox could hardly walk. With or without the Elders' maa, how would he defeat the Mage?

"I'll manage it," he snipped, as though I had uttered the thought out loud. "Just let me rest a moment." He sat heavily.

Light was trailing along the bank. It crested the river.

"The Mage won't pause while you catch your breath," I reminded him.

Métis tried to rise. His legs quivered and he thumped back down. "All right, all right . . ." He tried again. *I wasn't like this before. You should have seen me. I was swift and powerful. I was silver.* He gave his head a shake. With grim determination, he rose to his paws. He managed only a few steps before collapsing again.

"Come on, Métis. Come *on*." I urged, beckoned and shunted. He would go a few steps before stopping, breathless. My tail twitched. "We can't be far from the Elder Rock. Don't give up now."

"I'm not," he snapped back. I could see what the effort was costing him.

"Let me give you more maa."

"No!" he panted. He added more softly, "I won't do that. Last time I nearly killed you. I nearly killed us both."

The sun was peaking in the distance, the top of an orange circle. There was a strange murmur beneath the shingle. I wondered if I should leave Métis there while I ran to find the Elders. What if something happened to him? I'd promised to get him to the Rock.

My head whipped back towards the sunrise. Was someone moving over the shingle? The figure paused. A fox! He'd seen us. My heart started thumping. It was getting bright now. It couldn't be one of the Taken. But what if it was a Narral? "Métis," I hissed. "Someone's coming!"

The figure started running.

The Black Fox looked along the bank. He reared up, flashing his teeth. "Get behind me."

I obeyed, though what could the old fox do? I clenched my paws. At least there were two of us, I reminded myself. I wouldn't give up without a fight.

The fox was getting closer. He glided over the shingle, elegant and powerful. His long brush bounced behind him. There was something about his fluid advance that seemed familiar. His red coat gleamed in the morning light.

My heart leaped. "It's Siffrin!"

The red-furred fox bounded past Métis and slammed to a halt. "Isla!" he panted. "I thought I'd lost you for ever this time." His huge eyes gleamed with light. I had never seen a more beautiful fox. "I've come to the bank every day. I've walked each furrow and crag in search of you." He shook his head. "And look at you now. You've grown up."

I ran to him. Our brushes twined.

I smelled the sweet, rich scent of his coat. "I was in the Snowlands. I missed you so much." The words flooded out of me unbidden. "Pirie wasn't there after all. He's in the Darklands. The Mage has captured him! It was Métis – Métis was in the Snowlands. He pleached with a wolf and his maa is hurt."

Siffrin gasped and turned to the Black Fox. "Métis . . . I didn't recognize you."

"I don't recognize myself," said the Black Fox bitterly. "Siffrin, we need to reach the Elder Rock. It is imperative we get there before the gloaming."

Siffrin dipped his head in understanding. "Maa-sharm?" he offered.

Métis looked at Siffrin. I sensed him assessing the young fox: the gleam in his eyes, the power in his brush. Métis sighed. "I am a parched stream, a dug-out furrow. No amount of maa can save me. But perhaps in the short term . . ." He gave a small nod. "Yes, maa-sharm. Only enough to get to the Rock."

*   *   *

The Elder Wood had transformed in the time I had been in the Snowlands. Fruit hung in the leafy branches. Birds warbled in their nests. The earth's beat thumped against our paws, stronger through the soil than it had been through shingle.

The amber shana danced around the Rock, a ring of protection woven by the Elders to banish intruders. As we entered the circle of ancient trees, its colour rose to scarlet.

Siffrin stepped forward, clearing his throat. "Elders, it is your messenger. I come with Isla and the Black Fox."

The shana started to melt. I made a move forward, but Métis stopped me with a tap of the snout. The look in his eyes surprised me. Rueful, almost nervous. It made him seem much younger.

"I wanted to say something," he whispered. "I have been hard on you. At first I saw only a naïve foxling from the Greylands. I was wrong. I wanted to say . . ." He dipped his head. "You are a friend to the Elders. And you have been a friend to me. I wouldn't have made it back without you."

I was lost for words. As Métis raised his muzzle, his green eyes glittered. Back and forth darted those pointed ears, ever alert. I wished I'd known him before, when his maa was as bright as the sun.

The mist of the shana unfurled.

The Elders spoke with one voice.

Métis.

The Black Fox shook his head. "I have failed you," he whimpered bitterly. "You already guessed that I pleached with a wolf."

I saw Jana on the Rock, with the other Elders behind her.

At first we weren't sure that it was you. Keeveny is master of pleaching – he was drawn to its potent allure. We know now that he is the Mage.

"I must fight him," said Métis.

Jana frowned.

Step on to the Rock.

Métis heaved over the stones. Already, Siffrin's maa was fading. I remembered what the old fox said. *I am a parched stream . . . No amount of maa can save me.*

I followed Métis, with Siffrin close behind me. As he stepped on to the Rock, the Elders were chanting.

Come together, rays of light; comfort me in deadly night. Weave a wall of thickest mist; every fiend and foe resist.

The chant was lead by Shaya, the stern auburn fox. The Elders ran appraising eyes over Métis, then me. I recognized grey-furred Jana, an expert in wa'akkir. Then there was the tiny ginger-and-white vixen, Mika, mistress of pashanda. Brin, the large slimmering fox, blinked at me kindly. He and Shaya had disagreed with Jana.

They hadn't wanted to trick me.

Kolo cocked his head. As he murmured the chant, I

spotted the gap where one fang was missing. I remembered how he'd karakked, whipping up the air, shaking the branches of the ancient trees.

There were two other foxes on the Rock. They sprang towards me, their tails thrashing.

I could hardly believe my eyes. "Simmi! Tao!" I bounded towards them. "I thought you were in the Free Lands."

Simmi nipped my shoulder affectionately. "We went. We spread foxcraft among the skulks."

"But we had to come back," added Tao, touching my nose, then turning to Siffrin. "We saw the yellow dust rising over the Darklands."

"We couldn't stay away," said Simmi. "The Mage killed and pleached our family. We're going to fight him."

"The Mage has Pirie," I told them. "I will fight him too."

The Elders had stopped chanting. The shana whirled around the Rock, a deep orange fog. Jana turned to us. "We must all fight, however we can."

I glared at her. "You tricked me." From the corner of my eye, I saw Brin look at Shaya.

"Yes," said Jana. "We found hope in you. Who else could have rescued our lost Elder?" She didn't even apologize. She turned to Métis. "We didn't know what to expect. Métis, old friend, I am glad it's you. I never really believed you'd be the Mage. But when you didn't come at malinta . . ." Deep furrows appeared between her ears. "You are changed."

"I won't let it stop me," said Métis. "Tonight I leave for the Darklands."

For a time, the Elders were quiet.

Shaya sniffed him, then stood back. "You won't make it. I have sensed your maa. You are damaged beyond repair." I was shocked by the brutal frankness of her words.

Métis nodded. "I must use the last of my strength to challenge Keeveny."

"I know you long to," said Jana. "Yet you cannot. Stay at the Rock, pleached alongside us. Your gift for gerra-sharm cannot be rivalled. What maa you have can make all the difference. Share your talents through our circle of blood. You will still be part of this final fight."

"That isn't enough," he protested.

Jana's jaw was set. "Listen to me, Métis. You are not strong enough to challenge the Mage. This isn't about old rivalries."

"You think that's it? That I want to win against Keeveny?" To my surprise, Métis threw back his head with a cry. "I won't let our freedom be stolen! All that I have known and believed in, all we have stood for as the Elders. It is for *me* to fight him. I am the Black Fox, the fox of legend. I alone can repel the evil that rises in his lands." He collapsed against the grey stone. His burst of sorrow had exhausted him. "I am the Black Fox," he repeated in a cracked voice. "I have failed . . ."

My heart swelled with compassion. I padded closer to

lick his long ears. "You haven't failed," I told him. "You saved Farraclaw. You protected the Bishar. You've already done so much."

Métis raised his head. Light danced in his green eyes. "But our own kind will fall."

"No." I clenched my jaw. "Not when there are foxes prepared to defend them."

"We won't let the White Fox control us," agreed Simmi.

Siffrin's tail was swishing. "We'll stand against him, whatever it takes."

Jana watched us. I saw her tail-tip glow. One by one, the tails of the other Elders glowed too. They were talking to one another in gerra-sharm, sharing thoughts that we couldn't hear.

"It should be me!" Métis blurted out.

Jana looked at him with meaning. Her tail pulsed brighter. It fell into rhythm with the thump of the gloaming. Then the light faded and she turned to Siffrin. "You will go to the Darklands." Her gaze trailed over me, Simmi and Tao. "The four of you. It is a dangerous mission, one you may not survive. Yet there is no one left to do it, for we are only six, and we must stay to pleach. Without the power of our maa and the strength of our gerra, you will never reach the Mage's lair." She cocked her head, her grey eyes returning to me. "Isla already understands that her brother is there. That others too have been captured. Their maa is the key to Keeveny's power."

Shaya spoke in a low voice, though the shana weaved its protective wall around us. "It is not enough to free the young captives. One of you will have to kill Keeveny. He is the White Fox's link to the physical world. Destroy Keeveny before the gloaming's fire light meets the crimson stones. If you fail, the White Fox will rise."

I ran my tongue over my muzzle. The thought of killing another fox horrified me. But the Mage was the one who had summoned the demon. He was the one the Taken called "Master."

Brin stooped his head. "He was a friend once."

"That was a long time ago," said Jana wistfully.

Shaya's stare was intense. "You'll confront pleached foxes in untold number. You may meet the Narral . . . There are eleven of them now, since Karka died in the Greylands. Believe me, eleven are more than enough. They see any who resist the Mage as traitors. Evade them as best you can. Do not confront them, as you cannot win." She licked her muzzle. "You will have to enter Keeveny's lair before the last sun of the longest day lapses into darkness. The fire light of the gloaming is potent in maa. Its power is beyond our fathom. Listen well, young foxes – the light *must not* touch the crimson stones. It is enough to breathe life into the White Fox. He will be unstoppable."

Kolo's voice was brittle. "Kill Keeveny and you thwart the White Fox."

He made it sound simple.

Little Mika spoke suddenly. "Help comes from unexpected places." She raised her delicate muzzle. "Use pashanda where you can. 'Eye of gerra, inner-glance, share your secrets through my trance.'"

I dipped my head, silently repeating the incantation.

"Elders, it is time." Jana looked at Métis. "You will not enter the Darklands in the way you intended, but in pleaching you shall play your part."

"It wasn't meant to be like this," Métis sighed.

I thought of Ma, Fa and Greatma. I thought of our patch, and all that I'd lost. "Nothing is. But that doesn't have to be the end of it. We're not giving up."

Brin glanced at Jana. "You were right about her."

Jana let out a long breath. "You will be valuable on the journey, Isla. But most of all, we need Siffrin. He is strong and capable in foxcraft. He will join us in pleaching. The depth of our gerra and the warmth of our life source will run through his blood for as long as the pleach is true." She met his eye. "You have trained for this moment all your life. You will be the one to enter the lair. You must kill Keeveny for the good of us all."

Siffrin tipped his head. "I will do it, if you wish me to." He was quiet and calm. Only the twitching of his tail-tip betrayed his nerves. Métis was staring at him. Catching his hard gaze, Siffrin blinked back at the Black Fox. "You don't, do you?"

Métis frowned. His ears twisted back and forth. "You are the obvious choice. Yet my instinct tells me you are not the right one." His gaze shifted to me. "Isla should do it."

My eyes widened. "But I don't know how."

"No one does," said Métis. "You want honesty? You must be prepared to hear it. When you're a cub, you think of adults and believe they have the answers. When you grow up you discover that there are no answers."

Beetles of unease scuttled through my belly. "So why me?"

"Yes, Métis," said Jana, an edge to her voice. "Why Isla? She is young and inexperienced."

"I have walked with her. Heard her thoughts. I have shared her maa." Métis cringed, drawing his injured paw closer. He looked exhausted. "If it cannot be me, it should be her."

Jana's ears swivelled back. "Siffrin, what do you think?"

Siffrin raised his muzzle. "I don't want to send her to such a fate . . . But it's Isla's choice. I can only say this – she made it out of the Graylands. She survived the Snowlands. I can't think of anyone more determined than Isla. If her brother is in the Mage's Lair, she should have a chance to free him." Siffrin looked at me fondly. "Métis is right. Your maa is dazzling."

Beneath the light, I brushed against something fierce and powerful, like . . . like the water that thunders along the Raging River. There is strength within you, Isla.

232

I blinked at Siffrin, touched by his words.

Silence fell within the shana, a silence so profound that chirping ceased in the surrounding trees. The shana deepened to crimson. Then the light shifted back to amber and I heard the call of a bird.

The Elders all looked at me.

It was Jana who spoke. "Métis believes you should go in his stead. Are you willing to enter the Mage's lair? To do whatever it takes to resist the White Fox?"

I couldn't think about the Mage, his army of Taken, or the Narral . . . I couldn't imagine the White Fox. But Pirie was in the lair. There were others, free foxes, captured and leeched. I drew in my breath. "I'll do it."

19

It was twilight in the Wildlands. A long day had passed in rest and preparation. We had eaten, talked and slept. Now the shana dispersed and we trod on to the cool stones, down to the forest floor.

The Elders gathered at the blood-bark tree. Métis took the lead, his weary paws digging a trench in the soft earth. Siffrin rested his muzzle on my shoulder. Fear fluttered at my heart, but his presence comforted me. Soon, we would enter the Darklands. Soon, I would see Pirie.

If we make it.

My ears flattened. "We will make it," I said out loud.

Simmi glanced at me. At her side, Tao was focused on Métis. As he finished digging, the Elders formed a circle around the patch of earth. In turn, each raised their tails and closed their teeth over the white tips. Eyes closed, they wrenched out several bristly white furs. Métis was the first to lower his tail hairs into the trench. Jana was next, followed by Shaya and Brin. Kolo nosed his hairs on to the others. Little Mika was last. She tamped down the mound of fur with her paws.

Métis turned to me. "Your turn, Isla."

I padded between him and Jana, where the Elders had shuffled along to make space. Shutting my eyes, I drew in my breath and tugged out some hairs from the tip of my brush. A quiver ran through me.

"Now put it with the others," said Jana.

I opened my eyes. The Elders watched as I padded between them to add my fur to the small mound. I stepped back to join the circle as Métis gently covered the mound with soil. A short distance away, Siffrin, Simmi and Tao watched in silence.

The covered trench was between us, underneath the branches of the blood-bark tree.

Métis started chanting. "Your thoughts are mine, my will is yours. You are my eyes, I am your paws."

The rest of the Elders echoed his words.

Your thoughts are mine, my will is yours. You are my eyes, I am your paws.

Their tail-tips glowed.

With a shiver, I joined them.

"Your thoughts are mine . . ."

The thump of the earth grew stronger. A silvery light rose from the buried cache. It twinkled like stars. I watched, entranced. Longing wrenched at me. It was as though all the beauty and desire of the world was wrapped in that thrumming silver mound. It grew, levitating in the middle of the Elders like a silvery sun.

Métis turned to me. "Isla, come into the circle. We will channel our gerra and maa towards you."

The other Elders kept chanting.

I felt a chill of fear. What was I doing? Was it too late to back out? I noticed Siffrin from the corner of my eye. He cocked his head at me in encouragement. I thought of Pirie. I started forward.

I stepped into the circle of Elders, into the silvery light. Warmth leaped through me, from my paw pads to my whiskers. The light danced inside me. Colours spun loops in my mind. I had the sensation of floating. For an instant, I was the great bird gliding high over the Wildlands. The land lay before me. I spied the outline of the Elder Wood, the border of green treetops. There was a path beneath the cliffs that led straight to the valley where the grass no longer grew. From there, I saw a forest, so gnarled that the branches wove through it like the bars of a cage. Deeper, deeper, there was a tunnel of rock, a maze of dark angles and scarlet stones.

The chanting faded.

236

I looked up to meet bright green eyes. "You have seen the path you must follow."

I nodded slowly. Behind Métis, the branches of the blood-bark tree were swaying. Red sap ran over the gnarly trunk.

The tree weeps. The foxcraft is complete. The Elders spoke with a single voice. *We are pleached now. We are one. Until the pleach is broken, our gerra flows freely. The circle of our maa will not fade. Until the end of the gloaming, our maa will run through Isla's blood. Our thoughts will join with yours. Though you enter the Darklands, you will not walk alone.*

"She isn't alone," said Siffrin.

Jana looked at him with soft eyes. But the voice that replied came from all the foxes.

Bold Siffrin, you are right. Look after her, and yourself. Together the Elders turned to Simmi and Tao. The young foxes watched them in wary fascination. *You are all part of this now. Be shrewd. Watch out for the Mage's tricks. Protect each other.*

"We will," said Simmi shyly.

The Elders looked up, their heads moving in harmony. It reminded me of the glittering wolf in the tundra, when the Bishar of Claw had woven together in the shape of a great beast. *It is almost dark*, they said together. *The Taken will stalk the Wildlands. We must raise the shana one last time.*

We watched the Elders climb back on to the Rock. Brin,

Kolo, Jana and Shaya. Little Miko took great bounds to land on the grey stone. Métis was the last to step on to the Rock. I watched the amber light swallow him up.

The blood-bark tree still wept, its dark sap trailing to the floor of the wood. Where it touched the earth, the beat of the gloaming seemed to grow stronger. My paws quivered with its intensity. It was all I could do to keep still.

My body trembled with silver maa. "We must follow the path beneath the cliffs."

"I know the way," said Siffrin.

I turned to Simmi and Tao. "Are you ready?"

"Ready," they murmured.

"Good," I replied. We had a long way to go.

I started to run.

Light flitted between the trees. Cicadas chirped, awakening the night. I ran east through the wood, my paws barely touching the earth. They moved with their own momentum. Only with an effort did I slow down to let Siffrin lead.

We followed the red-furred fox, looping south below the cliffs.

He knew the untrodden tributaries between the leaning trunks, and passageways long hidden by ferns. Sprays of blossom hung in the branches, already giving way to leaves and fruit. Petals littered the ground, silky against our paws.

The earth thrummed with the beat of the gloaming.

Musty heat hung in the Elder Wood, like the Elders' breath against our backs, willing us on.

I had to coax myself to stop running ahead. My paws scarcely grazed the earth, as though riding on air. From whiskers to tail-tip, my body felt limber and strong. I pulsed with maa. It fizzed along my spine and tingled my ears. Colours leaped to my eyes. The world was brighter. Sounds were sharper. I heard earthworms shifting under the soil, the flutter of a moth. When I strained my ears, I was sure I caught the distant gush of the Raging River, and songbirds landing on the shingle. Was that possible?

We slipped through a tunnel of bracken at the edge of the Elder Wood. The bowing leaves closed over us. The earth was rich and damp. Eventually the bracken led to the stream, where we drank thirstily. Then we swam through the cooling water to the far bank.

Siffrin started washing, smoothing out the fur of his glossy tail. As I shook my coat, Tao padded up to me. "Did you really meet wolves?"

"Yes. Farraclaw leads a Bishar in the Snowlands."

"Weren't you scared?"

"I was terrified at first, but he helped me. He and another wolf called Lopclaw came with me to free Métis. Though at the time I thought I was looking for Pirie."

Siffrin dropped his tail. His amber eyes were troubled.

"You must think I knew Jana's plan, but she didn't tell me anything. She probably guessed I couldn't keep it secret from you."

"I know." I had wasted too much time being angry with Siffrin. "It doesn't matter now. I wouldn't have gone if I'd known it was Métis, but I'm glad I did."

"Even though you saw wolves?" asked Simmi.

"More so because of that!" My tail wagged as I thought of Farraclaw and Lop. "There are too many misunderstandings between our kinds. We only think about the differences that divide us. But we share a lot too."

"Like what?" asked Tao.

Siffrin gave himself a shake and started between the trees.

I nudged Tao with my nose. "Later. When all this is over, and we're in a meadow in a beam of sun. When the world is at peace." I hurried after Siffrin.

"She means never," grumbled Tao.

The trees above our heads were different on this bank. Instead of thickset trunks there were slender firs swathed in ivy. The breath of the Elders was softer, but I still felt their presence. They were part of me now, in every pawstep I took, in every flick of my ears.

The Elders spoke together, but one voice rose over the others. Métis, the Black Fox.

Be on your guard. You are close now.

"This is your home. Where you saw Liro."

I hadn't meant to say the words aloud.

"Liro. Of our skulk?" asked Simmi.

I glanced at her. "I think he's in the Mage's lair with my brother."

"Why would he be there?" asked Tao.

A sharp scent caught my nose and I swung back to Siffrin. He had paused up ahead and was sniffing the earth. His fur had risen along his back. I padded to his side. Yellow mushrooms with purple speckles were clustered on the forest floor.

A chill crept over my fur.

Up ahead, I saw more of the foul bulbs pushing up from the soil.

"We're still a ways from the Deep Forest," whispered Siffrin.

I drew in my breath. "Eye of gerra, inner-glance, share your secrets through my trance." For an instant, I saw this land as it used to be, rich and wild, bursting with blossom and fruit. The image melted into the rotting remains of the Ghost Valley.

The words that escaped my mouth came from Métis. "Not as far as you think. His realms are growing."

We walked slowly, our snouts low to the earth. The beat of the gloaming still rose from the ground, but it felt distorted, muffled by the clammy soil. I approached the nearest fir tree. Brown fungus sucked at its decomposing trunk.

Several others were splintered or had toppled on their sides, as though struck by a storm.

It wasn't long before the firs petered out. Up ahead, there was open land that reeked of decay. A low mist seeped over jumbles of yellow mushrooms.

"The Ghost Valley," hissed Tao. "It's come much further than it used to."

My head shot around. Had I heard the scrabble of claws over earth, long claws beneath a fox's weight? I glared into the darkening firs. It was already dusk. The Taken wouldn't fear to tread here. I watched a long time after the others had passed. They were gingerly treading between the mushrooms. The scrabbling had stopped. I turned back to the valley and followed.

Dead shoots were silent beneath our paws. A thorn hooked on to my tail and I ripped myself free in a flurry of fur.

"Be careful," urged Siffrin.

We made for the broken black trees of the Deep Forest. But as we came closer, a groan rose from their twisted trunks. My mouth stung with bile. The mushrooms swivelled their yellow heads towards us.

Simmi and Tao had fallen behind. Only Siffrin kept moving, but his lurching steps betrayed his confusion. "What's happening?" he mumbled.

A dark sense warned me to look back towards the firs. A moment later, I heard the gekkers. The screech of the Taken cut through the Wildlands. They couldn't be far – perhaps at the stream. They'd be here soon.

Run, Isla. You mustn't tarry in the Ghost Valley.

The voice of the Elders echoed through me, but my mind felt foggy. I paused, sniffing the air. The scent of cinders prickled my nose. A vine slowly coiled around my foreleg. I knew I needed to pull away but somehow I didn't, my thoughts blurring.

The gekkers ripped over the firs, closer now.

My vision became hazy. Everywhere I saw yellow mushrooms. I looked over my shoulder in confusion. What was I meant to be doing? I couldn't remember.

A fox burst out from the firs. I knew instantly that he wasn't one of the Taken. He moved quickly, head low, but with nervously twisting ears.

He could still be one of the Narral, warned the Elders. *Get out of there, start running!*

My jaw felt sticky, meshed together. I worked hard to free my voice. "Siffrin!" I warned as the fox approached. I tried to rear back but my paws were planted to the earth.

Panic fluttered at my chest, but my body was frozen.

"Blink!" yelped the fox as he ran closer. "Draw upon your maa! Breathe deep and slow. It's a trap!"

I stumbled backward in shock. A vine entwined itself around my hind leg. Haiki was running towards us, his grey tail bobbing. I hadn't seen him since he'd fled from the Elder

Rock – since he had betrayed me. Suddenly he was barking in my face. "Snap out of it, Isla! The Taken are coming! Do what I say if you want to survive."

20

I stared at Haiki, dazed. I wanted to pounce at him but I couldn't seem to move.

"I know I'm the last fox you want to see," he said quickly. "But I'm here to help you. What you're feeling isn't real. The Mage calls it kia-sharm. It's really just shana-sharm reversed, tu-shana-sharm. You're being drawn into his trap!"

Siffrin stumbled around to face the grey-furred fox.

"Get away from me!" I tried to lift my forepaw but it was firmly woven to the earth by vines. I started to panic, tugging at my paws. The vines only gripped tighter.

"Listen to me," begged Haiki. "Breathe deep and slow, like you're going to slimmer. Try not to panic. Tell yourself it's a trick." Haiki was whiskers away from my face.

The Elders seemed to hear him through my ears. Their voices rose. *The grey is right. It's foxcraft.*

Siffrin snarled and shook himself free of the vines that were clutching at his paws. He bounded towards us. Haiki flinched, his ears flattened. But Siffrin didn't attack the grey fox. Instead he set to work on the vines around my legs, gnawing and yanking.

"You aren't trapped," he told me. "You just *think* you are. It's like Haiki said, some kind of foxcraft."

"Breathe slowly, blink often," said Haiki. "Remember, it isn't real."

"Do as he says," Siffrin managed between gritted teeth. He pulled the vines loose.

"But Haiki lied," I gasped. "He was acting for the Mage."

"Slow your breath, Isla." Siffrin gave me a shove. I stumbled, my legs free. *It's foxcraft. It isn't real. It's foxcraft.*

My vision grew sharper. My mind became calm. I turned to Siffrin, but already he was running away from me to help Simmi and Tao.

I met Haiki's eye. *"You."*

His tail curled around his flank. "Why are you here? It's so dangerous! This is the last place you should be." His voice dropped to a whisper. "The Taken are coming." I caught the whites of his eyes.

I wanted to scream, *What's it to you?* I wanted to tell him that he could rot. But I found myself saying, "I need to reach the Mage's Lair."

Haiki's open mouth was a rictus of fear. "But that's in

246

the heart of the Deep Forest."

Siffrin was bounding towards us, with Simmi and Tao close behind. The gekkers of the Taken split the air. Yellow dust hissed over the valley and I started to grow confused again.

"I know the way to the lair," said Haiki suddenly. "I've been there. I can show you." Darkness crossed his eyes. "I've been there," he repeated in a strangled voice.

"Forget it!" I warned. "Leave us alone."

"Don't be hasty, Isla," said Siffrin.

I stared at him in amazement. "You *never* trusted Haiki."

Siffrin's whiskers bristled. "He was right about the foxcraft."

"No way!" cried Tao. "He led the Taken to our skulk!"

"I didn't know they'd attack," Haiki whimpered.

For an instant, the five of us were frozen, as through the vines had seized us all once more. Indecision gnawed at me.

Shrill gekkers leaped over the valley.

"You won't find the lair without me," said Haiki quickly. "But are you sure you want to go? The Taken swarm the red rocks and the Narral are always on patrol. There are swamps and—"

"Take us!" I snapped.

Haiki gave a quick nod. He turned and bolted into the Deep Forest as the red-eyed foxes arrived in the valley. We bounded after him. The branches arched over our heads and darkness filled the sky. The air was a heavy fog, thick with yellow dust. The slimy earth slipped beneath my paws.

Pirie's been here, I realized. *The Taken dragged him through the forest on the way to the Mage's Lair.*

I ran alongside Siffrin. I could only see a few tail-lengths ahead. The impulse to stop gnawed at me.

It isn't real. It isn't real!

We tripped on fallen branches. Behind us, I heard Tao curse as he bumped into a tree trunk. Only Haiki ran with assurance, as though the foxcraft didn't reach him.

Perhaps it doesn't.

I remembered my first visit to the Ghost Valley. While I'd frozen, bewildered, Haiki had seemed untouched by the valley's grip. He'd found it impossible to slimmer, but he'd been the first to identify the foxcraft in others. On the rainbow cliffs, he'd guessed the enchantment.

Was he using this skill for sniffing out foxcraft to lead us to the Mage? I was haunted by the memory of his betrayal. Remembering how I'd led him to the Elder Rock, my legs lost their footing.

"Don't stop," urged Siffrin, "the Taken are behind us!"

I picked up my pace. I could sense them, the thump of their paws.

"This way," whispered Haiki. He cut sharply between two bowing trunks. Thorny bushes sprang to block our way.

He edged along them, sniffing. Finding a gap, he scurried under. We dived after him.

We shuffled low, our bellies brushing the slimy earth as thorns grasped our tails. My thoughts raced, but I forced my breath to slow down. Haiki was right: it helped to block the Mage's enchantments.

We crept out from under the bushes and ducked into a massive, hollowed-out tree trunk. In the cool chamber, we cowered in darkness. My ears flicked forward and back. I could still hear the Taken, but their pawsteps were fainter now.

For a time, none of us spoke. A groan rolled through the forest with the dust. No birds sang in the branches, no insects chirped on the forest floor.

"This is a dead place," I said quietly.

Siffrin huddled close beside me. The musky scent of his fur seemed to ward off the acrid trees. "The Marshlands are like this now. It's how all the Wildlands will be if the Mage succeeds."

"It's true." Haiki's voice was soft. "I let him use me. I wanted my family back . . . But what I did . . ."

"I hope it was worth it," I hissed.

His eyes flashed in the darkness, then his muzzle sank. "No," he whined. "It wasn't. All the time I was helping him, my family were already dead. They weren't even pleached. Koch killed them."

I drew in my breath.

"He's the one who attacked our skulk," spat Tao.

Haiki sank to his belly. "I couldn't believe what he'd done. I should never have got involved." His muzzle dropped. "I was a coward . . . I was too scared to stand against them on my own." His eyes flicked up, then down to his paws. "Isla, please don't hate me. The Mage *made* me spy on you. He said he'd free my family. He promised he wouldn't hurt you." His paws crossed over his eyes. "I know none of you will ever forgive me. I wouldn't forgive me." His voice was no louder than feathers on grass stems. "Everything I did . . . I just wanted my family back."

His sorrow tugged at me. I didn't know what to say. Didn't know what to feel. It was hard to stay still. I thought of the Taken, all captives to the Mage . . . Were foxes no better than the furless with their beast dens? Than the snatchers who rounded up foxes to be killed? Pain pinched at my chest when I remembered the foxes in those cages. I'd escaped, but I'd left them behind. *I couldn't help*, I told myself. *There was nothing I could do.* My thoughts echoed Haiki's words.

My body still trembled with maa. I sprang to my paws. "Before we confront the Mage, we must free the Taken."

"Free them?" murmured Haiki in disbelief. He lowered his paws from his eyes. "That's not possible. They don't even want freedom. They aren't like us."

"They were once," I said. "They could be again." I sensed Siffrin tense at my side. As the words slipped out of my mouth, I knew they were right. "We need to find a tree."

"A tree? We're in a forest," said Haiki slowly.

Siffrin shifted beside me. His thick coat brushed my shoulder. "A red tree," he said. "Huge, ancient with heavy branches."

I glanced at him and he met my gaze. His amber eyes gleamed. *He was pleached once.*

"The tree that weeps," said Haiki. "Like the one next to the Elder Rock?"

"Exactly." I rose to my paws. Maa was rushing through my limbs. "A blood-bark tree. I know there must be one in the Deep Forest."

Tao cocked his head. "Why do you want it?"

My gaze was fixed on Haiki. "Do you know where it is?"

Haiki ran his tongue over his muzzle. "Follow me."

We clambered between the pointed briars, deeper into the forest. The call of the gloaming struggled against the suffocating pall of the Mage's yellow dust. Sadness washed over me. So many foxes lost. *Ma, Fa, Greatma . . . Rupus, Flint, Karo, Mox . . .* Far beyond the dust and knotting branches, the stars still shone. The moon rose over the Wildlands. But down on the forest floor, there were only shadows.

Several times I paused as the others watched me, murmuring the pashanda chant.

"Can you hear the Taken?" asked Siffrin.

I dipped my head in acknowledgement. I could hear further, see deeper than the others, now that I pulsed with the Elders' maa. "Too many to count." My tail twitched anxiously. "Most are behind us. They know we're in the forest but they haven't found us yet."

Tao sighed. "I hate this place. Can you feel it sort of . . . I don't know, sucking something out of you?" His head drooped. "I've never felt so sad."

Simmi turned to him. "I can't stop thinking about Mox."

Siffrin lowered his muzzle. "I know just what you mean . . ."

Haiki's eyes tracked between the tree trunks. Pale tendrils rose through the yellow dust. "It's the White Fox."

I didn't like to admit that I felt the same. A wordless sorrow had crept into my heart. *You'll never find your brother*, it whispered. *You cannot succeed. The time of the free fox has passed.*

"Isla?" Haiki was staring at me. He must have caught the anguish in my face. "Don't let it in."

It isn't real.

We walked through the dark trees. Yellow mushrooms bobbed up from the rotting earth. Their acid tang stung my throat.

My nose crinkled. I smelled grit and festering dirt. "There's something up ahead," I warned.

Haiki glanced back at me. "We're nearing the Bottomless

Swamp. It used to be part of the Marshlands."

My eyes flicked to Siffrin. Wasn't that his home once? The red-furred fox kept walking, his eyes set forward.

Haiki continued. "When we enter the swamp, walk slowly. Don't stop, or you'll sink. Whatever you do, don't run."

"Can't we go around it?" asked Simmi.

"The only other way is through the Narral's den." His ears pressed flat. "You can't imagine a group of foxes more dangerous or better schooled in foxcraft."

I tilted my head. "The Elders." They had spoken through me. *We are more dangerous. We are the masters of foxcraft.* But the Elders were back at the Rock. Could they really help us so far from their own base of power? The fur rose along my back. "Wouldn't it be best to run through the swamp? It would be quicker . . ."

Haiki swung around to face me. *"Don't run,"* he begged. "The more you run or fight, the stronger its grip on your gerra. It will suck you down. The swamp is like the belly of the White Fox. It thirsts for you, for your maa . . . You must trust me on this, please."

"How can I trust you?" The words escaped as a whimper. *I thought you were my friend.*

The Elders replied, *You don't have a choice.*

My tail flicked uneasily. My ears pricked up. The crack of a twig, the scuffle of claws. "The Taken! They've turned around. They're coming . . ." I craned to hear. I could pick up the footfalls of six foxes . . . seven . . . eight . . . I lost count.

"This way," said Haiki.

We padded quickly through the forest until the trees thinned out. The land ahead of us looked unremarkable. Flinty pebbles covered the ground. Grey clouds stretched over the sky. Only the strange whiff of grit betrayed the swamp.

"Remember," warned Haiki. "Move slowly but don't stop. Whatever happens, you mustn't run."

We glanced at each other.

Crossing the swamp meant breaking cover. "Follow me," said Haiki. He stepped into the mulch. His forepaws started sinking but he kept moving, carefully pulling out each paw and squelching it down into the earth. His tail hovered behind him. Step by step, he advanced over the swamp.

Siffrin waded in after him. The mud clung to his paws, but he gritted his teeth and pressed through, his long ears flat against his head.

Simmi and Tao paused by my side, sniffing the dank mulch.

Siffrin glanced back at us. "Are you coming?"

My ears pricked up. The pawsteps of the Taken were drawing closer. "Move," I hissed. Simmi and Tao stepped out over the swamp together.

Haiki and Siffrin were the first to reach the far side. I was relieved to see the red fox climb out. He licked his paws

254

urgently, ridding them of the filthy muck.

As Simmi and Tao padded ahead. I took a first cautious step into the mud. The cold earth grasped at my paws. I felt it seep between the pads. Its touch was acidic, and the stench this close was rank. It singed my skin beneath the fur.

It was all I could do not to recoil. I trod forward, breathing as slowly as I could, edging my way over the swamp. I followed a short distance behind Simmi and Tao, keeping an eye out for the Taken. I could hear them advancing, their claws scratching against twigs.

The red-eyed foxes appeared between the trees.

My heart started thumping.

Don't panic! Walk slowly.

"Get them!" snarled one of the Taken.

They bounded towards us, a wall of foxes.

Don't run . . .

I forced myself to slow down, even as the Taken sprang into the swamp. Even as teeth snapped close to my tail.

"Tao, stay calm!" begged Simmi.

I looked ahead to see the young fox batting at the mud with his forepaws. To my horror, he began to sink.

"Breathe slowly," I called. Fighting to stay calm myself, I worked my way alongside him. The young fox was already dipping. Simmi was tugging helplessly at his fur as the mud rose up his neck. In a moment he'd be swallowed whole. "Look at me!" I commanded.

255

Tao's terrified eyes met mine. I gazed at him, willing a bolt of maa to pass between us. Then I blinked and Tao gasped. He drew in his breath and lifted his head. Moving slowly now, he raised each foreleg from the mud in turn and managed to hook his paws over the edge of the swamp. Siffrin clamped his jaws over Tao's scruff and tugged him out as though he was a cub. Simmi scrambled out alongside her brother.

"Over here, Isla," said Haiki. He tried to help me out but I shoved him away, slipping backward and losing my footing. The cold grip of the swamp oozed over my tail. Panic jagged through me. I released a slow breath, fighting against it, and heaved myself out of the swamp. But before my tail was clear of the deadly mud, I felt jaws snap at its tip. With a yelp, I tugged it around me and turned back to the swamp. One of the Taken was whiskers away, his forepaws scrabbling as he reached for me. The mud was rising along his flanks. A red-eyed vixen was struggling after him.

"Don't let them escape!" barked the vixen.

The nearest pleached fox started batting his paws. He was nearing the edge of the swamp, but not quite close enough to find purchase.

"Don't struggle," I found myself saying.

"Isla, we should go," said Haiki. "Before one of them makes it across, or others cut us off up ahead. This way, hurry!"

256

I could hear Haiki bounding between the dead trees, and the shuffle of paws as the others followed.

Not all the others. "Isla, you can't help them." It was Siffrin. Mud clung to his belly and flanks. A splash had caught the brilliant red fur beneath his eye. He ignored it, staring at the Taken in the swamp. His face was stricken. I remembered his shock when one of the Taken had fallen from a roof in the Snarl. "You can't help them," he repeated, more to himself.

"Isla! Siffrin!" barked Haiki up ahead.

We turned and ran after him. We didn't stay to watch as the swamp claimed its victims.

21

The trees on the far side of the swamp crowded close to one another. Spidery vines drooped down from their leafless branches. Even the faintest contact left an acid tang on our fur.

Haiki advanced beneath trees. Despite everything, there was still a bounce in his gait. I wondered what he'd been like before – when he was back with his family in the Lowlands. *Happy-go-lucky.* Something of his old spirit remained in his bobbing tail.

"How did you get away?" I asked suddenly.

Haiki turned. Simmi, Tao and Siffrin paused, watching us.

The grey's eyes were wary. "What do you mean?"

"You were spying for the Mage. What changed?" A ripple of fear ran along my back. My ears pricked up. Even now, were the Taken coming closer? Was this part of a trap?

Haiki winced. "At malinta, when the Taken stormed the Elder Rock . . ." He lowered his head, shaking his ears. "I couldn't stay and watch. I tried to escape but Koch caught up with me. He mocked me. He said that my family were long dead. So I ran. I didn't know where I was going or what I would do. I just ran."

Simmi squealed with rage and charged at him. She pounced on his back, throwing Haiki to the ground. "Coward!" she spat before sinking her teeth into his neck. Haiki recoiled, doing nothing to fight back. "You ran and let the Taken attack. You led us to harm. You didn't warn us!"

"I wanted to," he whimpered. "I came close."

Simmi dug her teeth deeper and Haiki yelped.

"Enough," said Siffrin. He sprang forward, butting against Simmi and pushing her off Haiki.

"He deserves it!" snarled Simmi. "He deserves worse!"

"Maybe," said Siffrin. "But we need him unharmed. He's the only one who knows how to find the lair." He looked Haiki in the eye. "But first, there's something I don't understand. If you ran from Koch, why are you back here? Why stay at the edge of the Darklands where you're bound to get caught?"

I glared at Haiki. "Why *are* you here?"

Haiki's ears pointed out at the sides. "Because I felt terrible for what I'd done. I wanted to help make it better." He dropped his muzzle and added. "And I had nowhere else to go."

Sympathy fluttered at my fur. "This isn't part of a trap?"

"No," said Haiki. "I won't forsake you. Not this time – never again." He dropped his head. "I thought of hiding away for ever. But the yellow mushrooms were everywhere, more and more of them every day. And I realized that it doesn't matter if you choose not to fight. Sometimes you don't have a choice. Because . . . because foxes like the Mage don't care what you want to do." He looked up. His eyes were wide. "I started walking the border of the Darklands, waiting for my chance."

Siffrin frowned. "Your chance for what?"

"To do something right," said Haiki quietly.

Tao stared at him. "So the Mage doesn't know you're here."

"I'm sure he does by now," said Siffrin ominously.

"Probably . . ." Haiki's tail crept to his flank. "But I'm not working for him. Not any more."

I flexed my paw. If that was true, the grey was taking a huge risk.

"There's nothing left for me," said Haiki quietly. "My home is gone, my family are dead. I've let everyone down . . ."

My ears twisted restlessly, forward and back, forward and back, like Métis. Had I heard something? My tail shot up. "The Taken are near."

"Quickly," said Haiki. "Through Petris Wood. It isn't much further to the weeping tree."

"What's the Petris Wood?" asked Tao.

Haiki hesitated. "The trees are ancient, frozen by time into marbled stone."

Siffrin tensed. "I've heard about petris trees. They're older than the earliest settlement of furless. They were here before the White Fox first claimed its stake on our world. It is said that shadows from the past stick between their branches like flies in a web. There are tales of visions, apparitions."

Haiki dipped his head in acknowledgement. "I've passed between the petris trees untouched, but enchantments don't seem to affect me." He cocked his head. "If you see anything strange, just remember it isn't real."

My ears flipped back. "What sort of visions?"

"I don't really know," said Haiki.

I wanted to hear more, but there wasn't time. I could just catch the pawsteps of the Taken. They had picked up our scent.

The ground lurched downhill as we sprang forward. The grainy earth scattered beneath our paws. It seized my nostrils, sharp with decay. Fear coursed through me and I looked around. Was it too late to escape the Deep Forest?

I pictured Pirie playing in the wildway. Remembered how we'd chase each other. How he'd slimmer – though I had no name for it then. How I'd karak.

There was no way back.

Darkness still hung over us, from branches and latticing vines, but as we bounded downhill I could make out great grey objects. The petris trees came into view, standing as rigid as rocks. Closer up, I could see blue veins running through their dark trunks.

The fur was sharp down my back. I felt it instantly – there was something strange about this place. A few paces ahead, I saw Siffrin draw to a halt, his tail puffed up. Simmi and Tao exchanged wary glances.

"I think we should go another way," whimpered Tao.

Haiki was already striding between the trees. "It's too late for that."

The yellow dust was drifting towards us. I could hear the cackle of the Taken.

I stepped between the petris trees.

Their branches were jagged and broken. It was stale between their ancient trunks. Airless. I drew in my breath.

I sniffed and looked up. Grey clouds shifted overhead. The others had disappeared. I was alone.

"Siffrin?" I called. A fox was moving up ahead. I could see the outline of his body. "Haiki?" I said more warily.

A shiver of grey light. A silver-and-gold dappled brush. My voice cracked. "Greatma?" But the fox was too small to be an adult. "Pirie . . . ?"

He peered at me from around the trunk of a blue-veined petris tree. His eyes were two globes of light. Then he darted away, into darkness.

"Pirie, wait!" I started to run. I could hear him

zigzagging between the trees. My footfall followed his. Each paw instinctively fell where his pads had left an imprint in the soil. My breath came in gasps. Long grass tugged at my legs and I glanced back to catch a flick of my mottled tail.

Pirie's tail.

I am Pirie.

Isla was hiding. I could hear her breath as she crouched on the far side of the fence. I sniffed, reached under the wood with my paw. I could smell her ginger coat, could sense her triumph. I imagined the tilt of her head, the bristle of her whiskers.

I knew this fox like my shadow.

I broke through the fence in a shower of wood chips. I drew in my breath and steadied my mind. In an instant, I disappeared from sight. Silently, I was gaining on Isla. My tail twitched in amusement. But a moment later, my heart crashed at my ribs as a bird shrieked overhead. My trick was spoiled and I lost my footing.

The cawing stopped. I looked up, head cocked. Then it struck me. *It must have been Isla.*

She was getting too good at that! I picked up speed, racing towards her.

"Enough!" she hissed.

"Not till you beg for mercy!" I pounced on her. "Say it!"

"Never!" she spat.

263

"Say it! Say it or else!"

"Or else what?"

"Or else this!" I covered her with long lashes of my tongue. We wrestled and nipped each other, curled up together until Ma, Fa and Greatma arrived in the wildway. As they left to move the cache, Greatma looked at me. She didn't say anything – she didn't have to.

No more foxcraft. That's what her dark eyes told me.

I did my best to look innocent. *Foxcraft? Me?*

Isla slipped off deeper into the wildway. I saw her ginger tail floating between the grass stems. *Naughty foxling*, I thought, my own tail wagging. Well, I couldn't blame her. I wasn't going back to our patch either. Not just yet . . . I padded to the broken fence where I'd run after Isla. I'd promised Greatma, but a little more practice couldn't hurt. When I was sure I was alone, I closed my eyes. I drew in my breath and my heart beat slow. My mind was silver. A familiar warmth flowed through my paws. I opened my eyes, my jaw falling open. Colours swirled overhead. I'd seen them before, but not like this. Gold through violet and green. Was I really the cause of those beautiful colours? Even the sunset couldn't rival them.

I thought of Greatma's warning.

You never know who might be watching.

Guiltily, I released my breath. The colours dissolved, first as rainbows and then into clouds. When they had passed, I felt a change. A deep chill crept over my fur.

A breeze is rising. It is touched with river and ice.

The bitter tang of acid. The shuffle of paws along the fence. The dark shape of foxes, stark against the crimson sunset. Their heads were dropped, their jaws were set. The vixen in the lead was enormous. Her thickset legs strutted towards the fallen branch that led to our patch.

"The colours of his maa were very close," snarled the vixen. "His patch must be here. Find the cub!"

I watched in horror as they poured over the branch and into my patch. Would Ma, Fa and Greatma be there? What would the foxes do? I turned towards the wildway. I had to warn Isla. But as I hurried through the grass, I couldn't find her.

A sharp voice stopped me in my tracks. "There!"

I spun around. The male who had spoken was only strides away from me. Others stood behind him. Their eyes were red-rimmed and veiny. A strange tang rose off their fur.

"What do you want?" I murmured.

The foxes didn't answer. Instead, their lips peeled back, green froth clinging to their fangs.

Terror ripped through me. I turned and ran into the night.

*   *   *

I ran blindly, scrambling between the blue-veined trees until they gave way to arching black vines.

Karka and the Taken came . . . and it was Pirie's fault!

I smacked against something solid. "Careful!" cried Simmi.

Blinking rapidly, I looked up. Yellow dust was drifting between the trees, hissing towards us. Overhead, the cloudy sky betrayed no murmur of Canista's Lights. I gulped for breath. "The memory . . . Pirie's memory. The Taken arriving at our patch. He ran." I shook my head. "But I know they caught up with him and brought him here."

"I thought of the first time we'd swum in the stream," said Simmi. "Me, Tao and Mox. Mox was so small . . . Dexa and Mips didn't want him to swim, but he insisted. It was so much fun." Her tail crept around her flank. "I'd forgotten all about it."

Haiki padded towards us. "Are you all right?" He cocked his head. "Did you remember sad things?"

"You're lucky it doesn't affect you," I said quietly, as Tao burst out between the petris and ran to Simmi.

"I remembered stuff I had forgotten even happened!" he exclaimed in a rush. "Swimming in the stream—"

"The way the water cooled our fur and the sun on the bank," said Simmi.

Tao stared at her in wonder. "We had the same memory!"

I hardly took in their words, my mind running over Pirie's memory. Métis hadn't understood how the Narral had learned of Pirie's gifts. Greatma had warned him not to play

266

with foxcraft.

"Oh, Pirie . . ." I sighed. "Why didn't you listen to her?"

He never meant to hurt anyone. He had no idea. How can a cub understand the brutalities of this world? He longed only for adventure.

Métis . . . His voice in my thoughts rising over the words of the other Elders.

Do not blame Pirie. He did not create the Taken. None of this is his fault.

My muzzle sank. "I don't know what to do," I whispered.

Do not tarry – it is what Keeveny wants. Even now, his army of pleached foxes closes in. Can't you sense them? Very soon, it will be too late.

My head snapped up, my ears twisting forward and back, forward and back. Métis was right! The Taken were running towards us. I felt the thump of pawsteps up ahead, and others behind us.

"We need to go. Where's Siffrin?"

"Here!" he replied. He moved quickly through the yellow dust, but his eyes were pained.

"What's wrong?"

He shook his head. "Nothing."

My tail-tip twitched. He looked haunted. "What did you see back there?"

"Nothing," he repeated. "I reached for my memories, for

something of my ma, of my brothers and sisters. There was darkness."

I wanted to comfort him, but there wasn't time. "The Taken are close."

"The weeping tree is up ahead," said Haiki. "It isn't far now."

There are Taken up ahead.

I could sense them, their acrid fur. I could almost see their dead eyes upon me. But what could we do? The Taken were coming from all directions, swarming over the Deep Forest.

"We have to get to the blood-bark tree before they do!" The Elders' maa was rippling through me. I could run faster than the Taken, but what about the others? I remembered how I'd slimmered over Farraclaw. Thinking of him brought back the hunt.

A single beast, a single heart . . .

"Stay close to me!" I urged. Simmi and Tao stood alongside me, with Haiki ahead and Siffrin just behind. I unfurled my maa like a silver pall, letting it wrap them in its power. Our paws slammed over the broken twigs, our legs pounced over the yellow mushrooms. While the gloaming hummed beneath the soil, the Mage's dust hissed through the Darklands.

Five sets of forepaws, five floating tails. Five pairs of pointed ears.

Yet we were more.

We were the power of the pack, the breath of the Bishar. I knew them then, and they knew me. I'd felt the bond between Simmi and Tao. Sensed the self-doubt beneath Siffrin's strong will. Touched the despair of Haiki's fragile heart.

I didn't need to ask the way. I could see it clearly through Haiki's thoughts.

Betweeen grasping vines, under briars and ivy, over upturned roots and burrs, till the bowing trees split to reveal a giant trunk. We burst towards it so fast that we smacked against its weeping bark and tore apart, five foxes once more.

"How did you do that?" gasped Tao.

Simmi's tail was thrashing.

"You found it!" gasped Siffrin in amazement.

Haiki yelped in delight.

But I could not rejoice. My ears heard further, my sight saw deeper. I threw out my senses in pashanda and caught an icy breeze as it cut through the Darklands. *The Taken are close*, it told me. *The Taken are coming.*

The Taken are here.

22

"Start digging." My voice was a low growl. "Now!"

Simmi and Tao stared at me. Haiki's tail fell. Only Siffrin snapped into action, throwing himself at the earth beneath the blood-bark tree. He started shovelling dirt with his paws.

"The Taken," I yelped, joining Siffrin under the great tree. "We need to find the cache! So many foxes have been pleached. It must be a great mound of fur."

This was enough to jerk Simmi and Tao from their confusion. They scrambled under the tree and started to dig. Haiki stood still, head cocked and ears flat.

"Don't you want to help?" I snapped. "Still not sure which side you're on?" I kicked up earth. I couldn't see Haiki's face but I guessed at the anguish that passed across it. I swivelled my head and our eyes met. "To free the Taken,

270

we must unearth their buried fur. It will be under a mound of white hairs from the Narrals' tail-tips."

"Is that how he does it?" Haiki's brown eyes glinted. "I'm on your side," he added quietly.

I blinked and returned to the earth under the blood-bark tree.

Haiki started to dig.

Gekkers pierced the quiet of the forest. I jerked up my head. Between the black trunks there were silhouettes. Long tails and pointed ears.

I leaped to my paws. "Simmi, Tao, don't stop! Remember there'll be two lots of fur, with a much larger stash below. When you find them, whisper across them: 'Run fast, be safe, live free.' Be as quick as you can!" I refused to think about the scale of the pleach. Could this really work?

What would we do if it didn't?

Simmi and Tao converged on the trench, digging furiously. They had lost their ma and fa to the Mage's ghoulish army – I knew what this meant to them. My eyes darted around the dark forest. The yellow dust was thickening. It rose in the air, mingling with the mist.

The Taken were on the move. Like shadows they appeared between the trees. I had never seen so many, even at the Elder Rock. The contour of numerous pointed ears loomed out of the forest. They were legion, an army, and we were only five. The mist trembled and arched, drawing tighter and dispersing in sickening waves.

Beneath the muffling hiss of the Mage's dust, I sensed the call of the gloaming. "Siffrin, help me hold them off."

The red-furred fox leaped to my side. I heard the mumble of his voice.

"I am the fur that ruffles your back. I am the twist and shake of your tail. Let me appear in the shape of your body: no one can tell; others will fear; dare not come near."

Siffrin sprang forward. In midair, he whirled around, a flurry of fur and violet light. He thumped down hard on the forest floor in the shape of a savage dog. His muscles bulged beneath taut flesh and a brindle coat. His muzzle was blunt, jowly and wet. With a snarl he revealed his enormous fangs.

The Taken cowered to a halt. A couple whined, their tails wrapping around their flanks.

"Dog!" barked one, stumbling backward. "A dog is here!"

Siffrin stormed towards them and they dispersed. Then their eyes started glowing. A moment later the Taken webbed together. Terror showed in their drooping tails and flattened ears.

"The Mage is controlling them," I hissed beneath my breath. "He won't let them run." I had always suspected that the Mage was watching, but now, surrounded by pleached foxes, the realization gripped me. We were in his lands, like mice scampering through a cat's hunting grounds. He would never let us escape.

Four of the Taken sprang at Siffrin. I threw back my head and karakked, showering them with the shrieks of coyotes. The terrified Taken reared, smacking into one another, as Siffrin slimmered. He reappeared beneath a tree, still in the form of the brindle dog.

But the Taken were coming in ever-increasing numbers. Tens of red-eyed foxes strode shoulder-to-shoulder. I wheeled around to see others nearing the blood-bark tree, dangerously close to where Simmi and Tao were wildly digging up fur. I hadn't tried wa'akkir since I'd mimicked the great bird – since I'd plunged into the Raging River.

I tried to calm my racing heart. "I am the fur that ruffles your back. I am the twist and shake of your tail. Let me appear in the shape of your body: no one can tell; others will fear; dare not come near." To myself, I added, "I am Isla. I am changing. I am King Farraclaw Valiant-Jowl." A bolt of maa shot through me so fast that I lost my footing and almost fell to the forest floor. My forepaws throbbed. I glanced down – they were enormous. White fur was dusted with flecks of grey. My body pulsed with power.

"Get away!" I growled, pouncing towards the pleached foxes.

They cringed from me, smacking into one another. But a moment later they stalked forward again, their red eyes trained on Simmi and Tao.

"There it is!" cried Haiki. He pressed between them,

revealing a ball of white hairs. "Isla, what do we do?"

Hope shot through me. "Keep digging!" I barked. "You need to find the Takens' fur!"

One of the pleached foxes reared on his haunches and dived at Haiki. Simmi was closer. She crashed into the fox's shoulder, knocking him to the ground. Haiki turned back to the cache and resumed his furious digging. In a moment, Tao was at his side. I lost them under a storm of soil. Beyond it, I spotted Simmi again. Her lips moved in incantation as she started to slimmer. I could just make out the edge of her paw as she slammed it into one of the startled attackers. Confusion was breaking out among the Taken, but still they kept coming, more and more red-eyed foxes. On the other side of the blood-bark tree they were overwhelming Siffrin. I saw him wrestle and leap, shifting into different dogs, slimmering and karakking, but it was a losing battle. There were too many Taken.

A tawny fox turned and looked at me. Light quivered in his red-rimmed eyes. Longing tore through me unexpectedly. As though the voices of untold foxes had risen in fear and confusion and were scratching at my thoughts.

Help us!

Free us!

Bring us back!

Then I saw it – the giant ball of long white furs raised preciously in Haiki's jaws. He set it down between his forepaws.

"The chant!" I yelped. "Say it over the fur, again and again."

Tao's voice was shaking. "Run fast, be safe, live free!" he yelped.

Haiki echoed his words, standing above the balls of fur. "Run fast, be safe, live free."

Nothing happened.

I heard Siffrin cry out and my heart leaped. I could no longer see him over the heads of the Taken. They strode towards the blood-bark tree with gloomy purpose. The yellow dust rose in the forest. Ahead of me, I heard the snap of teeth. One of the Taken had dared step closer and was straining to land a bite on my leg. Others flanked her, baring their fangs. A wall of red-eyed foxes enclosed us.

I karakked again, raining down coyote shrieks. The Taken only paused a moment before starting forward again. They had closed in a ring around the blood-bark tree.

Don't waste maa on wa'akkir! It was Métis's voice.

The Elder was right. My disguise could not repel them. "I am King Farraclaw Valiant-Jowl. I am changing. I am Isla." With a spasm, I was myself again, scrambling away from a fox's swipe.

Simmi and Tao were chanting. "Run fast, be safe, live free!"

Silently, I repeated their words. *Run fast, be safe, live free.* The Elders' voices joined my thoughts. *Run fast, be safe, live free.*

Pain shot through my flank. One of the Taken had pounced, snapping his jaws around my leg. Another threw her forepaws on my back. I twisted in time to see her yellow teeth as she bore down on my throat. My eyes clamped shut in terror as she tugged me up from the ground.

Abruptly, she dropped me, and I fell with a thud. Daring to open my eyes, I saw the vixen had rolled on to her side. The fox who had bitten me released my leg and staggered backward. Cautiously, I rose on to my paws. The Taken were everywhere, a mass of foxes, but the redness in their eyes was fading. Some were shaking, collapsing to the forest floor. Others stood still, their ears pricked in shock.

Haiki ran to me. "Isla, are you all right?" Behind him, Tao was gaping. Simmi flickered back from her slimmer.

"They're changing," I said slowly.

I looked to the bundle of fur beneath the blood-bark tree. It had gone.

Something was happening to the tree. Its bark trembled, cracking into deep grooves that etched a familiar shape – the mark of the broken rose – the same mark that the Taken bore on their forelegs. The tree's red sap channelled down the furrows of the rose's petals. The bark shifted, swallowing all traces of the mark. The last trickle of red sap dried along its trunk and vanished.

"They're free," I said in wonder.

Dozens of foxes blinked into the dark forest, glancing at their paws and staring at each other in shock. A vixen squinted at the male beside her. "Aril? Aril, is that you?"

He blinked back at her. "Do you know, I think that is my name." He shook his fur. "I lost myself . . ." He lapped his muzzle. "Nirap?" The two foxes touched noses. Tentative tails began to wag.

Our army of attackers had been transformed into a mass of confused foxes. Some ambled between the trees in shock. Others were drawing in great gulps of breath.

A brown-and-white vixen was looking about, her head tilted curiously. "What is this place?"

"It's the Darklands," I told her. "The Deep Forest. The Mage kept you prisoner, forcing you to be his slave. He stole your will, but you're free now. You can go home."

"I can go home," she murmured in wonder. Her eyes strayed to the mark of the rose, still darkly etched against her foreleg – a permanent reminder of all she had been through.

"We can go home!" yelped another of the Taken.

Excitement fluttered through the freed foxes.

They started to disperse, hurrying between the trees. I watched them, hoping they would make it – that enough of them still had skulks to return to. That somehow they'd piece together the fragments of the lives they had once known.

"Ma!" gasped Simmi. She pushed past me, making for one of the Taken. I recognized a vixen with a pointed snout and a slim red tail. As Simmi and Tao butted and nipped her affectionately, Karo seemed to melt back to herself, like a thawing stream. "My cubs," she gasped. "I thought I'd never see you again." "Karo?" Flint staggered towards them. The four foxes pressed into a huddle, overwhelmed to be together again.

I tugged my gaze away. It wasn't my moment to share.

I thought of Pirie. With the Taken freed, it was time to enter the Mage's Lair. I could feel the gloaming tugging at my paws, struggling against the muffling yellow dust. "Siffrin?" I called.

He was limping towards me, lame in one back paw. I noticed spots of blood.

"You're hurt!"

He glanced behind him. The yellow dust was clotting in mustard knots. The white mist was uncoiling, spreading into long sheaths like claws. A hint of grey touched the sky. "It's almost dusk."

I dipped my head quickly in understanding. "Do you need maa-sharm?"

Siffrin lowered his gaze. "I'm all right," he said stiffly.

Haiki was standing behind me. He had watched in hushed amazement as the Taken returned to their senses. "I didn't know this could happen," he mumbled, breaking his silence. "I didn't know they could come back."

"I came back," said Siffrin quietly, his gaze dropping to

the old scar on his foreleg.

"Do we need to go that way, through the trees?" I asked. "Towards the rising mist?"

"Yes," replied Haiki. "If you're sure you want to go to the lair." He dropped his voice to a whisper. "They say the Mage is invincible. He—" The words died on Haiki's tongue. At the same moment, I caught the scents of other foxes. Almost a dozen.

Koch appeared from the yellow fog, surrounded by the rest of the Narral.

The freed foxes who were still by the blood-bark tree fell back in terror. Several fled, others started keening and trembling.

Koch glanced at Siffrin, who stood at a distance. Then he ran his small eyes over me and Haiki. "How *dare* you free the Master's army? You had no right." The Narral behind him shape-shifted into coyotes. More foxes shrieked in terror and ran. Only Koch retained his shape, his blunt snout sniffing the air, his greasy auburn fur slicked back. Somehow, it made him even more sinister – a fox leading a pack of coyotes.

Fear hammered at my chest. They topped us in number. They beat us in foxcraft. They would see through any art I tried; they would outstep any move I made. Even with the Elders' maa, I knew I couldn't win.

Koch shot forward. My mouth flew open but no words

would come.

Pirie! I thought in despair.

But it was Haiki who sprang into Koch's path. "You murdered my family!" he cried. "I won't let you hurt Isla!"

Koch's eyes flashed green. "Oh, won't you?"

Haiki was quaking, his small ears pressed back. Still, he stood his ground. "You'll have to kill me first."

Koch pounced without warning, seizing upon Haiki. He threw him roughly to the earth. Yellow dust encircled them. A flurry of grey forepaws. A shower of dirt. The cracking of bones.

The Narral fox stepped back. Blood clung to his maw. It happened so fast, in the blink of an eye. "That was always the plan," he spat.

Beneath the choking yellow dust, Haiki slumped on his side. The fizzle of escaping maa, a sharp tang in the air, and he was gone.

23

With a yowl I sprang into the air. "I am the fur that ruffles your back. I am the twist and shake of your tail . . ." As I thumped against Koch, my outstretched paws were the black dog's. We rolled on the ground in the dust. Koch snapped his teeth near my ears. "Foolish foxling, you can't beat me!"

Maa thrummed through me. "Can't I?" I slammed him hard against the earth, slimmered and jumped, springing down on his chest and gnashing his shoulder, tasting blood. He snarled in rage and threw me off. An instant later we were both on our paws, squaring up to each other.

I can do this. I can beat him.

My brush shot straight behind me. Siffrin was running to my side. From the tail of my eye I saw a Narral fox block his path, still in the shape of a coyote. They started sparring.

Simmi and Tao confronted two other attackers, backed up by Flint and Karo and a few of the freed foxes.

But other freed foxes ran to defend the Narral. The ones who had been pleached too long, whose crusty eyes and spit-caked mouths told of the harm they'd suffered. They turned on Simmi and Tao, and the foxes who tried to protect them. Chaos broke out under the twisted branches as freed foxes turned on one another.

Coyotes closed around me. They stared at me with the flaming eyes of the Narral.

A sneer contorted Koch's face. "You didn't expect a fair fight, did you?" He took a swipe at me, knocking me off my paws and breaking the wa'akkir. I was a small fox once more, outclassed and outnumbered.

A deep roar ripped through the forest. The yellow dust recoiled. An echo of howls joined the first. Each was imprinted with a wolf's rich voice. Could this be one of the Mage's tricks? Were the wolves really here?

"Farraclaw!" I cried.

A thunder of paws and they stormed into view, the snow wolves with King Farraclaw in the lead. He took in the scene at a moment's glance. Powerful and fearless, he crashed through the Narral. Coyotes juddered back to foxes, dwarfed by the lofty wolves. I spotted Norralclaw and Rattisclaw, Briarclaw and Lyrinclaw.

"Don't trust their foxcraft!" barked Norralclaw. "Sniff

them out and hunt them down!"

The wolves lost no time: they set upon the Narral before they could karak or slimmer, slamming them to the ground. Freed foxes panicked, crashing into one another and spinning in circles.

Farraclaw seized Koch. The fox gasped in terror as the wolf clamped his jaws at his throat. With a shake, he was dead, his head drooping from his broken neck.

A moment later and Farraclaw was beside me. "Isla, are you hurt?"

I buried my head against his ruffled mane. "You came! But it's the Eve of Maha . . ."

"I was wrong," he said solemnly. "I put tradition before friendship." He nudged me with his muzzle. "Our ancestors would understand."

I looked up to gaze into his moonlit eyes.

Cattisclaw and Lop bounded towards us. Lop dropped in a deep bow before me. "Isla! You're safe!"

Huddled between the wolves, I drank in their confidence and strength.

Then I caught the sky between the branches. The clouds were dividing, revealing slivers of grey. "The gloaming is almost at its peak!" I yelped in alarm. I jumped to my paws. "If the White Fox rises we will never defeat it. I must reach the Mage's Lair. Only in killing the Mage can we stop the White Fox."

"This way!" called Siffrin. Already he was limping between the trees. The wolves were still circling the Narral, rounding them up like bison and smacking them to the ground. I saw Thistleclaw toss a brown-furred Narral into the air and I turned away with a shudder. Some of the freed foxes were fighting one another, rolling in the yellow dust. But most of the former Taken had already fled.

As I stepped around Koch, I saw Haiki's body lying still in a pool of blood. Too late, I remembered Mika's words.

Help comes from unexpected places. Know kindness for what it is.

Sadness clawed at me. Sometimes good foxes made bad choices. In a dangerous world, anyone could.

I swallowed hard and called to Simmi and Tao. "Stay here until the battle's done."

Flint and Karo had chased away one of the freed foxes who fought for the Narral. Already they looked much more like their old selves. There was no sign of spit at the corners of their mouths, and their eyes were clear and bright. They glanced fearfully at Cattisclaw, who struck down one of the Narral.

"Do not fear the wolves," I told them. "They're here to help us. Make sure the remaining freed foxes are safe – that they know how to escape the forest. They mustn't run through the swamp." My ears twisted forward. "Welcome back," I added softly.

As I ran through the Deep Forest, I could hear the howl of wolves and the dying cries of the last of the Narral.

But as we followed the choking yellow dust towards the curls of white mist, an eerie silence fell. Echoes from gerra-sharm leaped to my mind. Pirie had passed through this forest, heart racing with fear.

I'm in trouble, Isla. There are shadows here, and trees with branches that catch like claws.

Siffrin limped alongside me, gritting his teeth. I longed to share my maa with him but I understood why he'd refused. Who knew what lay ahead . . . Behind us, Farraclaw, Lop and Cattisclaw kept an easy pace. Even as the forest seemed to tangle around us, I felt safer for their company.

The dust tumbled into our path, rising as high as my belly. Where flecks reached my throat, it stole my breath.

Not far now, I told myself.

Between blackened tree trunks, I spotted an arch of knotted briars. The dust gushed out of it and I coughed, staggering back a few paces. I looked at Siffrin.

"The entrance to the lair," he whispered.

Beyond the thorny arch was a spiral of great red rocks as tall as the treetops. The hole beneath the briar was only slightly larger than I was. I darted around the outside of the rocks, sniffing and coughing. There was no gap between them. The white mist rose high over our heads. It was grow-ing, taking shape. One moment, it seemed no more than stray tendrils. The next I saw great ears, a muzzle, a billowing tail. A dim light touched the outskirts of the forest. The thump of the gloaming grasped at my paws.

We'd run out of time.

I dashed to the others. "There's no other way." I met Siffrin's eye. "We'll have to go alone."

Farraclaw thumped down a huge paw. "You can't do that!"

I reached to touch noses with the wolves. "We wouldn't have made it past the Narral without you. We'll be back soon." I shuffled beneath the briars before Farraclaw could stop me.

I sensed Siffrin right behind me, shoving through the knot of thorns. The yellow dust enclosed us. I felt it sinking into my nostrils. In its acid clutch, it was hard to breathe. My heart started sprinting, *ka-thump, ka-thump*.

You can slimmer can't you? Métis's voice. He was right! I didn't have to breathe the dust. I forced my heartbeat to slow down and lingered on my drawn-in breath.

Kaa-thump, kaa-thump.

I wouldn't think of how long that breath could last, of what the poison of the yellow dust might do . . . Already I felt it pawing at my thoughts. *Be part of something, Isla, something greater than yourself. Offer your maa for the good of your kind. A new order is coming. Bow to the rule of the White Fox.*

I set my jaw. *A fox has no ruler.*

It's what set us apart from the tan-furred coyotes, from the dogs of the Snarl who served the furless. It's what made us different to our wolfish cousins. No king, no slaves, no under-fox. All equal beneath Canista's Lights.

The red rocks closed over our heads in a low tunnel. I trod blindly. The Mage's dust stung my eyes. The thump of the gloaming had left my paws, but I felt it through the Elders as blood that pumped behind my ears. The gloaming was inside me.

Good, said Métis. *I knew I was right about you.*

It wasn't much, but it gave me strength. A surge of feeling rushed through me for the old fox. A longing to finish what he had started.

A groan rose through the dust and I faltered, reminded of the horror of the Ghost Valley. But beyond it, very faintly I felt a tug. As though a part of me was buried in the ghastly yellow fug. A part of me long lost.

A choked gasp behind me.

"Siffrin?"

His voice was a crackle. "I can't breathe!"

I wheeled around awkwardly in the tight space. The dust was so thick I could scarcely see him. I came close enough that our noses brushed and his whiskers tingled against mine. Blinking hard, I caught the black outline of his amber eyes. I sensed his breathless despair.

A shot of maa passed between us. A ripple of warmth.

"Thank you," he murmured.

I turned back towards the yellow dust, remembering the amber glow of the sky. The thick dust muffled my senses. But against it, a familiar scent fought through, tantalizingly close. The groan of the Mage confused my thoughts while the beat of the gloaming urged me on.

All of a sudden, the yellow dust dropped. The tunnel opened out into a domed cave of red rock. At the centre, the cave gaped, revealing the sky. White mist swirled overhead, winding and splitting.

Sitting beneath it was a fox with acid blue eyes.

My muzzle wrinkled. "Where's my brother?"

The fox rose. I noticed that instead of a tail he had a stump, gnawed off before the white hairs began. A fox who could do that to himself would think nothing of maiming others. I swallowed down my terror.

"Your brother is far away."

My heart sank. The yellow dust shifted and I staggered, dizzy from its dark enchantment.

"He's lying," snarled Siffrin. "Look over there!"

I squinted beyond the spinning mist. I could make out the drooping shape of five young foxes. My gerra leaped towards them. *Pirie, are you here?*

There was no reply.

"Far away in every sense that matters," said the Mage. He took a step forward. A whisker of light glanced through the mist to hide behind a bank of cloud. The gloaming thumped in my ears.

Siffrin trod towards him. "Your terror is over, *Keeveny*. The Taken are free, the Narral felled by wolves. There is no one left to fight for you." He used the Mage's real name, reminding me he was just a fox. Siffrin sprang into the air, leaping high with his fangs bared. He flew towards the Mage. The Mage met him with outstretched claws. Though he scarcely brushed the red-furred fox, Siffrin jolted in mid-air, his legs in violent spasm. As though struck by a massive force, he crashed into the red stones and slumped to the ground.

"Siffrin!" I cried, darting to him. He was breathing rapidly, coughing blood.

I spun back towards the Mage. He had taken a step closer. His muzzle was low and his blue eyes shone with menace. "It doesn't matter about the slaves or the Narral . . . It's too late to stop us."

White mist looped around him, blurring the sharp outline of his pointed ears.

Siffrin scrambled to his paws. "I'll fight him," he whispered. His eyes were locked on the Mage, but his muted words were just for me. "Free Pirie – *go*."

I gathered the Elders' maa towards me and started along the wall. Siffrin was charging at the Mage again. While the blue-eyed fox was distracted, I darted around the mist.

It hissed in my ears. I heard Siffrin cry out, but only at a distance. Against the far wall, four young foxes stared blankly ahead.

There at the centre was the face I had seen in my memories. The patchwork of gold, grey, ginger and white.

My heart was crashing against my ribs. "Pirie!" I yelped, touching his muzzle. He stared ahead, unseeing. His breath rose and fell, but his mind was elsewhere. I pawed at him. "What's wrong with you?"

Pirie didn't reply. Like the other young foxes, his eyes were blank. I sniffed his mottled coat but found no injury.

I sensed the Elders pushing against the mist. It repelled their thoughts from my mind. I concentrated harder and caught a single word.

Pakkara . . .

Of course! I'd seen Métis use the foxcraft on Farraclaw. The Mage had put Pirie and the other young foxes under a trance. It made them powerless to fight back as he leeched their life source with tu-maa-sharm.

The reversal chant played at the tip of my tongue.

Through the mist, I heard Siffrin yelp, "Isla, look out!"

The Mage sprang at me. I ducked. Siffrin leaped on to his back, his claws grappling against the Mage's shoulders.

A claw . . .

Of course, that was it! I focused on Pirie. "When you

feel my gentle claw, you will be in trance no more." I touched his nose.

He shuddered to life. His muzzle trembled, and he blinked his eyes. "Isla! So it wasn't a dream . . ."

My heart burst with joy. "You're alive!"

Siffrin cried out. "The light's almost red!"

Destroy Keeveny before the gloaming's fire light meets the crimson stones. If you fail, the White Fox will rise.

There was so much I needed to say, but there wasn't time. I darted to the other young foxes, repeating the chant, touching each with a claw. As life flooded through them, I turned back to Siffrin. It was worse than I'd feared. Even through the mist, I could see that he was badly hurt. Blood was gushing from deep wounds. He was dragging his damaged leg – perhaps it was broken.

"I can't touch him!" he yelped.

The Mage was preparing to pounce once more. I knew from the red-fox's staggering gait – Siffrin wouldn't survive another blow. Cutting through the mist, I dived at the Mage. For a moment I flew through the air, as free as a bird. Then I slammed against a more powerful force. I felt the yellow of its touch as it thrust me back against the ground.

I fought for breath.

Get up, Isla! The Elders spoke as one. *The fire light is coming. There's no more time!*

I looked up and my belly clamped. Chinks of scarlet

broke through the pall of grey. The sun was setting on the longest day.

"Get the foxes out!" I barked. "Lead them to Farraclaw."

"I won't leave you," said Siffrin. "We have to kill the Mage!"

You can't. You'll die trying.

Pirie's voice in my head. He was edging along the red stones, leading the other young foxes.

"Please," I begged Siffrin. I'd lost too much – I wouldn't lose him. I rose to my paws, pulsing with maa. "I am one with the Elders. You have to trust me." He'd asked me to do the same once, to trust him when I'd lost all faith.

His amber eyes met mine. For a moment he paused, torn with indecision. Then he turned, dragging his injured leg. "This way!" he yelped, leading the wide-eyed foxes out of the tunnel. Relief coursed through me. Could they get away? If the White Fox rose, would they be safe?

If it rises, none of us are safe. Métis, reaching through my thoughts. *You* must *stop Keeveny. I know you can.*

The Mage took another step towards me. The mist wove around him like a shifting pelt. I reached for the Elders' wisdom. How was the Mage's maa so strong? How could I fight his unstoppable force?

The voice that replied was not of the Elders. *They act together.*

"Pirie?" I craned my head. He hadn't left with the others.

292

He stood behind me, almost close enough to touch. But he spoke silently, through my thoughts. With pakkara broken, he couldn't be overhead.

My mind whirred over Pirie's words.

They act together. He and the White Fox.

I thought of what Jana had said to Métis, back at the Elder Rock.

Keeveny is master of pleaching – he was drawn to its potent allure.

In that moment, I knew what Pirie meant. The Mage had pleached with the White Fox.

Yes, said Métis. *That must be it! That's why you can't touch him. You have to break the tie between them.*

"I can't!" I cried. How had the Mage pleached with a thing that wasn't even real? How could the foxcraft be undone?

I sensed Pirie reaching out for me. *Use your maa!*

Overhead, the scarlet light was glinting through the gap in the cave, trailing down the red stones. The white mist spun to life. To my horror, the Mage was growing. His body bled into the mist. Together they swelled, bursting towards me, spilling out of the gap in the roof. Rising into the air as a giant fox.

Now! cried a voice.

Pirie's voice. Métis's voice. The song of the Elders, pleached together.

293

I sprang at the Mage – the solid form beneath the mist. With a thud, I made contact, throwing him from the path of the light. With my body, I blocked the sunset as it brushed the cool earth. But I couldn't thwart it, not all of it – a razor of crimson light had broken through. The groan in the chamber rose to a scream, the thump of the gloaming deafened my senses.

The White Fox was rising, a twisted ghoul.

A thud beside me. The softest fur. The light cut out.

A rumble rose from the earth. The great red stones started quaking. I felt the force of the White Fox, the depth of its yearning, relentless ambition. It pounded us but we held firm. Its screech clawed wildly at our heartbeats. Its bodiless voice gasped against our maa. The earth split beneath us with a burst of heat. I threw my maa around us like a pelt, felt the Elders' silver force rush through me, protecting me and the fox at my side. Gathered together, our hearts beat as one.

Ka-thump, ka-thump.

Flames exploded through the cave. Their crackle and hiss rose over the gloaming. The Mage was running, his fur alight, a blur of red and burning hair. The earth rocked into darkness as smoke blackened the world. Colours bled from the eye of my thoughts. The groan of the Mage was swept away, until all I could hear was the beat of the gloaming, falling in step with our hearts.

As the smoke unwound, the cave was empty. No sign of the Mage or the White Fox remained. Only the two of us, coated in ash.

Me and Pirie – together at last.

24

Métis was dead. I sensed it even as my maa unravelled from the Elders – the fading of a brilliant light. Through force of will, he had fought on, lending what strength he had to repel the White Fox. He had kept his promise to guide me to my brother. It wasn't the way he had wanted it, but he had played his part. I hoped he'd known peace at the end.

We gathered by the blood-bark tree in the Deep Forest. Farraclaw, Lop and Cattisclaw had waited for us with some of the other wolves. Siffrin was there with Simmi and Tao, Flint and Karo. A few of the freed foxes had also remained. They welcomed the four who'd escaped from the Mage's Lair. Liro, Shri and Zilla. And Pirie – my brother.

The White Fox had gone. I pictured it, this knot of matter, a cluster of frustrated dreams, twisting in the air beyond the sun.

No trace remained of the Mage. The fire that rose in his lair had wiped him out. His choking dust had disappeared. The air in the forest was lighter. At last, I felt like I could breathe.

We slept through the long day that followed the gloaming, pressed against the earth like cubs beside their ma, feeling its comforting beat. The wolves surrounded the foxes protectively, though the threat of the White Fox had gone. Still, I slept deeper for their presence.

The next morning we rose, reenergized. We walked together to the edge of the Darklands, where the trees still dared to flower. We drank thirstily from the winding stream.

Pirie rested his head against my shoulder. "I knew you would come. Even when I begged you to stay away. You never were one for being told."

I gave him a gentle nip. "Neither of us are."

He looked beyond me, his ears rolling back. I instantly regretted my words. Was he thinking of our time back in the Snarl? If he'd listened to Greatma, Karka wouldn't have found our den. He was only playing – was just a cub. He hadn't created the Taken. He hadn't pleached with the White Fox. Métis was right – it wasn't his fault.

I nudged Pirie with my nose. "I know how to slimmer now," I said boldly. For a moment, I flickered in and out of view.

"Show-off!" He batted at me with a paw. In the wag of his

mottled tail, I saw the Pirie I used to know – my mischievous, loyal, affectionate brother.

Siffrin still limped but his wounds were healing. I'd offered him maa-sharm and this time he hadn't refused. It was only my own maa now – my pleach with the Elders had ended – but it was enough. I had never felt closer to the red-furred fox. As Pirie rested next to Farraclaw, I licked dried blood from Siffrin's coat. The mark of the broken rose was still there, half-concealed beneath his fur.

I looked up at him. "I was wrong about you, Siffrin. Do you forgive me?"

"There's nothing to forgive." He cocked his head. "I hope that you finally know I'm your friend."

I touched his nose. "Maybe you can be more," I said bravely.

His amber eyes glowed with light. "I'd like that, Isla." He twined his tail with mine and my heart beat faster.

I studied his face. "What did you see under the petris trees?" He'd looked haunted. What memory had the ancient branches shared with the red-furred fox? What had disturbed him so much?

Siffrin shook his head slowly. "I felt like I was tumbling back to my time as a cub. I saw the Marshlands as they used to be, the tufty grasses and watery ponds. I could smell the pungent fragrance of the floating flowers. But then . . ." He shook his head. "Nothing. That's what upset me. The memories have gone. The Mage stole them when he took my will." Siffrin looked down at his paws. "I am a fox without a past."

I couldn't bear to see him sad. "Red," I said quietly. I concentrated. "Your ma's fur. The deepest red I've ever seen. She was beautiful."

Just like you.

Siffrin looked up.

"She loved you so much," I said. "All of you. You were one of six! Such sweet little cubs. Your fa had died and she raised you alone. She managed it somehow. She was a great hunter."

Siffrin's mouth opened slowly. "Six of us . . ." His eyes widened in wonder. "I feel them. I feel the warmth of them." He stared at me. "She watched over us fiercely. She caught ground squirrels . . . I remember the ground squirrels!" His tail started wagging. "Isla, how did you know?"

"It was in maa-sharm at the Snarl. After the fight with the Taken, you healed me. I lost myself in visions. I didn't understand it at the time but now I do. I saw your memories – they were hiding inside you all along."

Dusk settled over the bank of the stream. It was here we would part with our friends. Simmi and Tao would return to their old meadow with Karo, Flint and Liro. It wouldn't be the same, but in time their skulk would grow. I pictured the meadow in full bloom, saw it alive with cubs. Could almost feel their fuzzy brown fur and see them gambolling near the nettles.

Some of the freed foxes would return to their abandoned dens, claiming them back from the Darklands. These lands had once been green and vibrant. They could be again. Thinking of the Lower Wildlands reminded me of Haiki and my tail drooped in sadness. I felt no anger for the grey-furred fox, not now that I understood him better.

The wolves would return to the Snowlands. Farraclaw padded up to me, flanked by Cattisclaw and Lop. My heart thumped with warmth for them.

"There is always a home for you in our Bishar," said Farraclaw.

"Please come," said Lop. "Even Storm Valley will soon be dotted with flowers, and the mountain hares are jumping. You'll be happy with us."

I nuzzled between Farraclaw and Lop, lost for a moment in their bushy ruffs. I would miss them most of all. "It's time for us to build a new skulk," I told them. "Far from here, and far from the furless."

"You won't go back to the Greylands?" asked Simmi.

I glanced at Pirie. "There's nothing for us there."

He trod alongside me. "We're chasing the rising sun," he said. "Fa told us of the lands by the sea, with their giant rabbits and beautiful valleys. We want to see them for ourselves."

"I'm coming too," said Siffrin. "So are Shri and Zilla. We'll find a new territory, build a new skulk." His handsome brush drifted close, the tip touching mine.

Lop glanced at Siffrin with knowing eyes, then his gaze shifted to me. His tail bobbed up with a curious wag and I looked away, suddenly shy.

Farraclaw sighed. "We will howl for your ancestors along with our own. We will say rites for those who have passed." He dipped his head. "For friendship. For honour. For ever."

I blinked at him gratefully. I pictured Ma, Fa and Greatma – their agile bodies and sparkling eyes. A fox had no rituals, no rites or laments. Yet it gave me comfort to know the wolves would keep our fallen in their thoughts. That somewhere, in a land of ice and flames, the memory of my family lived on.

The sun set in a twirl of pinks and reds. Beneath its fading light, we said our goodbyes. Simmi and Tao struck out west with their ma, fa and Liro. The other freed foxes headed south. The regal wolves ran north. As they faded from view, I heard their howls. The power of their maa rose through the trees. I dared to hope that in their wake green shoots would stir in the Darklands. That buds might form in the bowing branches.

"Come," said Pirie. His tail was lashing. "We've got a long way to go and those giant rabbits won't catch themselves!"

Siffrin hurried after, his gait loping with his injured leg.

Yet somehow he was still graceful. Shri and Zilla followed eagerly. We were all so young, scarcely more than cubs, yet cubs who had seen enough for a lifetime.

We would run through the night. Our journey would take us far, but not too far. Come next malinta, I'd return to the Elder Rock. I had a role now, one I would never outgrow.

The stream had cleansed the ash from Pirie's fur, but mine was for ever changed. For as I'd emerged from the ruins of the Mage's Lair, I'd stepped out with a blackened pelt.

The other foxes had stared in wonder. The wolves had looked to one another. And I had twisted around, taking in the raven furs that covered my back and swept down my tail. Only the tip remained white.

"You're the new Black Fox," Siffrin had gasped in amazement. "You're the fox of legend."

Young and from the Snarl. It hardly made sense. Yet Métis had known it before the rest – Métis had touched my maa with his own.

The other foxes ran ahead. I paused, taking in the music of the night, my ears rotating forward and back. I heard the chirping of cicadas. The hooting of an owl. The distant murmur of the earth.

The sunset had faded, leaving the black mantle of the sky. Canista's Lights shone over the Wildlands. Wolves and foxes, from the Snowlands to the Snarl, fought to survive beneath the same bright stars. I thought of Métis, who had put so much faith in me. Who had given his life in the name of our kind.

"Farewell, old friend," I whispered. "Run fast, be safe, live free."

THE END

⟫ GLOSSARY ⟪

FOXCRAFT

KARAKKING

Imitating the call of other creatures. The technique allows the fox to "throw" his or her voice, so it appears to come from elsewhere. Used to attract prey or confuse attackers.

SLIMMERING

Stilling the breath and the mind to create the illusion of invisibility. Prey and predators are temporarily disoriented. Used to avoid detection.

WA'AKKIR

Shape-shifting into another creature. Misuse of wa'akkir can lead to injury or death. Its practice is subject to ritual and rites that are closely guarded by the Elders.

MAA-SHARM

Maa is the energy and essence of all living things. Maa-sharm transfers maa from one fox to another. Used to heal frail or wounded foxes.

GERRA-SHARM

Gerra is the thinking centre of living beings – the mind. Gerra-sharm allows foxes to share their thoughts. It is a rare foxcraft – a forgotten art – and can only be performed by foxes with an intense, intuitive bond.

PLEACHING

The weaving of minds (gerra) with another creature. Pleaching is to the mind what wa'akkir is to the body. Its practice is perilous, as the stronger will can overwhelm and dominate the weaker.

PASHANDA

A trance state where knowledge is summoned from the winds. Used to sense the approach of friends or foes.

SHANA-SHARM

The fusing of wills to weave shana. Used by the Elders to protect the Elder Rock during malinta and the gloaming.

❧ REVERSE FOXCRAFTS ❧

KIA-SHARM

Reversal of shana-sharm. A powerful field of maa draws victims towards it, trapping them. Also called tu-shana-sharm.

PAKKARA

Reversal of pashanda. A trance is forced upon another, leaving them helpless.

TU-MAA-SHARM

Reversal of maa-sharm. Maa is leeched from the body of an unwilling victim.

❧ TERMS ❧

BISHAR

A mysterious title used by snow wolves to describe their packs. Little is known to foxes of these creatures or their ways.

BLACK FOX

The ultimate master of foxcraft. An honorary title bestowed on the wisest fox – there is only one Black Fox in any age, and he or she is traditionally an Elder.

CANISTA'S LIGHTS

A constellation of stars that are the basis of a fox's maa.

DEATHWAY

Also called the death river. These are roads, but to foxes it appears as the deadliest trap of the furless.

ELDERS

A secret society of foxes dedicated to keeping foxlore and foxcraft alive. Each Elder is a master of a particular type of foxcraft – while the Black Fox is master of them all.

FOXCRAFT

Skills of cunning and guile known only to foxes. They are used in hunting or to elude the furless. Only gifted foxes will master the higher arts, such as wa'akkir.

FOXLORE

The fox's age-old struggle to survive the torments of the furless is captured in stories of resistance against all efforts to tame or destroy the fox. This lore distinguishes foxes from other cubs of Canista. Foxes understand dogs and wolves only in terms of their treachery. On one side, dogs are slaves to the furless; on the other, wolves are savages that howl to warlike gods. Foxes stand between them, answering to no one.

GERRA

The seeing, thinking centre of living beings – the mind.

GLOAMING

The gloaming occurs between twilight and dawn on the longest and shortest days of the year. A time of great magic.

MAA

The energy and essence of all living things.

MALINTA

Malinta occurs twice a year, when day and night are of equal length. A time of magic.

MANGLERS

Cars. To foxes they appear as fast, growling predators with shining eyes.

SHANA

A protective field of energy.

⟩ PLACES ⟨

GREYLANDS

The city. Also called the Great Snarl. Filled with manglers, dogs and many other dangers.

WILDLANDS

The countryside, where many foxes live, including the Elders. Isla's fa is from here.

SNOWLANDS

The frigid northern realms where the snow wolves live, hunting in packs known as Bishars.

ACKNOWLEDGEMENTS

I have run with the foxes for several incredible years and am grateful to those who have shared my journey.

First and foremost, I would like to thank my editors – Zachary Clark, Abigail McAden, and Samantha Smith at Scholastic – for insights, encouragement, and the best fox gifs the Internet has to offer.

Thank you to Team Fox at the Blair Partnership, including (but not limited to) Neil Blair, Josephine Hayes, Jessica Maslen, Georgie Mellor, and my fabulous agent, Zoe King.

Sincere gratitude to my family: my son Amitai Fraser Iserles, the light of our lives, who has shared our passion for stories from the youngest age; my soulmate, Peter Fraser, for always having the time; my sister, Tali Iserles, for being the most considered, enthusiastic reader I could have hoped for; my mother, Dganit Iserles, for patience, support, and cake-baking virtuosity; and my father, Arieh Iserles, my oracle and adviser-in-chief for every book I write.

Thank you to Priscilla Barrett for your gimlet eye and unparalleled understanding of canid behaviour; to Naomi O'Higgins and Richard Mansell for being there from the beginning; and to the Charlotte Street Group for writing camaraderie. Deepest gratitude to every reader who has taken the time to write, tweet or dress up as a fox for World Book Day – your support means everything.

My friend Lee Weatherly has been my "trilogy twin" throughout the process of writing Foxcraft. Lee: You have helped me celebrate the highs and buoyed me in times of doubt. Thank you from the bottom of my heart.

Finally, I would like to acknowledge the foxes of Myddleton Square. One evening at twilight I stepped out of my old apartment in London to be greeted by a magnificent red fox. She looked at me with her amber eyes. *Come,* her gaze told me. *Come on an adventure . . .* She turned to hurry along the street.

I followed.

Inbali Iserles, Autumn 2017

ABOUT THE AUTHOR

Inbali Iserles is an award-winning writer and an irrepressible animal lover. She is one of the team of authors behind the *New York Times* bestselling Survivors series, who write under the pseudonym of Erin Hunter. Her first book, *The Tygrine Cat*, won the 2008 Calderdale Children's Book of the Year Award in England. Together with its sequel, *The Tygrine Cat: On the Run*, it was listed among "50 Books Every Child Should Read" by the *Independent* newspaper.

Inbali attended Sussex and Cambridge Universities. For many years she lived in central London, where a fascination with urban foxes inspired her Foxcraft trilogy. She now lives in Cambridge, England, with her family, including her principal writing mascot, Michi, who looks like an Arctic fox and acts like a cat, but is in fact a dog.